The grenades detonated almost simultaneously

The ground shook with the force of the blasts as Mack Bolan and his partner raced from cover, crouching and firing at the terrorists' positions, spraying the areas where the grenades had landed.

The two Estonians in the blast range had been silenced, either dead or too injured to return fire. That left just one man, who was forced from his position by the hail of gunfire that peppered his cover. He tried to run, but there was nowhere to hide and he was mowed down quickly.

Knowing that they had to claim the truck and clear the area before the Russian military on-site closed in, Bolan jogged to the vehicle and wrenched open its back doors.

For one moment the world seemed to lurch to a sickening stop. Several of the nuclear devices were stacked inside, the trigger mechanisms attached and the weapons armed....

**Other titles available
in this series:**

Don Pendleton's Mack Bolan®

Death Metal

A GOLD EAGLE BOOK FROM
WORLDWIDE®

TORONTO • NEW YORK • LONDON
AMSTERDAM • PARIS • SYDNEY • HAMBURG
STOCKHOLM • ATHENS • TOKYO • MILAN
MADRID • WARSAW • BUDAPEST • AUCKLAND

Recycling programs
for this product may
not exist in your area.

First edition April 2014

ISBN-13: 978-0-373-61568-1

Special thanks and acknowledgment to
Andy Boot for his contribution to this work.

DEATH METAL

Printed in U.S.A.

I call upon the scientific community in our country, those who gave us nuclear weapons, to turn their great talents now to the cause of mankind and world peace, to give us the means of rendering these nuclear weapons impotent and obsolete.

—Ronald Reagan,
1911–2004

No question the world would be a better place if nuclear weapons were rendered impotent. But they aren't and, until they are, when called upon, I'll lay my life on the line to keep them out of the hands of madmen.

—Mack Bolan

CHAPTER ONE

Shale rolled and slipped beneath the soles of Mack Bolan's boots as he half ran, half slid down the red dust and rock slope, leaning back against the incline so that he could keep an easy balance. Despite the speed at which he moved, he was breathing easily, hardly working up a sweat. That would come later, when the terrain became really hostile.

Cones and firs littered the surface of the ravine as he reached the shallow dip at the bottom, the creek showing a bed nearly dried by a long drought, the waters reduced to a narrow channel that Bolan traversed with one step. On the far side the rock rose sharply, the gradient harsher than the one he had just run. His pace slowed as he began something that was less of a run, more of a climb. In places he was almost vertical to the rock, using handholds to aid his progress.

His breathing came harder now, the lightweight tent and provision pack on his back starting to register where it had been insignificant just a few minutes before. His ordnance was stripped down: a Beretta 93R pistol holstered in the small of his back and a Lee-Enfield rifle slung across his shoulders.

The soldier felt a pool of sweat gather in the hollow beneath the holster, and his black T-shirt felt clammy. Despite the increased effort, he grinned; this was what he wanted, to push himself a little. The strain and burn in his thigh muscles felt good, and the relief when he reached the summit and was on level ground again was sweet.

Bolan, aka the Executioner, stopped and looked around him, drawing great gulps of air into his lungs. His gaze went back over the ravine and across the plain that he had run since pitching camp that morning. Ten, twelve klicks? Not bad. It was still before noon, judging by the blazing sun that had not yet reached the summit of the sky. He checked his watch and nodded to himself.

He had chosen this part of Colorado because the climactic conditions at this time of year were not that far removed from sections of North Africa and the Middle East. A lot of his work had taken him there in the past few years, and he figured he could use some conditioning for future missions.

Bolan shrugged the Lee-Enfield and the backpack off his shoulders. He had kept his water in the pack as a test of endurance. On his belt it would have been too easy to take in when his dry throat demanded. Secreted in the pack, to yield to temptation would have meant a break in his progress, and that was enough to keep that lure at a distance.

As he took out the water and swallowed a long drink to quench the burning in his throat, he amused himself with the thought that Walt Whitman was getting to him. The soldier rarely found himself with downtime to read anything other than documents and books that were mission related.

So when Aaron "the Bear" Kurtzman, cyberwizard at Stony Man Farm, had downloaded *Leaves of Grass* to the soldier's smartphone with the recommendation that he should break training each evening with a few stanzas appropriate to the landscape he had chosen, Bolan had been skeptical. He had to admit, however, that the nineteenth-century poet had tapped into something eternal about the American landscape. Bolan had been able to push his body and rest his mind.

Choosing this place had given him that luxury. Secluded, isolated and well off the beaten track for any military or civilian activity, he was unlikely to be interrupted. A quick satellite scan from Stony Man before he arrived had confirmed that. It was exactly what he had wanted. Usually Bolan spent his entire life as taut as a wire—something that could not continue indefinitely without that wire snapping. He needed to rest that part of himself, from time to time, even while he pushed his body.

Throughout the morning, unconsciously as he ran, his ears had been tuned to the sounds of nature around him. Each snap of a branch beneath his feet, each tumble of shale, the distant call of circling birds and the rustling of mammals shying away from his intrusive presence. All of that had registered and had been processed by his mind, analyzed and dismissed as non-threatening as he had passed by.

He needed to switch off a little. It was time to play with the present that Barbara Price, mission controller at the Farm and his sometime lover, had given him the last time he had seen her.

"It's not my birthday," he had murmured when she had handed him the package.

"It'll be a long time before it's your birthday again,"

she had replied knowingly. "Just trying to get a little culture into you," she had added.

"You've been talking to Bear…" he had said cryptically, not bothering to explain as he had unwrapped the MP3 player.

"It's been loaded with a whole lot of stuff. Put it on Shuffle—you'll find out there's more to life than Springsteen, Sinatra and Mellencamp," she had stated.

Now, out in the wilds, he did as Price had asked, and slipped the buds into his ears before setting the MP3 playlist mode and looking at the vast deserted expanse around him. His grin broadened as the first piece of music swelled in his head, seeming to fill the very air around him, even though the forest's perfect stillness and silence remained, should he choose to pull the buds from their resting place. He recognized the piece as being by Copland, one of his mother's favorites, and there was nothing—and no one—who he could think of as more appropriate to his surroundings.

Bolan stood perfectly rigid against the sky as the music took him on a journey that relaxed his mind so that he could feel the tension slip from his body, only the loose elasticity of his easy-but-still-animal-alert muscles betraying anything other than complete relaxation.

Suddenly a charging surge of bilious, overamplified and distorted guitar chords blurred into a white noise punctuated by a barrage of bass drums shot through with a bass guitar so low that it was barely audible— more felt than heard. Smashing through this, like an insistent pickax to the head, a snare drum beat a rhythm that had all the swing of a boot camp parade ground and threatened to spear Bolan's frontal lobe with a viciousness that felt like a migraine.

As the rhythm became more disjointed and jerky, something that might have been a human voice—but only by association—joined the mix. It sounded for the world as though someone was either belching or hurling or maybe both. Singing was hardly the description Bolan would have used for it, but as there seemed to be syllables that were vaguely related to words somewhere in there, he could only guess that this was the purpose.

"What the—" Bolan pulled the buds from his ears and looked at the face of the MP3 player. It told him that this shapeless and formless mess had a title—so was presumably intended to be a song—and even had a band that was prepared to hold up its hands and claim ownership.

The "song" was appropriately entitled "To the Gates of Oblivion," and the group claiming credit for this little masterpiece—and on reflection he guessed it probably was in its own way—was named Abaddon Relix. Which was what? A reference to some old demonic mythological figure? Bolan had a vague recollection of the name Abaddon from somewhere, but the Relix bit? Who knew?

One thing was for sure, it was such a testosterone-fuelled racket that Bolan very much doubted Price was responsible for placing it on the playlist.

He was pretty sure he knew who, though. He hit a speed-dial number on his smartphone as he killed the noise—now tinny and hollow at a distance—before dropping the MP3 player on top of his pack.

"Striker, you're supposed to be chilling out and

working that musculature," Kurtzman said with some surprise. "What's up?"

"Barbara's MP3 player," Bolan replied flatly.

"What? Don't like the tunes?" Kurtzman asked.

"I'm guessing that you maybe had a say in what she loaded onto it."

"Aah," Kurtzman said followed by a pause. "Which little aural delight has tickled your ears, Striker?"

"Abaddon Relix," Bolan said.

"Interesting little band, isn't it?"

"That's one word for it. I know you all think I have limited tastes, but when I hear something like that, I think that may not be such a bad thing."

"I was just trying to broaden your horizons a little. You'd be surprised at what I put on there without her knowing."

"I don't think so," Bolan replied. "It doesn't really go with the landscape. Good call on the Whitman, Bear, but I wonder if you may need to get a hearing test."

"Admittedly it's not to everyone's taste," Kurtzman conceded. "There is one thing, though. It wasn't entirely for leisure or for the sake of shaking you up a little that I put that band on there. They were on my mind, as the name has cropped up in some unlikely places of late."

Bolan's interest was piqued. "Unlikely as in work related?"

"Could be. When you pitch your tent for the night, take a little time to look them up on YouTube."

"I'm guessing you're not expecting me to be drooling at the thought of concert footage?"

"There's plenty of that but no—the more recent video uploads have been of a radically different nature.

Tell me, Striker, what do you know about black metal and death metal?"

"There's a difference?"

"Musically, yes, if you like them. If you don't, then the similarities mirror the closeness that exists in their worldview. Maybe you should surf a little. It'll while away the twilight hours."

"Homework? You think something could be that imminent?"

"I have a hunch, and you know how that works."

Bolan looked at the sun high above him. If he set out now, he could be at his map objective well before dusk. It looked like he needed to be; it may well prove to be a long evening.

"Oh, yeah, I know how that works," he eventually replied.

IT WAS A LONG AND DULL drive from Helsinki to Karelia. Baron Kristalnacht—or Arvo, to his mother and father—sat in the rear of the car, slowly sinking the level of his bottle of vodka while his moaning became a lower rumble in his throat.

He was just the drummer, was he? Everyone made fun of the drummer. Drummers were stupid; they knew nothing; and all they were good for was hitting things. That was what the rest of the band thought. He knew that, and he was slowly getting more and more pissed off about it.

"You think I'm some kind of moron, right?" he slurred in a louder voice.

Severance—Uhro to his parents, who hadn't realized he was taking the car when he told them he was going out—frowned through the windshield as he leaned over the wheel, trying to see through the sleet that the wipers were barely touching. Arvo was a prick, but not because he was a drummer. He was a prick because he had a big mouth. Severance didn't need this kind of hassle. He had enough problems, more pressing concerns.

"You're not answering, man," the Baron admonished him, gesturing with the bottle and cursing when some of the spirit threatened to slop out of the neck. "Who found it in the first place? Why does that idiot Mauno want to take the credit?"

"Because he has an ego as big as your drinking problem," Severance replied. "That's why he went to Norway and we're here, keeping an eye on things. And that's why he took Jari with him—because he's a big lug who hits first and asks questions later."

The Baron smiled with the absent humor of a drunk. "Man, that Jari, he really is stupid. He should have been a drummer, if not for the fact he can play a guitar like an angel. A dark one, of course," he corrected himself.

He stopped, looked puzzled for a second, then continued. "Sev, you write the words. You can death grunt better than Mauno, and his guitar playing is shit. Jari could do it all in the studio, and it's not like we gig that much. Why is Mauno in the band anyway?"

"Because," Severance said through gritted teeth, "he's the one with the vision and the drive. That's what he keeps telling me, anyway. I just wish he'd kept it to the music."

"Man, that's our turnoff," the Baron interrupted, gesturing recklessly with the bottle as they approached.

"I know," Severance growled. "I'm not a drummer. Now just sit back and shut up until we get there. I need to concentrate in this crappy weather." He wondered briefly if he should get the Baron to check their guns before they arrived on site, just in case, before figuring that asking a drunk drummer to check firearms in the enclosed space of a car was not a good idea.

They entered the province of Karelia, headed for a spot in the north where the region ran into the border with the old Soviet Union. Severance felt his guts churn. He wondered how Mauno was getting on in Norway.

FLASH BOMBS EXPLODED on stage and reminded Mauno of the sight he had beheld the previous evening. A small wooden church with a stone foundation, fifty klicks from Trondheim, in a tiny village whose name he couldn't even remember now.

Five young men had invited Jari and himself along to witness their dedication to the cause. Mauno suspected that it was also to test any nerve that he and Jari might have. He would never have admitted it to anyone, but his bowels turned to water during that night. Jari, now, he was another matter. He was a Neanderthal who knew no fear because he had no sense.

They had driven out of the rehearsal warehouse in Trondheim that Asmodeus used as their base and through the pitch-dark night at frightening speed. The band had played its entire set in practice for this night's show and had ingested large amounts of whiskey along with fat lines of amphetamine sulfate. That had already pumped them up, long before the anticipation of what they were about to do had increased their adrenaline levels.

"It's been too long since churches and Christians

were put in their rightful place, yes?" Ripper Sodomizer, the bass player, had chuckled.

Just as the rest of the Norwegian band, he was built
like a bodybuilder, his face streaked with white and
black face paint—they preferred to rehearse as they
would play live—that had run with heat and sweat,
making him look like a ghostly clown. The band members were known to Mauno only by their stage names,
just as he was known to them only as Count Arsneth.

Despite the fact that his identity was also unknown
to them, he felt alone and very small as he watched the
brawny men—now dressed in black from head to foot
with their face paint removed—take explosives from
the back of the car, prime them and move in planned
formation to plant them. Once they returned to their
vehicle, they waited in silence as the timer fuse played
out. Then they celebrated with high fives as the night
air was shattered and split by the sound of timber and
stone being blown into fragments, fire catching on
what remained and lighting the night sky.

Jari had joined them, but Mauno had kept his distance under the guise of studying the carnage with
approval. When Arvo had told the rest of the band of
his discovery, Mauno had seen a way of using this to
improve their standing in the underground world of
black metal.

For too long, he had told them, there had been bands
that only talked and did not follow through on their
words. Not like the old days, when the music had been
young, and the likes of Count Grisnacht and Euronymous had been willing to walk the walk.

When Arvo pointed out that Grisnacht was serving a life term and Euronymous was dead, Mauno had

brushed that aside. He had learned from the mistakes of those pioneers, so they would not be caught.

No one knew their real identities, after all. They did not register their songs; they never signed anything except in their band identities, and even their friends—most of whom had no interest in black metal—didn't know who they were. They were the four geeks into metal, but that was all. It was like being a superhero and having a secret identity. The secret, hugged close to the chest, was what mattered.

Except that now Mauno was beginning to wonder about that. The Norwegian band had played up a storm, and their fans in the small subterranean club were going nuts. The sound had been deafening, even before the flash bombs. It wasn't like this in Finland.

Down here, everyone knew who the band members were, called them by real names, not made-up ones. Most of the audience was also part of a band and, from the introductions made earlier in the evening, were also church burners. After a long hiatus, the bands had taken up the attack once more.

It was still small-time enough to be a local phenomenon. As yet it hadn't been noticed in the rest of the world, though the shell-shocked Norwegians were alert to its implications, and the rest of Scandinavia was catching up. What the metallers wanted was something that would really catch the eye of the world and get them taken seriously.

This was something Abaddon Relix had…and how. That had been their calling card and their bargaining tool to get into the scene.

The problem was that, as the band and the audience drank more and talked more, greeting Mauno and Jari as old friends and new heroes, it struck Mauno that he was getting them all in a hell of a lot deeper than he could cope with.

Eventually the crowd began to disperse and the band collected its meager share of the door money before starting to pack its gear. Jari helped them eagerly, though it didn't escape the notice of Ripper that Mauno was less than keen.

"You didn't enjoy yourself, my friend?" he asked.

"Of course I did. It's just that I have things on my mind," Mauno hedged.

Ripper eyed him shrewdly. "So have we all. Your discovery and your offer were something that none of us expected. I have to confess, you are not what I expected, but I put that down to you being a thinker rather than doer—a planner and strategist, if you like.

"Now Jari here," he added with a laugh, clapping the guitarist on the shoulder as he walked by with a Marshall amp in his arms, "he is one of us through and through. If not for him, perhaps I would not have trusted you so quickly. Plus, of course, he plays like a bastard devil." He shot the guitarist a grin, which was returned.

Ripper left his bandmates and the giant Finn, moving over to Mauno and putting a protective arm around his shoulder as he led him away from the others. He spoke softly but with a firmness that made Mauno's blood run cold.

"What you offer to us is something that can change the way the world looks at us. They will realize how serious we are about our aims and the purity of our vision. This is not just about music, as you know. We have friends throughout Eastern Europe who were under the

Communist heel for far too long and have no wish for liberalism to let that in again by the back door.

"Nor do they wish those same liberal fools to spread miscegenation across lands that have remained true to their own. Like us, they have struggled to be taken seriously. You have given us the tools to make that happen, and for that we will always be grateful, and you will always be heroes of the cause. The name of Abaddon Relix will live on for more than just their excellent music and lyrics."

"That's very good of you to say so," Mauno said, trying to keep the tremor out of his voice but wincing as he heard himself and realized that he had not been entirely successful. He was also painfully aware that Ripper had spoken at great length, not just because he wanted Mauno to hear his views, but so Ripper could carefully guide Mauno into a darkened corner of the club, where two men sat at a booth.

They were dressed in black, much as the audience had been, but where those young men had almost prided themselves on their length of hair, these two were proud to sport the cropped version. They had the look of men with a military or paramilitary past. There was a hardness to their chiseled features and defined muscles that spoke of more than being the gym rats the Norwegian band were. These guys were the real deal.

While Ripper introduced them as Milan and Seb, Mauno knew that these were not their real names. They were hiding behind their pseudonyms much as he and his band—and the Norwegian band—hid behind their own more outrageous tags. They shook hands without standing and gestured to Mauno that he should be seated. The firm pressure of Ripper's arm on his shoulders, pushing him down, allowed him no room for dissent.

"You're a lucky man," Milan began without preamble. "You're in at the start of a glorious revolution. Fate had chosen the four of you to be our figureheads. Of course you'll need guidance, which we can give you. You rock. We fight. We'll show you what you need to do. There is just one thing…"

"What's that?" Mauno asked through a parched throat.

Milan leaned forward. His voice was little more than an impression of a whisper, yet to Mauno it was as loud as the night's performance.

"You'd better not be lying to us…."

CHAPTER TWO

The clear, star-filled Colorado night was peaceful and still as Bolan sat by the fire he had built near the lightweight tent. Contained by stones, the fire needed hardly any brush to start the flames and was designed to cause as little disruption as possible to the environment while he heated his meal and the water for coffee.

It would have given those who opposed him and what he stood for pause for thought if they could have seen him. For the soldier it felt good to leave as little impact on the immediate environment as possible, seeing how many of the actions he was forced to perform during his workday missions used vast amounts of resources.

There was, however, one form of pollution that he could not avoid. As he lay back under the stars with the remains of the coffee and relaxed in his sleeping bag, noise pollution rent the air as he used his smartphone to browse YouTube.

Kurtzman may have had a sense of humor that left some people baffled, but even allowing for that, Bolan knew that there was no way Kurtzman would want Bolan to endanger his hearing on Abaddon Relix unless there was good cause.

For a band that he had never heard of, they had a hell of a lot of material on the internet. There were clips of them in rehearsal and fewer of them performing in front of a crowd. It took Bolan a while to follow link to link, unpleasant blasts of guitar chords and drum beats spilling tinnily into the otherwise quiet night, before he came to the material that Kurtzman had intended him to find.

It began with some jumpy and hard to follow footage of the four—three of them in view, the other holding a phone or camera—trekking through a clump of forest that was thick and overlain with a carpet of fern and grasses. Their breath misted, and—checking the date uploaded—it had been a recent trip.

The clip then jump cut to an entrance to a bunker. It was too dark to see clearly, either because night fell or the entrance was buried in some way. Bolan paused the clip, made it full screen and was sure that there were earthen walls around them.

Hitting Play, he watched while the three men in front of the camera opened the doors into the bunker. They yielded easily, and the men knew what they were doing. They had been there before. Too young to have been serving soldiers in their lifetimes, it had to be that this was another visit after their initial discovery.

Wherever it was in Finland, it had to be well hidden. Bolan wondered how they had chanced on it, then dismissed the thought from his mind. How was irrelevant. It was what happened from here that was important.

As they hit the lights and the camera whited-out for a second before readjusting to the new levels, the soldier knew that they had been able to scope out the bunker fully on their previous visit or visits. The assurance and speed with which they made their way through the corridors confirmed that.

They were talking rapidly in Finnish. Bolan had only a smattering of it—Finnish wasn't a language he had ever been required to pick up quickly at any time—and so most of what they had said was lost to him. One thing was for sure: they were excited by their find, and as they showed the rooms to the camera—and so to the outside world—Bolan's sense of unease began to grow incrementally.

He recognized the design of the bunker. It was Soviet—probably built sometime during the 1970s to judge by its design—and occupied up until the fall of the USSR by border patrols.

Despite the fact that the Soviet authorities had always denied to the free West the existence of such bunkers along all of their borders—and those of any Eastern Bloc country—enough proof of them had turned up since the dissolution of the USSR to prove otherwise. Documentary evidence was scant, but some had been found, along with eyewitness accounts, to stamp the truth into history.

Now it looked like these guys had found yet another bunker. This one was fairly well preserved. The dust and dirt that would gather over a twenty-year period of desertion was there, and the walls were stained with dampness that had seeped through the neglected construction and insulation as the long Finnish winters had taken their toll.

The thing that concerned Bolan most of all was that the bunker had been deserted pretty quickly, rather than with a structured withdrawal. There were still maps, posters, pinups and notices on the walls. The bedding in the dorms had been left on the cots, some still in disarray as though men had risen that very morning and just walked out the door.

There were books scattered about, personal belongings that were either neglected where they had been placed twenty years before or were smashed where these four young men had had some fun before getting bored.

Boredom was something they seemed to get with ease. As those thoughts passed through Bolan's mind, the video had reached the kitchen of the bunker. Even here twenty-year-old dirty dishes lay in stagnant greasy sinks, covered with scum and accumulated dust, while the fridges still hummed. How the power plant had kept working for so long was a mystery. Leaving maintenance aside, there was the question of fuel for the generator.

If the bunker did not rely solely on its own power source, then it had to be linked in some way to a main supply. Running a cable out to such a remote spot was no easy undertaking.

Bolan watched uneasily while the members of Abaddon Relix took food from the fridge, threw it at each other and made disparaging remarks about Russian food as they did so. Bolan's Finnish was just strong enough to pick out a few cuss words—the golden rule of any language being that the first thing you learned was to curse—and as much as he wanted to fast forward to what he feared was coming, he did not want to risk missing anything important.

So he remained patient and watched as they fooled around, moving out of the kitchen and down another winding corridor until they were outside a metal door that the Executioner recognized all too well. Their mood had sobered now, and they were talking in more subdued voices. There seemed to be some argument, and then the camera jerked and swooped as it was handed from one to another, the man behind it so far now coming out in front of the camera.

He stared into the lens, his eyes seeming to bore into the viewer. He was undoubtedly the leader of this group—the way in which they had deferred to him seemed to bear that out—and whatever this group had to say, he was damn sure he was the man to say it.

He coughed as he stood in front of the door, and when he spoke, it was in faintly accented English.

"Hey, world. I am Count Arsneth. We are Abaddon Relix, and we are not just a band. Everything we sing and write about has a meaning. All you fools out there think that metal is just music and that we'll grow out of it. It's a way of life, and you need to get over it. Our beliefs, along with those of our Norwegian brothers, are about the return of the old ways.

"Men need to make a stand for the purity of their people and their culture. We have evolved a way of life that is true to nature, and is the only way to live honestly and free. Religion just seeks to oppress you and keep you down. Keep you small. You need to think big, man. You are your own destiny. You control yourself when you are a man. We want our nation to be this way and not take any of that other shit from other cultures.

"We don't want to integrate with people who know nothing about culture other than the weak crap they want to foist on us. Screw them. The time has come to fight back. Already the weak-willed Christians are suffering once more at the hands of our Norwegian brothers. We will take it one step further. We will help them to take it one step further. We will show you all that we are for real...."

He stopped ranting and turned to the door. Bolan had noticed that this Count Arsneth had not blinked once during the machine-gun rattle of his delivery, as though he had learned it by heart and was delivering it like the lyrics of their songs. Only this time he didn't sound like he was vomiting.

Leaving aside the puerile and adolescent nature of much of what the leader had said, there was an underlying, if unreasoned, streak of extreme right-wing racism in some of his assumptions that put the band perfectly in line with what Bolan knew of black metal politics—even the most cursory search at Kurtzman's behest earlier in the evening had shown Bolan this, before he had braced himself for the metal onslaught—and placed these four, given their location, firmly in the frame for the extreme right-wing terrorism that was a bubbling undercurrent throughout Eastern Europe.

Given what Bolan was sure these guys had found behind that door, this could never be a good thing.... As he watched, Arsneth opened the heavy metal door and revealed an armory that was fully stocked with boxes of twenty-year-old Russian army–issued SMGs, revolvers, rifles, ammunition and grenades. It had been a fairly large bunker—maybe up to a dozen men at full complement—and the armory reflected that. But there was more. Toward the rear of the room there was another door, which had an electronic locking system that was keypad activated.

Without the key there was no way they should have been able to get into that room, but Bolan knew how the minds of bored, fatigued and jaded soldiers worked.

Over time, the code would be forgotten; changing it would be a royal pain in the ass; and so to avoid the hassle, someone would scratch the code into the metal plate above the keypad. After all they were left to their own devices, and the chances of actually having to use the room were so remote...

Bolan cursed the lazy mind of the career soldier left to rot by his government as Arsneth keyed in a series of numbers with confidence, the rusty door creaking and yielding. The concrete frame had shifted in the earth, and the door caught on the floor with a grinding noise as it opened. But open it did. Arsneth walked through, followed by the other band members, with the new cameraman at the rear.

Bolan cursed again under his breath. This time it was because he saw what had excited the band members so much, and made a bunch of teenage misfits with a chip on their shoulder and a fetish for the devil so dangerous.

The room contained a row of squat gray cylinders with painted noses, as well as a sealed safe in one corner, which Bolan knew from its design and his experience was lead lined.

Why the Soviets had desired to stash a small arsenal of nukes on the Finnish border was a mystery. Had they been in transit, in storage, or had there been some contingency plan for defense or attack that had been lost in the ensuing decades? It didn't matter. The fact that their presence could not now be explained was another irrelevancy. What mattered was that the arsenal was there—and that they had been discovered by one of the least likely and most volatile parties that could have stumbled onto them.

The upload ended with a lingering shot of the gray cylinders. Arsneth had been pretty restrained, as had the other members of the band, and had said nothing, letting the room speak for itself. It was likely that those few souls who actually liked the band for their music—Bolan couldn't imagine them offhand but was willing to concede that they may exist—would be unable to recognize the missiles for what they were, even though the rest of the armory was pretty identifiable. Viewers might even think the whole thing was a setup, some kind of promotional gimmick. They weren't the ones who concerned the soldier.

He had little doubt that the kind of right-wing fascist terrorists that Abaddon Relix's music, geographical location and politics brought them into contact with would be able to identify the missiles and the veracity of the bunker's contents with no trouble at all.

And they would be all over the teenage metal band like a rash of the worst kind.

A sense of foreboding came over Bolan. So much so that, for a moment, he did not register that You-Tube had brought up a menu of associated clips on the screen. Most of them were of the same band and were clips that he had already dismissed. There was, however, one that he had not seen before: burning a church with Count Arsneth. He looked at the date. The video had been uploaded only the day before.

Bolan set the clip to Play and watched the bombing of the Norwegian church that had taken place less than thirty-six hours before. He recognized Arsneth and the giant who had thrown food in the bunker and played guitar. Their other two band members didn't seem to be there.

Of more concern was the fact that another group, the members of a Norwegian band, instrumental in attacking the church, seemed a whole lot more businesslike. They spoke to the camera forcefully yet calmly. Their rant differed little from that of the previous band, except that it was somewhat better reasoned and a tad more mature in that it lacked the juvenile chip on the shoulder.

Bolan watched their exultation as the church went up in flames and smoke, and noted that, although the giant seemed happy to join them, there was something about Arsneth that was subdued and nervous.

Was he regretting getting in that deep? Posturing was one thing; taking your actions onto the battlefield and into combat was quite another.

Hitting the back button, Bolan ignored the clip of the bunker as it played again. Instead, he looked at how many hits the clip had received and at the comments below. Already it had racked up ten thousand hits, and there were over two hundred comments.

Ignoring the sound track, he read through them. Some were unintelligible, either because they were in Finnish or Norwegian, or because their English was so poor that it was hard to work out what they were trying to say. But some were chillingly comprehensible, messages of white power, of Aryan culture, and of support and even offers of assistance or to buy the weapons from the band.

Bolan put down the smartphone, the clip still reeling, and stood up, walking away from the fire and feeling the chill night air pluck at his skin. The dark outlines of the distant mountains and outcrops were black against the wine-dark sky, its stars distant beacons of light in the wan glow of a crescent moon.

In the name of their supposed freedom, the men who had appended those messages would take away the freedoms and even the lives of others. Bolan believed in freedom and democracy, but not at the expense of someone riding roughshod over others because they didn't fit Bolan's view.

Democracy was a funny thing. The rage and hate against others he had just seen was allowed to go unchecked in that name. Didn't anyone moderate that kind of crap? He guessed they would eventually, but by then, it would be too late. It might already be. How many terrorist groups were after Abaddon Relix, whether the band sought them or not?

Bolan thought about it. Kurtzman had had a hunch, and his hunches were usually informed by a little more than just intuition. He had picked up something and was ahead of the wave, as usual.

The Executioner allowed himself a chuckle. The whole point of being out here was to train and acclimatize for those climates most likely to be points of duty.

It looked like he might be doing a 180 on that and sooner than he would have thought.

CHAPTER THREE

"This is a very nice place. You're not from here, are you? You must be pretty well loaded."

Count Arsneth nodded. His mouth was dry, and he felt unable to actually speak in the presence of the two short-haired men. Every word seemed to carry an undertone of threat, to be loaded with a number of meanings. Maybe he was just overthinking things. That was driven from his mind by Jari's response.

"The Count, his parents, are plenty loaded, man. That's why he's in the band—we couldn't afford shit without his parents."

Arsneth could have hit him, hard, except Jari was a hell of a lot bigger and would have hit back harder. That wasn't the only reason Arsneth was angry. He wanted these people to know as little about him as possible. He also didn't want them to think he was some kind of dilettante—though he was, frankly—as it would put him at a disadvantage in what was to come.

Which, to judge from the way Ripper, Milan and Seb were looking at him, was not going to be good.

"You rent this in your own name then?" Milan asked as he went to the fridge and took out two beers, tossing one to Seb with an implied assumption of ownership that made his point well.

Arsneth nodded. He couldn't think of himself as

Mauno. Mauno was a scared kid; Arsneth was a rock star with a cause.

"Your real name?" Ripper asked, astonished. "You used that? What kind of a idiot are you? You know how easy it will be to trace you back to us?"

"Chill, Rip," Milan said easily, taking another beer from the fridge and tossing it to the Norwegian musician. "You guys are a lot more careful. The trail stops with a band that doesn't officially exist. This guy's a dead end, in more ways than one."

Jari had thrown himself over the couch into a seated position and had hit the remote for the big-screen TV. He was already in another place, watching a porn channel. But even he could catch the drift of the conversation and was torn away from the grinding on-screen.

"Hey, what did you say to Mauno?" he asked, anger flashing in his eyes. "You screw with him, you screw with me, asswipe."

Seb grinned. "You can chill, too, big man," he said, handing Jari a tumbler of Jägermeister poured directly from the bottle. "We just mean that he needs to show us the goods, or we won't believe him. Anyone can fake a movie set, right?"

Jari took the glass and polished off half of it, before saying, "Hey, Mauno doesn't lie, and neither do I. Listen, dude, you can come with us to Karelia and see it for yourselves. That's what we're here for, right?" Then he finished off the rest of his drink.

"Shut up, Jari," Mauno snapped in a tight voice.

"What?" Jari queried, his eyes glazing and his brow furrowing. "It is, isn't it?"

Mauno gave him a look that veered from withering to pitying and back again. It was wasted, a little like

Jari. Even as he stared at Mauno, Jari's eyes rolled, and he began to pass out.

"A little something extra in the drink, just to make sure," Seb said with some satisfaction. "When he comes around, he won't remember what happened, which will be useful in more ways than one."

"You drugged him?" Ripper asked. "Why? He's supposed to be—"

"He seems like a good soldier," Milan interrupted, "and he's a strong enough guy. But he's loyal to this one—" he indicated Arsneth "—and that makes him dangerous right now. We need answers. We need them quick, and we need to move before we're beaten to it."

"Now wait," Ripper said, stepping between Arsneth and the two terrorists. "Listen, man, he came to us, right? He wants what we want."

"Does he really?" Milan snapped. "Look at him. He's a stupid boy playing games who got lucky. They all are. Your men have proved their worth and their dedication to the cause, more than once. These?" He gestured again to Arsneth and to the semicomatose Jari. "They're kids, rich ones playing at being daring, trying to piss off their parents and leaving a trail that puts us all in danger. It stops now, agreed?"

He eyeballed Ripper, who tensed. Behind him, Arsneth hoped for a moment that the big man would protect him, but this hope was strangled as he saw Ripper's shoulders slump, and he stepped to one side. Milan stepped into the space and came close to Arsneth, so close that he could smell the sour sweat and the beer on Milan's breath. When the terrorist spoke, it was softly and with a menace that made Arsneth's blood run cold.

"You're going to tell me the location of the bunker.

How to get there. And you're going to tell me where the other two members of your boy group are right now, so we can stop them talking."

Count Arsneth would have stood up to these men, would have gone down fighting if necessary, never betraying his secret.

Except that Mauno wasn't Count Arsneth. He was Mauno, a scared nineteen-year-old who was out of his depth and had no escape route. Except that, just maybe, if he told them what they asked, then he would be safe. If he showed them he could cooperate...

In a trembling voice he spilled the location, told them exactly how to get there by road and how to negotiate the woods. Told them that the Baron and Severance were there waiting for Jari and him. And even as he spoke, he knew that it would not save him.

"He's told you all he can. Let's just leave him and get on," Ripper said when Mauno had finished.

"Can't be done," Seb said flatly. "He's gutless. We got that out of him without even having to torture him. He would say anything to anyone. Can't risk that."

Mauno felt his stomach flip and his vision blacken at the edges. Hell, it felt like he might have a heart attack and spare them the effort of killing him.

"Don't worry, little boy, we'll make it quick," Milan murmured. Even as the words left his lips, a cheap switchblade knife, palmed as he spoke, found purchase beneath Mauno's rib cage and drove upward, twisting as it thrust. Mauno, taken by surprise, yielded easily to the blade and doubled over at the force of the blow, his eyes wide in shock. Blood bubbled to his lips as he chokingly tried to scream.

He collapsed onto the floor at Milan's feet as the

terrorist withdrew the blade and let it fall beside the body. He held out his hand and snapped his fingers. Seb passed him a heavy brass horse's head that had been standing on the mantel. Milan looked at it for a moment and shook his head.

"Shit furnishings and fittings for the price he must have paid," he muttered before bending and smashing the heavy object on Mauno's head three times, each blow cracking more of the skull and spreading hair, bone and brain across the carpet. Milan then stood and tossed the brass into the lap of the now comatose Jari.

"What was that about?" Ripper asked, stunned.

Milan shrugged. "The police will figure it out soon enough, but anything that will delay them will give us the time we need."

"But when Jari comes around—"

"He won't," Seb cut in. "He'll be dead in a few minutes. It will look like alcohol poisoning. At least for a while it will just look like he drank too much, argued with this idiot and then killed him in a drunken rage. By the time they figure it out, we'll have picked up what we want from the base, gotten rid of the other two kids and be well on our way."

Ripper shook his head sadly. "He was not a bad guy, this Arsneth. It's a pity, but…I guess the cause has to come first."

"It does. And we look after our own," Milan said coldly as he led them out of the apartment.

As they left, Seb made sure the door was secured so that no one could stumble on the corpses before strictly necessary. The shattered body of Mauno and the slowly dying Jari were left with only the writhing images on the porn channel to show any sign of life.

BOLAN TOOK OUT his anger by pushing himself harder when the sun came up. The beauty of the Colorado landscape around him did much to take his mind from the idiocy he had seen the night before.

As a soldier he was used to coming up against ideologies that were opposed to his own in the course of combat. That was fine; that was war. He was used to the venality of the criminal mind that would seek to oppress others for its own end. That was fine; there had always been men like that, always would be, and that was why he kept fighting. But the kind of irrational stupidity that he had seen, shapeless and formless, that could almost by accident threaten the innocent and unsuspecting? That was something that angered him.

He ran all day, breaking for water, food and rest at regular intervals. His anger spurred him on so that he covered fifty klicks more than on the day before. He used it to drive his body and tried not to think. That was the worst of it. On a mission he was working to an end. With the Abaddon Relix situation, he had no input; although if Kurtzman was right, it might not be that way for long.

When he settled for the night and made camp, it was still playing on his mind. He waited until he had eaten and was ready to bed down for the night before once more breaking the silence of the Colorado evening with the noise pollution offered by YouTube.

The clip of the bunker was missing. No amount of searches called it up. Most of the nonmusical Abaddon Relix material had also been taken down. He found references to the clip of the burning church, but that too had been removed.

Someone had wanted all evidence of the bunker and

of Abaddon Relix's connection with the Norwegian group to be wiped. The question was who?

Oddly he found this calmed his mind. Something out there was happening, and no way was it good. From frustration he found a sense of purpose flow through him.

It looked like Kurtzman was on the money again.

BOLAN AWAKENED SHORTLY after dawn. No sooner had he started to rekindle the ashes of his campfire than he was interrupted by his smartphone.

"Striker," Hal Brognola said when Bolan accepted the call. "Something's come up. Something urgent. Bear tells me you might have an inkling."

"Scandinavian climes, Hal? Good morning, by the way."

"Is it?" the big Fed growled. "I'm not so sure."

"I couldn't see a link to the U.S., Hal—how the hell can we justify getting involved in this one?"

Brognola chuckled. "Bear told me you weren't a fan of death metal or black metal."

"I wouldn't have put you down as one, either," Bolan replied.

"You've never met my nephew," Brognola said, sighing.

"A metal fan, obviously, but what has he got to do with this?"

"Short answer? I buy him stuff, and it's amazing how much you learn from product description. Florida has been a hotbed of this crap for years. Now they tend not to be the head-case political end of the spectrum down there. More the kind who have just watched too many gore films. But some of them get curious, and there have been tentative links to the far-right bands involved, which kind of links us to the far-right terrorist groups."

"That links it to the U.S.A., I'll buy that. But a bunch of rivetheads and survivalists in the swamps aren't a real threat."

"Of course not. But the Russians are. Word is that the Russian president has been ranting about how that bunker could have gone unrecovered for so long and how he wants that ordnance back where it belongs."

"With him, naturally—and we don't want that, do we?"

"We certainly don't, Striker, and we also don't want this to be official. I've had Stony Man GPS your cell phone, and there should be a chopper for you within an hour to bring you to Washington for a briefing. Maybe you should have taken that training schedule up to Alaska."

"Yeah, funny, Hal. Don't give up your day job."

SEVERANCE AND THE BARON were cold, tired and bored. There had been no word from the Count or from Jari— like everyone, they could never think of the Neanderthal by his band name, no matter what—and they had been expecting to get at least a call. Severance had tried to call them, but their cell phones were switched off. That could be for any reason.

In truth what had actually gone down had never occurred to them. As they sat and shivered in the bunker, raiding those sections of the kitchen that Jari hadn't trashed, running over possibilities between themselves, they figured that the silence was due to security and that the first they would see of their bandmates was when they walked through the bunker doors with the Norwegians.

In between this speculation they moaned at length about how everything else in the bunker seemed to be working except the heating system. Any attempt to get it turned on did nothing more than set the air conditioner to chill the area even more. So they huddled in their blankets, drinking and waiting, hoping that the time would pass quickly and that they would be greeted as heroes by the Count, Jari and the Norwegians.

It didn't quite go as planned.

Thirty-six hours after they had entered the bunker to guard it, they were awakened from a stupor by the signal that the entrance had been breached. They were sleeping in what had been the control room—a small office with a bank of monitors, only some of which were working, showing the interior of the bunker. Those connected to the outside cameras were blank, the weather having long since eroded their efficiency.

The signal was a regular pulse, accompanied by a flashing red light on the dash. Severance pulled himself to his feet, groaning, and shook the Baron, who was a touch more testy as he awoke.

"They're here," Severance muttered.

"Shit. I feel like shit," the Baron remarked with a tenuous grip on comprehension. "You sure it's them?"

Severance nodded, wishing as he did that he hadn't. "They used the right codes."

The Baron was on the verge of commenting that they could have read them from the scratch marks in the pad—which was what he had done—but refrained as he remembered how long it had taken him to actually locate them—and even then by chance.

"Come on," Severance continued. "Kitchen. Coffee. They'll need warming. We need it anyway."

The two youths made their way to the kitchen area and were in the middle of brewing coffee when Milan, Seb and Ripper entered.

The Baron tried to look past them, expecting to see the Count and Jari, and the other members of Asmodeus.

"Ripper, who are these dudes?" he asked thickly, indicating the short-haired terrorists.

"Where's Mauno?" Severance added, more to the point. He didn't have a good feeling about this, though he doubted that his fears had penetrated his companion's denser brain at this point.

"The Count is dead," Ripper replied in a monotone. "So is Jari. The rest of my band won't be coming. This is more serious than that."

Severance said slowly, "What could be more serious? What do you mean Mauno and Jari are dead? What's been going on?"

"A lot," Ripper said as flatly as before.

Severance and the Baron stood facing the three men in silence for a moment, not knowing what to say. Ripper had offered them no explanation; they didn't know what to think.

"What's going to happen?" Severance asked quietly.

"I think you know, my friend," Milan said, speaking for the first time. "What you have found will be invaluable in furthering our cause. Our good friends in Norway know this, which is why they forged these links."

"Why is only Ripper here, then? And how did Mauno and Jari die?" the Baron persisted. "Do we have enemies we need to guard against?"

Severance looked at his friend. Funny, he had always looked at the Baron as a pain in the ass, but now he realized that the drummer was the only friend he had in the room. The only friend he had in the world, now that Mauno and Jari were gone.

"It's too late to guard against them, Arvo," he murmured. "They're already here."

"You're a bright boy," Milan commented. "Pity your friend had a big mouth. He was a liability. He put you all in the firing line. Maybe you could have been educated and trained, like Ripper's men."

"Who says we can't be?" Severance said desperately.

"Me," Milan replied simply. "It's too late. But what you have here will be removed and put to good use before anyone else can get to it. Letting the world know by YouTube was stupid. That kind of idiocy can't be justified."

Severance felt his bowels turn to jelly as Milan added a final statement.

"It'll be quick."

CHAPTER FOUR

The chopper picked up Bolan from the Colorado Desert, then dropped him in D.C. A waiting unmarked sedan whisked him to the Mall for a meeting with a grim-faced Brognola and Aaron Kurtzman via a conference call on a scrambled line.

After the briefing Bolan had hitched a ride to Bremen with a U.S. troop transport. From there another U.S. service flight had brought him to Oslo on a routine NATO business mission. One thing was for sure. The continued U.S. military presence—even though the Cold War was long dead and buried—was a useful cover for him in hopping around Europe.

The Norges Statsbaner train had taken him from Oslo Airport to Trondheim, this water-surrounded city, the fourth most populated in Norway. Bolan got off the train and felt invigorated by the cold air blowing on his face. After the central heating of the train and the flight that had preceded it, he was glad to feel something sharp on his skin. It refreshed him and reminded him that he was alive.

The hotel he had been booked into was only a short walk from the station, and he took the opportunity to get some air and a feel for the city as he made the journey on foot.

The buildings were a mix of old and new—some

clean lines and little exterior decoration with a functionalism that made it of less interest to the tourist than Oslo; plus the city was quieter than Oslo. Maybe that was why the black metal activists preferred to live here rather than the capital.

Even going about their everyday business and keeping their heads down, anyone who looked like the guys Bolan had seen in the videos would be noticeable. Long-haired metal fans were a minority; even without their face paint, these guys would have the tattoos and piercings that would set them apart.

As Bolan checked in and went up to his room, settling in, he went over the briefing he had received before leaving the States.

"IT'S STRANGE HOW I suddenly became an expert because of tastes that got me laughed at the rest of the time," Kurtzman had remarked. "Black metal is a strange beast, Striker. For such a macho and posturing music, its protagonists can be surprisingly mild mannered. Either because they're kids compensating for adolescent feelings of inferiority, or because they realize all their aggressive tendencies through their chosen art form—"

"Like Polynesian traditional theater or Japanese Noh theater," Bolan interjected.

"Hey, you do read some of those books I leave in your quarters," Kurtzman commented.

"It's interesting how people work out their aggressions," Bolan said. "If more people did that, there would be a whole lot less work for me to do."

"You're not about to become redundant," Brognola growled, cutting across the conversation. "Can we stick to the point?"

"Of course," Kurtzman said. "My point, in the middle of that discourse, was that the minority of people in these bands—and it's primarily a male preserve, as you might expect—are committed or obsessive enough to follow through on their beliefs, to take action to realize the aims they profess. But when they do, they can be incredibly destructive."

"I saw the clip of the burning church," Bolan commented, keeping the disgust out of his voice. "It's been a while since they were doing that."

"Yes, but sadly that's not the only instance in recent times. However distasteful we find that, though, it's not the real problem. Since the pendulum started to swing right in Eastern Europe, the bands and followers who take their views seriously have found a lot of people who are willing to help them realize their fantasies and in turn enlist their help."

"What do the locals have to say about this?" Bolan asked, turning to Brognola.

"The police in Trondheim are attributing the murder to the dead guitarist, who apparently died from acute alcohol poisoning."

"If he could kill someone with the force and direction indicated by the medical report you emailed to me, then he can't have been that drunk when he did it. Why keep on drinking? Why not try to get away?"

"Indeed," Kurtzman said with a sardonic edge. "Particularly as an inventory of the apartment doesn't seem to indicate there was enough booze there to actually induce the condition. Let alone account for the evidence that at least two other people were there around the estimated time of death."

"So the locals are happy to tie it up regardless of any evidence to the contrary. Nice."

"They're embarrassed about the churches, and it took a long time to recover from the damage the black metal deaths caused back in the nineties."

"There were links to far-right groups in Trondheim?" Bolan queried.

"Only after that nut-job metalhead—what's his name—was banged up," Aaron Kurtzman replied. "And the Norwegian security services have no evidence of any real links between far-right groups and the bands beyond a few messages of support between the two on websites. There are no documented meetings between the factions, and no communications that can be traced."

"That says more about the Norwegian security services than anything else," Bolan remarked.

"You were never the most diplomatic of men, Striker," Brognola murmured, "but I can't fault your logic. These rogue groups get smarter all the time."

Bolan sat in silence for a moment, then said, "I guess there's no point in relying on any local liaison to fill me in. On the other hand, there's no one to get in my way, and I won't be interfering with any official lines of inquiry, as there aren't any. A clear field…it could be a hell of a lot worse."

BOLAN WENT OVER this intel to date as he showered and changed before hitting the streets. He had brought with him currencies for both Norway and Finland. The trail began here in Trondheim, but he figured that it would rapidly take him across the border to the lost bunker. The last thing he wanted was to waste time on logistics.

He carried his favored Beretta 93R handgun in an underarm holster, and a micro Uzi SMG clipped to the belt of his blacksuit. Some spare magazines and a couple grenades—smoke and fragmentation—completed his immediate armory, though he had some in reserve in his case. The convenience of using USAF transport was that he could ferry ordnance across borders with no problems.

Stashing his case, he left the hotel, the blacksuit covered by a winter jacket and baggy ski pants, his combat boots not appearing out of place in this cold environment.

Searches by various intelligence services—those of the U.S. and Finland, plus Stony Man's own resources—had yielded no background on the band Asmodeus, whose members had been at the root of the church burning, and who were known contacts for the dead Finns.

The only proof of their existence entailed email addresses and a website domain—paid for with a credit card that was then paid off in cash and billed to a P.O. Box under the name of a man who had been dead for seven years. Even their music and related videos had no material presence, bought solely on download. Their few local shows seemed to be organized by equally shadowy men under aliases that disintegrated under close examination.

Whoever they were, these ghosts were adept at covering their tracks. In their everyday lives they would be unable to hide their allegiance to a certain type of music because of their looks but would probably pay lip service to a less controversial form of the music. But they had to rehearse somewhere. Sure they would be using other names, but because of the nature of what they played, they would want some privacy.

This was the Achilles' heel that the Stony Man intel team needed. It was a relatively simple task for them to isolate all rehearsal spaces in Trondheim, or other locales that were hired and used for such a purpose, and whittle down the possibilities.

All the conventional rehearsal spots for musicians could be dismissed out of hand. These would be used by a number of bands, of varying types, and so would be too open for such a necessarily secretive group.

Of the warehouses and spaces remaining, there were eight: two of them were along the dock, and were in areas that were well populated during the working day but deserted at night. The other six were within the city itself, and could hardly be said to be private or isolated at any time.

Bolan opted to check out the isolated venues first. If either of the dockside warehouses were used by Asmodeus, then night would be the best time to scout them out. The band would not wish to be seen by day. As it was now early afternoon, it gave Bolan time to navigate the city and check out the businesses surrounding these prime targets. He was pretty sure that one of the two dock locations would be his objective, but it would be politic to double check.

The first site was not one warehouse but a collection of them. The first two businesses were closed, but a few discreet questions in adjoining shops elicited the information that one warehouse was used by a progressive rock band that spent entire weekends working on complex arrangements that—per the bartender who sold them beer during their breaks—had so far never seen the light of a stage.

A second warehouse in this segment was used by a traditional folk group who threw the space open on weekends for dances and cultural events celebrating Norwegian folk traditions.

The soldier found that the next space was used by a young punk band that was bankrolled by one member's father—a wealthy lawyer who would do anything to keep his son off the street and out of trouble. That came straight from the lawyer himself, who Bolan encountered helping the band lug its gear into the warehouse.

That left three spaces. In two he found a caretaker—one lugubrious, but the other glad of the chance to stop and talk and let go his mop—from whom Bolan learned that one spot was used by a Norwegian beat group from the sixties who got back together as they hit retirement and sought a hobby, using the space for themselves and also for any musical endeavors of their children and grandchildren. The other was used by a covers band that was working in Denmark for a month, and tended to use the space in concentrated periods to work up an ever-changing set between engagements.

By the time Bolan reached the last space, he felt he knew more about the musical habits of the Norwegians than he really wanted to. He had drawn a blank, but in a sense that was exactly what he wanted. The two locations he would scout tonight were, he was sure, where he would find his prey.

The group he found working in the last space taught him something more about this country of seeming opposites. They were a radical Socialist rock group and theater company, with lyrics that—from his basic knowledge of the language—were clearly enunciated and were about the inequality of capitalism and the need for redistribution of wealth within a free state. With mime, which he could well have done without.

Nonetheless, as he left them to their earnest endeavors, he was reminded that this was a land where the people dealt in extreme views. When they had been invaded by the Nazis during WWII, many had fled to fight in the U.K. for the exiled Norwegian king. Others had formed a resistance at home. And yet around fifteen thousand of the population in this small country had chosen to join the Nazi armed forces, many of them opting for the Waffen-SS, the most feared and vicious of units, as well as the most loyal to the Nazi ideal.

As Bolan made his way down to the docks, night fell with the suddenness common to Scandinavia. In a few hours, he had narrowed possibilities to two, only about fifteen minutes apart. He mentally tossed a coin to decide which one to check first, as one was just as viable as the other. There were no clues to give him any indication otherwise.

The Executioner hurried through the deserted dock area, the cranes and warehouses now empty, apart from a few late workers loading trucks that would hit the highway for all-night drives to their destinations. Bolan kept to the shadows so that the few workers heading to their homes did not see him as they passed. There was plenty of cover, and the workers were intent on their own journey, so it was easy for him to keep hidden.

When Bolan reached the location of the chosen warehouse, he knew he had been directed to the wrong place before he was even within close proximity.

Two cars were drawn up outside the warehouse,

and one of the large gated doors was hanging open, letting the noise from within filter out into the quiet evening. As he watched from the cover of an adjoining building, a third car roared along the dockside, pulling up with an exaggerated squeal of brakes and a hand-brake turn that was designed to impress the squeal-ing girls, clad in leather and lace, who spilled out of the battered vehicle, followed by two young men in denim and leather, both clutching a number of liquor bottles. They had long hair, sure, but they were a little more colorful—as were their women—than the men he sought. They were certainly less than discreet.

At a distance he followed them. They yelled greet-ings as they entered the warehouse, and Bolan could see that they had arrived in the middle of a full-scale party. There were around twenty people inside, in-cluding three men on a raised dais made from pallets. Two of them wielded guitar and bass, while the third sat behind a drum kit that dwarfed him. They pounded out a form of metal that was far more bluesy and—to Bolan's ears—more melodic that the black metal he was seeking.

As the new arrivals were greeted by those already drunk and partying, and the band broke off to greet them before falling into their loose groove once again, Bolan withdrew into the shadows.

Whatever recreational chemicals may be added to the alcohol, and whatever licentious activity may take place as a result, they were a relatively innocent group. The soldier could see why they had chosen such a place: isolated, with no prying neighbors to com-plain, they could celebrate all night and be as rowdy as they liked without fear of their party being broken up by the law.

It had to be the last location then. If not, he was back where he had started with no leads at all and time running out.

Moving with speed—but not so fast that he could not recon his surroundings as he moved across the dock area—Bolan reached the final location before the ringing in his ears from the last site had died away.

At first glance it seemed that Stony Man's intel was dead wrong. The warehouse front was as dark and deserted as any others at that time of night. Moving closer, Bolan could see little sign of life.

This was either not the location or he was too late and Asmodeus—and whoever they were allied to— had already moved toward their objective. Given the lack of intel he was working with, the soldier hoped not. The plan was to catch up with them and tail them to the location of the bunker before taking them down.

He would have to watch and wait tonight.

Fortune favored the stubborn as well as the brave Bolan decided, when, after hunkering down for half an hour and feeling as if his haunches would freeze, a black truck approached the warehouse and slowed to a stop. The windows were dark, obscuring how many people were inside. The engine was killed, and the vehicle sat waiting.

Bolan felt encouraged, more so when a second black truck pulled up less than five minutes later. As it drew near, the first truck chugged to life, its headlights illuminating the front of the warehouse.

The driver's door of the second truck opened as the engine died, and a heavily muscled man in black—with a flowing ebony mane and piercings that glinted in the light of the first truck's lights—got out. He walked across to the warehouse and unlocked the gated door with keys from a large bunch at his belt. He beckoned to the shrouded inhabitants of the first truck as two men spilled from his vehicle and jogged to the open warehouse door. They were of a similar appearance.

The other engine was shut off, and three men joined them from the first truck: a long haired man in black and two men with cropped hair. Bolan could almost smell the mercenary on them, even at a distance.

It looked like Lady Luck was with him, after all.

CHAPTER FIVE

The six men gathered in the warehouse. One central line of fluorescent lighting illuminated what had once been the central aisle, and was now a walkway to the stage area that the band members had created in the middle of the warehouse. It stood silent and brooding, the stacks of amplifiers and the large drum kit flanked by instruments propped on stands, leads plugged in and ready to go. It looked exactly like a set before the beginning of a gig, which was just how the band liked it. On either side of the stage area were flight cases, and boxes that held pyro and effects for the show. Crates for shipping amps stood behind those, fading into the shadows of the unlit warehouse areas.

Most of the building was empty, devoid of anything approaching cover for Bolan as he approached the open door and slipped into the dark interior. He had removed his outer clothing, despite the intense cold, and the blacksuit underneath allowed him to blend in to the dark with ease. He could only safely stay at the periphery, however. The lack of cover precluded a closer approach until he could recon the rest of the warehouse space. Provided, of course, that his prey stayed where it was and gave him that precious time.

Right now he wished that he had packed some of the surveillance equipment that Stony Man usually provided: a long-range mic would have solved this problem easily. Those were the breaks; he would have to do this the hard way.

While this ran through his mind, he was moving along the wall of the warehouse, to his left, seeking darker patches away from the central light where he could gain ground toward a cluster of packing crates that would allow him to close in.

The fact that the band had chosen such a large space and seemingly used so little of it was initially baffling, until Bolan remembered the last warehouse: private parties would be easy here for black metallers who wanted their musical preferences to remain secret.

Not just musical preferences. The privacy this location afforded could be very convenient for keeping political and terrorist activities under wraps.

By now the soldier had made his way to the cover of the stacked crates and could hear what the six men in the center were discussing in hushed tones.

RIPPER WAS THE BAND LEADER by virtue of having the strongest convictions and the most overwhelming personality. Milan and Seb had identified that about him from the beginning and so had made him their focus. But now that they knew the location of the bunker, they were unwilling to risk their own men until the ordnance had been safely removed.

The site had been secured, and they needed transportation. They were aware that the local police were treating Arsneth's murder as a closed case with the corpse of Jari providing a convenient scapegoat. But it was only a matter of time before someone questioned the scenario, and they did not want to bring their trained personnel into such a situation until they were ready to put their main plan into action.

This was just the preliminary stage. They might have been able to take any evidence of the bunker that could identify its location off the internet, but there had been enough time for interested parties to start assembling clues.

They needed cannon fodder, and they needed it now. Ripper's bandmates were known only by their assumed band names: Hellhammer, Visigoth and Emperor Hades. That was all they needed; as Seb and Milan stood in front of the stage and addressed them, they saw reflected back four dour and intense faces, serious about their task.

And their task this night was to learn about the weapons they may need if they encountered resistance at the bunker. Briefly Seb outlined the location they were headed to, and the formation they would take: two trucks, three men each truck, ordnance for a firefight if necessary and space to pack the mother lode, with Seb and Milan riding shotgun to each truck driver.

"We may not be alone," Ripper continued, walking over to the crate stack where Bolan had hidden himself. "Others may be on the trail. We are sure that Arsneth did not tell anyone else the exact location, but it may be that interested parties have worked out the map reference. We must be prepared. I know that you have explosives and small arms experience, and that some of you are used to hunting rifles. As far as I'm aware, despite shipping and storing these babies for us, you've never used them. Time to learn."

He cracked open a crate, pushing back the top to reveal a cache of Heckler & Koch MP5s, each wrapped in oiled cloth. He took one out and uncovered it, then tossed it to Emperor Hades, who caught it without an eyelid flickering.

Seb grinned at Milan; this should be simple.

BOLAN HELD HIS BREATH as the mercenary turned and walked toward the stack. Bolan had the micro Uzi SMG in hand—spray'n'pray may be his best bet if discovered at such close range, but he would rather not fire at all…yet.

He almost sighed with relief when the merc picked a crate at the front of the stack and then turned away. One of the musicians caught the weapon thrown at him and examined it while the leader returned to the crate and took another out, repeating the process.

With as much stealth as he could muster, Bolan drew back into the shadows, quickening his pace as he made his way toward the exit. He had heard enough to know their plans, and also that he had time to execute some of his own while the mercenaries ran through some basic weapons training for their troops.

Outside in the cold air with his breath frosting, Bolan located his thick coat and put it back on. He was going to be outside for a while, and he couldn't afford to slow down due to the temperature. He intended to follow the trucks and required a vehicle of his own. He had some ideas about that, but first he needed a way of tracking the vehicles if he lost visual contact.

His lack of surveillance equipment was an oversight that he couldn't let happen again, but in the meantime, he had the ingenuity to improvise. He had his smartphone on him, and that was fitted with a GPS tracker in addition to the one that came standard to the phone.

Keeping in the shadows with one eye on the open doorway of the warehouse, the soldier took the back off his phone and located the tracker where it had been fitted under the cover. He replaced the cover and hit a speed-dial number.

"Bear, don't speak. I've taken my personal tracker out of my phone and am placing it on a target vehicle. That one I want followed in case I lose it. I'll be on the network tracker."

"I'll adjust accordingly," Kurtzman replied simply before disconnecting. It was the least Bolan had heard him say for a long, long time, and despite the situation, it brought a smile to his face as he moved forward across the open space between his cover and the two vehicles.

He chose the one nearest him, the vehicle by the doorway providing him with some cover as he slid underneath the chassis and secured the tracker in a gap the bodywork gave him behind the rear wheel well. He rolled out, got to his feet and made his way back into the cover of the dark and silence.

The first part of his task was complete. Now for the second.

MILAN HELD UP A HAND to stop Seb as he was about to run through the action of the MP5.

"If we're going to run some targets, then we need to make sure we're not overheard."

"Man, we've played sets where we set off the full pyro and nobody cares. There's a trash band that has a warehouse down the block who have all-night parties with the doors open, and no one pays it any attention. Who will hear?" Ripper complained.

Milan smiled coldly. "You'd be surprised at how

gunfire can travel and how it can catch the ear when other things get ignored. It's always best to take precautions. Wait…"

The mercenary made his way from the pool of light and across the darkened floor toward the warehouse gateway. When he reached it, some instinct gave him pause. Cautiously he stepped out into the dark night, scanning the locale. Initially he could hear nothing, only the distant sounds of music and traffic carried on the freezing night air from the edge of the dock. There was an undertone to it that seemed out of place—a rustling of shale, footsteps on damp concrete?

It was then that he saw him: in the far distance, moving around the side of a warehouse, caught for a fraction of a second in moonlight that was bright enough in contrast to the dark shadows to highlight his figure.

He was moving in the opposite direction to where Milan stood, and the merc was pretty sure that no one had been closer, but nonetheless…

He closed the door, locked it and strode back to the center of the warehouse.

"Let's speed this up. The sooner we're gone, the better."

BOLAN APPROACHED THE TWO CARS outside the partying warehouse. Light and noise spilled out, with the occasional shadow cast as someone reeled close to the entrance. Voices screamed and yelled to make themselves heard, blending in with the noise of the band as they riffed endlessly on one chord, jamming loosely and covering any noise Bolan could make. If anyone came out while he was claiming one of the vehicles, he would have to disable him, but with the minimum of harm.

To look at, the two vehicles were suitably undistinguished: at least five years old, painted in drab colors and with no distinguishing marks. They both looked like they had been driven hard and recklessly, which wasn't good. Bolan was hoping for something reliable.

He tried the driver's side door of both. One had been left unlocked, and in the interest of saving time, he opted for that vehicle, as there seemed little to choose between them.

Hot-wiring a car—even in the days of sophisticated locking systems and computerized engine control that sometimes didn't require a key—was still a simple task for the soldier, and in a matter of seconds he had the engine purring into life. Luck was with him, as it turned over nicely and was in better condition than the bodywork had led him to believe. The tank was three-quarters full, which was a bonus. If his luck held, then he would be able to keep on the enemy's tail until they needed to refuel without losing ground.

He slipped the car into gear and pulled slowly away from the warehouse, heading back down the dock to a spot where he could keep his prey under surveillance.

THE MERCENARIES HAD completed their run-through of basic SMG training in double-quick time. The Norwegian band members were fast learners, and their prior knowledge of some armament was a bonus. Setting up targets, the mercenaries were soon satisfied that the four black metallers were proficient enough to hit a target well enough to stop it.

Milan divided up a crate of MP5s and spare magazines so that each man had a second SMG and enough ammunition to stop a division, let alone the handful of men that he was expecting at worst. He hadn't mentioned what he had seen to the others, but his fellow merc knew there was something wrong and took him to one side.

"It might have been nothing. I saw a man nearby. He was in the shadows, moving away from us. But my gut—"

"Is something I trust," Seb interrupted. "Was he here?"

Milan shrugged. "I doubt it. But the sooner we move, the less risk. And watch those shadows when we leave."

Seb nodded and joined the four musicians as they took their weapons to the trucks, splitting into pairs. Milan killed the light, shut the warehouse door and locked it. As he turned back to the trucks, where he would join Ripper and Hellhammer, he sniffed the air like a dog. There was something there, he was sure. But what?

"Is everything okay?" Ripper queried as Milan climbed into the truck.

"Maybe. Let's roll—but slow."

Ripper grinned. "You don't want us to draw attention to ourselves?"

"Something like that."

BOLAN HAD PARKED the car between two warehouses, looking out on the main road that led to the dock entrance. There was only the one way in and out of the complex, so the enemy would have to pass him. He sat in darkness, only the red lights on the dash illuminating the interior of the vehicle, the headlights extinguished.

He was jolted from his resting state to full awareness as one of the trucks pulled past the recess in which he was parked. The soldier prepared to turn the ignition and follow after a moment or two, but the second truck didn't show up.

He cursed. It was an obvious precaution, and he should have expected it. Despite that, the tension still gnawed at him as he waited. Should he follow the first truck and risk discovery, even though the second truck may not move for some time?

He knew from what he had heard that the mercs were in a hurry. Their nerves would be cracking right now, and he figured that they were likely to move the second truck sooner rather than later.

RIPPER GAVE MILAN a puzzled look as the mercenary directed him to turn off the wide road and head down the narrow gap between two warehouses. The truck behind moved past them. In his side mirror Ripper saw Hades stare at them as he passed, with the same puzzled stare.

"Seb understands. Trust me," Milan said.

"I don't get it. We have to leave the same way as them," Ripper muttered.

"Turn the lights out and take it slow," Milan said, ignoring him. He fingered the MP5 in his grasp. Maybe he would need it.

"I can't go any slower than this," Ripper cautioned as the truck moved at a crawl.

"Suits me fine. We can catch up with them," Milan murmured, his eyes narrowing in the dim light.

There was a maze of narrow roads between the warehouses that populated the docks. They were built in rough squares, so that each had some loading and unloading space to the front, with the narrow spaces between being purely for access. That made them hard to negotiate, and even harder to recon from within a moving vehicle.

"Got you," Milan whispered to himself as they passed the far end of the narrow passage where Bolan had parked. He indicated to Ripper to back up.

"Who the hell is that?" Ripper asked as he put the truck into Reverse.

"Don't know, don't care, won't ask," Milan said softly. "Turn down there and hit full beam," he added, racking the SMG. "Let's flush him out."

BOLAN CURSED WHEN he saw movement in the rearview mirror. It was a momentary darkening of an already black space, but it was enough to make him realize what the second truck was doing.

He had been certain that he had not been seen. Maybe his luck wasn't as good as he'd thought.

Bolan opened the door, slipping out and letting it fall back so that it appeared to be closed. He moved in front of the vehicle, edging toward the wide ribbon of road. If nothing else, he was pretty sure that would now be secure.

He edged around so that he could see down the narrow alley as the black shape passed back again. The soldier racked the micro Uzi SMG.

Any moment now…

CHAPTER SIX

The night was rent by the sharp and deafening chatter of SMG fire as the headlights of the truck illuminated the car while Milan—having slid out of his seat and resting the barrel of his weapon on the doorsill to steady it—sprayed an arc that spewed glass and acrylic paint chips across the ground and the backseat of the vehicle.

As he ceased fire, the silence was oppressive, closing in suddenly as the SMG fire echoed swiftly away. Ripper and Hellhammer were transfixed in the truck, staring at the damage inflicted on the sedan.

"What the hell..." Milan left the cover of the door and moved forward quickly, MP5 held at waist level. He peered into the interior of the vehicle, gun barrel up and ready. He had expected to see his enemy, incapacitated if not dead. Instead there was just empty space.

He turned angrily as he heard Ripper laugh nervously.

"An empty car, man. No big deal."

"Then what is it doing here? Why—"

"Hey, it doesn't matter. Now come on, let's get going before they get too far ahead."

Milan gestured to the giant to be quiet, angrily scoping the ground in front of him. He couldn't see anything, but he just knew that the car's driver was out there. Waiting...

BOLAN PULLED BACK as the lights of the truck winked on brighter and heard rather than saw the barrage of fire. His gaze narrowed at the thought of being detected that easily.

It was no longer safe to be in the area. Gunfire in the open would attract attention, and he didn't want to have to answer awkward questions and get tied up in red tape. One of the trucks was headed for the bunker. If it was the one he had fitted the tracker to, then things were good. If not, he needed to pick up the trail as soon as possible.

He heard the exchange between the Norwegian and the merc, and could picture their relative positions. He had seen two men in the front of the truck that had passed him. That meant one, maybe two more at most beside the pair he had heard.

Bolan stepped out across the line of the alley, snapping off three short bursts of fire before stepping back.

MILAN WAS DISTRACTED for one full second, yet it was enough. He knew that the enemy was close, but when he had heard Hellhammer mutter to Ripper, he turned back to silence him. It was an instinctive move and an error.

The merc's head was turned away when Bolan appeared behind him. Milan had time to register Ripper's expression, but no more, before the first short burst stitched him across the ribs and spine. By the time the second and third bursts had shattered the truck's headlights and damaged the fender and open door, he was out of the game.

The return fire had panicked the two musicians. Hellhammer was yelling at Ripper to get the truck in gear and out of there. In his panicked state, the driver was grinding the gears, the truck jolting forward with a sickening lurch and crunching into the rear fender of the car before hitting Reverse and screeching backward with rubber burning smoke on the concrete.

Bolan moved down the alley, hurrying past the car and the prone mercenary, needing only the most cursory of glances to see that he was no threat. He snapped off another burst at the dark shape that the truck had become as it reversed and skidded sideways. He wanted to take out the windshield, maybe take down the driver. A burst of glass signaled that he had taken out the side window on the driver's door, but the Norwegian must have ducked and got lucky as the truck continued on, skidding wildly across the confined space and smacking into the warehouse on each side, the front fender screeching and buckling under the impact.

The vehicle slowed, the agonizing sound of scraping metal betraying that the wheel well had closed in on at least one of the front wheels. But still it moved forward. The soldier could come out behind it and take out the tires, or he could go for a frontal assault, if he was fast enough.

He gambled that he was. Running back past the now useless car, he came out onto the main ribbon of concrete at the dock and ran hard. In his mind's eye he could see the layout of the warehouses and the narrow alleys between the open squares as they were clustered.

The mercs were headed for the sole exit, and there was only one way they could get there. If Bolan was quick enough, he could get there before the enemy.

He cursed as he ran full-out into a straggling group of drunk and stoned metalheads who had wandered from their warehouse, attracted by the noise of the firefight. They were spread over the road, and Bolan would have to take evasive action to avoid running into them. That was rendered unnecessary when one of the women realized through her stupor that he was carrying a gun and screamed in fear. It had the effect of making them scatter, some of the young men grabbing women and pulling them away, sheltering them with their bodies.

The Executioner was past them, cutting across and down an unlit passage, when he heard an angry voice raised above the confusion. The owner of the car he had hot-wired had discovered its final resting place.

No time to worry about that now. The soldier had cut across an angle in the wide road as it took a curve at the dock and was now at a point where the crippled truck would have to come out if it was to head for the dock entrance.

In the gloom of the overhanging warehouse walls, Bolan could hear rather than see his prey as it approached. He could also hear distant sirens. One of the partygoers obviously had had sense enough to use his or her cell phone. He took a moment to reload his Uzi SMG.

It was time to bring this to a close, Bolan decided. As the dark shape of the truck closed on him, the shrieking of metal setting his teeth on edge, he aimed low and with two short bursts took out the front tires. Whatever control the driver had over the damaged vehicle was gone now, and it swerved wildly within the narrow gap, cannoning off the walls with showers of sparks where metal scraped concrete and more metal.

Bolan wanted to advance and finish the confrontation quickly, aware of the rapidly closing authorities, but he was stymied by the erratic progress of the truck. He didn't want to risk being caught and pinned in a confined area.

The truck slewed to a halt, sliding around so that it became jammed at an angle between the two walls of the alley. It prevented anyone from exiting the back doors as they were constrained by one wall, but it did leave Bolan on the wrong side of one cab door if a person chose to run.

The soldier snapped off another burst, shattering the window of the driver's door. He had wanted to take alive the men inside, so that he could question them, but circumstances altered that plan.

He closed in on the truck, micro Uzi SMG held at shoulder level.

"Out. Now. Facedown," he yelled in English, which was one of the main languages of the nation.

In the relative silence, now that the engine had coughed and died, he could hear moaning from within the truck. There was no faking the sounds he heard. The impact of the crash and the results of his gunfire had disabled the threat within.

Weapon still leveled, he yanked open the driver's door and stepped back quickly as the driver's unconscious body spilled out onto the ground. He was covered in blood from wounds that were superficial and caused by glass. Somehow the burst of gunfire had miraculously missed his head and torso, but he was still out of the game.

Stepping over the musician and vaulting into the cab, Bolan found a figure lying across the back of the vehicle. He was the only other person in the truck.

Bolan had a slim penlight in one of the slit pockets of the blacksuit, and with its aid he could see that the long-haired man lay at an odd angle, his arm twisted beneath him where the impact had dislocated his shoulder. His eyes were half-closed, unfocused.

There was no way he could get any intel from this man, either, not in the time Bolan would have. He pushed at the far side door; it was jammed solid. No chance of making an escape into the shadows then. He would have to risk the open road.

As the Executioner scrambled out of the truck, he was aware of approaching footsteps and turned to find some of the young men from the warehouse party, armed with wooden pallet stakes and chains. They stood at the head of the alley. Bolan could see that they had taken the women away from the area of conflict before arming themselves and, despite their obvious nerves, were sticking together.

He had to admire their courage, which he wouldn't have expected, but there was no time for explanations or niceties.

"You speak English, right?" he barked as he leveled his weapon at them. "If I set this on rapid fire, you all go down before you take two steps. You back off, and you're fine."

He waited, muscles tense and straining to move as he heard the sirens grow nearer. The young men did not answer him; glances among them betrayed their fear.

Bolan stepped forward slowly, allowing them time to react. For a moment he thought he would have to fire a warning burst to convince them, but as he got closer, they melted away, backing off.

"Wise move, guys. They're alive back there. Get the police to ask them about Count Arsneth."

Moving backward so that he could keep his face to them, the soldier moved down the road. He was heading toward the sirens, but he was banking on his words having an effect on the group.

Curiosity, bewilderment and the subconscious desire not to risk death held sway. The group of young metalheads moved toward the truck.

With relief that he hadn't needed any more punitive measures, Bolan turned and ran, angling toward the next narrow alley leading onto the main drag. His progress was not being watched, and the authorities were not yet within sight. With luck—something that had treated him erratically this night—he could melt into the dark and effect an escape.

It was risky trying to direct the police to Arsneth's real murderer but inevitable. He was sure that once the authorities found the corpse of the merc Bolan had taken down, then the dead guy's true identity would open up a whole can of worms.

Time was getting tighter.

BOLAN MADE IT BACK to his hotel room without further incident. The gates to the docks had been manned by the authorities on their arrival, but the rest of the perimeter fence had been ignored. Weaving his way through the dark side roads until he was as far from the gates as he could get, he had easily scaled the fence. There was a risk it was wired to set off an alarm, but the area was so quiet that he could take that chance. Police patrols had not spread out, allowing the soldier time to blend into the town without being observed.

Now he showered. There was little point in hurrying. He had no vehicle and would have to wait until morning before hiring a car. If the truck that had escaped carried the GPS, then Kurtzman would be on it. If not, Bolan was back to where he had started.

That could get complicated, and he might have to pull some strings. If he was going to get necessary rest before starting the next phase, then he needed to know. Once out of the shower, he hit a speed-dial number on his smartphone.

"Striker, you're in Trondheim, and your tracker isn't. What went wrong?"

Bolan filled him in on the evening's events. Bolan was already relieved, as Kurtzman's first words had determined Bolan's course of action.

A course that would be made easier by the fact that the target truck was headed for Oslo, and not on the main highway to the north and the Finnish border. Why? That was the question. It could be that the enemy knew they had suffered casualties and sought additional men for the raid on the bunker. If so, that might give the soldier a lead. He asked Kurtzman to send him any intel on far-right groups and black metal bands within the city, particularly those with some link to Count Arsneth's band.

It was a place to start. As Bolan settled to the complete blackout that was sleep, a fleeting thought crossed his mind: if the band needed that much manpower, then who were they expecting to meet on the way?

IT WAS EARLY MORNING when the black truck hit Oslo. The three men inside had made the journey in silence. No one in the second truck was answering cell phone calls, and the guys in the black truck had received no communication as to why.

Seb knew that Milan had been right. Someone had been spying on them, and whomever it was had in some way stopped the truck. Milan was good. Whoever had taken him out had to be a professional. It was imperative that they pick up more men.

It was only when they pulled up at a neat and tidy suburban house on the outskirts of the city that Seb finally spoke.

"We need another truck. Men, too. You need to know that, if they have stopped Milan and your bandmates, then they are good. You must be ready to fight."

Visigoth sniffed hard. "Maybe they will not be at the bunker. Maybe they need to follow us to find it."

Seb nodded. "That would make sense. In which case, we have lost them for now. At least we will be prepared."

The three men got out of the truck and walked across the deserted street to the front of the house. They were expected; the door opened before they were halfway up the drive. They were greeted by a shaved-headed man in black, with Celtic tattoos showing beneath his black T-shirt.

"Good. You are here. There's something you need to see," he said without preamble.

Seb realized what he meant when he saw the news channel tuned to on the flat-screen TV.

BOLAN SLEPT FOR a few hours, then rose and checked out of his hotel before renting a vehicle with a credit card under his Matthew Cooper alias. He tuned the car radio to a station that broadcast in English, but the altercation in Trondheim was not big enough news, so he selected a Norwegian station and struggled with the language before giving up and driving for a while in silence.

As he traveled, he thought about what he had heard in the warehouse before the firefight had kicked off. It was pretty clear that the mercs and at least one of the band members had been to the bunker. He thought it likely that the two remaining members of Abaddon Relix had been there and had joined their dead friends in Valhalla. In which case, why train the Norwegians for a firefight? Were they actually expecting opposition when they went back to the bunker to transport the ordnance, or was it precautionary?

The Russians were keen to get their weapons back. The fact that they hadn't gone straight in as soon as the first video had appeared on YouTube suggested that any record of its location had been destroyed—either accidentally or with force—when glasnost had happened. So they would be in the same position as the soldier: reliant on piecing together clues from what had appeared online, or else identifying and following the Norwegians.

He had been unaware of anyone else in Trondheim who could be following his line of thinking but could only preclude it at his own risk.

There were a lot of unknown factors at present: Who, if anyone, was following? What were the Russians planning? Who were the terrorist groups vying for the ordnance? Was the bunker manned or deserted? And if manned, then by whom? The big question hanging over all of this was simple: what did they want the ordnance for?

This made planning difficult. Covering all possibilities

for an offensive or defensive battle when the circumstances, the motives, were so ill defined was almost
impossible. The only thing he could do was to keep it
simple: follow and intercept at the point of pickup, dealing with eventualities if and when they arose.

Bolan would have been happier with a larger armory
at his disposal than the one he currently carried. If possible, he would gather more along the way.

He stopped for coffee and to call Stony Man when
he neared Oslo. Researching for the mission, he had
found that 90 percent of the population growth in Norway over the last decade was due to immigration, and
that the city with the largest portion of immigrants
was Oslo. This would explain the resurgence of fas-
cism in black metal activism and in general. Coming
from America—a land built on immigrants in search
of a better way of life—it seemed a strange attitude.
But Europe had always had pockets of insular thinking, and when times were hard, that thinking became
more hard-line.

Kurtzman was businesslike this morning. There was
no time for the usual pleasantries. He gave Bolan a GPS
setting to put in the rental car's navigation system that
would take him to where the black truck was parked.
Bear also informed the soldier that the Trondheim authorities were holding two men recovered from the
scene in connection with the death of Count Arsneth.

Bolan nodded to himself. The partygoers had understood Bolan, and his gamble had paid off. The warehouse used by Asmodeus had not been identified, but
the dead man had: Milan Millevich, a Bosnian by birth
who had long-standing right-wing affiliations, and was
linked to an Estonian group called Freedom Right.

"Any intel on them?" Bolan queried.

"We found out some small-scale bombings and bank raids in their homeland have been attributed to the group, but more recently they've been forging links in Scandinavia. Nothing big up to now."

"But this could be their entry into the big leagues," Bolan mused. "Not if I can help it, Bear."

CHAPTER SEVEN

"Why have we come here?" Visigoth asked. "Why not just head out and meet up along the way?"

Seb looked up from the laptop, which displayed maps of the northern Karelia region.

"We need to pick up another vehicle, plus additional men and brief them," he said shortly. "More than that, we need to make sure no one is following us."

"We didn't see anyone," Visigoth continued in a whining tone.

"Yeah, and now you know they were there when we left the warehouse," Seb said, sneering. "These people are professionals. You're not likely to spot them."

"So we wait and see if they attack us here?" Hades interjected. "Where we're in a position of strength and not in the open? Then move on?" He looked at Seb like an eager puppy, keen to prove his ability to think tactically.

"You know, you could learn a lot from your friend," Seb said, directing the comment at Visigoth. "He picks things up quickly."

Hades looked pathetically pleased at these words of praise, and Visigoth shot him a look of pure loathing, feeling as though he had obscurely been condemned.

Seb left them to their petty jealousies and returned to the maps. Milan had already planned their route, but he was dead and things had changed. If there were alternatives, then it would be good to have them as backup. And while Seb had understood the reasoning behind using the Norwegians for the pickup, that too had changed. Now there were only two of them and one professional. More bodies were needed for logistics, and the possibility of combat had made it essential that they were trained and experienced.

If anything Seb now felt that they would be carrying the Norwegians, rather than using them effectively. If only he could dispose of them without causing some ripples of discontent. Unfortunately the black metal scene in Norway was close-knit, and their disappearance without explanation would endanger links and lines of communication that were invaluable to Seb's group in their current situation. The brief given to Milan and himself had been simple: secure the ordnance, keep the locals sweet, but never lose sight of the bigger picture.

As they were in the house of Erik Manus, who owned and produced for the largest black metal specialist recording company, Seb was in exactly the wrong place to attend to that bigger picture.

Moreover, Manus—who was currently preparing a meal for them—was a relatively well-known figure in what was otherwise an underground and secretive scene. His status made him a key link in the chain, but his profile made him the most risky in circumstances like this.

Seb checked his watch. Thirty-three minutes had passed since he had called for backup. How long did it take them, for Christ's sake?

BOLAN DROVE PAST twice to get a good look at the place. This was a fairly affluent suburb, and the houses were spaced widely apart. Circling the block he could see that the houses had large yards and gardens that were not easily accessible. If he had to go in through the back, it would take time he could ill afford. However, that very space gave them a great deal of privacy. By now it was almost midmorning, and on each pass he noticed that there were few people about. So few that he was a little concerned that his car would be noticed on its second pass. He had chosen a nondescript vehicle in order to blend in as much as possible, but when there was nothing to blend with, then that became irrelevant.

The black truck was off to one side of the house, by itself. Bolan parked a couple hundred yards back and got out of his car, appearing to check an imaginary fender dent while he took a good look up and down the street.

Under his coat he had the micro Uzi SMG, Beretta 93R and grenades that he had carried the previous night. He also carried a Benelli M3T combat shotgun with folding stock that he had stashed in his case, and which fit nicely beneath the heavy overcoat covering his blacksuit. With seven rounds in the tube magazine and one in the chamber, its double O buckshot .33 caliber pellets, with twenty-seven in each round, made it a weapon that was less than subtle but extremely useful in enclosed spaces where he may be outnumbered.

Bolan didn't want to engage this enemy; he wanted to tail them to the bunker. Somehow though he doubted they would be that obliging if they knew he was here.

He strolled past the house on the opposite side of the street. At a distance the large glass windows on the ground and upper floor seemed opaque, and as he couldn't see in, so he couldn't be sure he wasn't observed.

The Executioner turned and headed back to the rental car.

He would have to sit and wait.

"I DON'T LIKE THE LOOK of that guy," Hades murmured as he watched Bolan walk away. The Norwegian stood up and walked to the window, looking out from one side so that he could not be observed. Bolan had walked just out of his sight line, but not enough so that he could not see the soldier get back into his car.

"What is it?" Seb frowned, looking up. Hades beckoned him over and explained what he had just seen.

The mercenary nodded. "Good job. Might be nothing, but we can't be too sure." He took out his cell phone and dialed a number. After the monosyllabic answer, he said, "Dark blue sedan a couple hundred meters from objective, parked opposite sidewalk. No other vehicles within a hundred meters in either direction. Prejudicial action required."

BOLAN WAS WATCHING the house. Minutes dragged by, but he was prepared for that. A stakeout was sometimes a tedious task but necessary. If he was to obtain his objective, he had to stay focused on the long-term goal.

The locale was quiet enough that he heard the truck approach the end of the road before he saw it in the rearview mirror. It turned the corner, and he could see that it was another black truck with tinted windshield, an obvious replacement for the one eliminated in Trondheim.

What it did next was not so obvious. As it traveled

down the road, the gears suddenly ground and whined as it notched up and gathered speed, angling across the road so it was unmistakably heading for the soldier's vehicle.

He could jump out, but that would leave him exposed and also without transport. There was only one thing he could do: he hit the ignition and cursed as the engine took forever to fire up. He cursed again at the stick shifts in Norway as he had to throw it into gear before the vehicle pulled itself away from the curb with agonizing slowness. The truck on his tail slewed around to catch him as he moved, its back wheels bumping up on the curb, causing the driver to lose control and skid, the tail of the truck spinning through sixty degrees.

It bought the soldier just enough time to get his vehicle fired up to pick up speed. He was able to put several hundred yards between himself and the black truck by the time the driver had gained control of the vehicle and was gunning for his tail. Bolan took the corner on two wheels, pulling hard to keep it tight and gain valuable distance.

He would need to put enough space between himself and the house so that he did not engage the men in the house. Allowing them to continue was paramount. If they used this as cover for their own exit, then at least he still had the tracker on them.

The truck on his tail had been their backup; he had no doubt about that, but he had been spotted. Now he was marked, and he had to either throw them off or engage in a firefight.

Neither option would be easy. Bolan was headed toward the center of Oslo, and the traffic—both vehicular and pedestrian—was starting to build up around him as he began to weave in and out of other cars to keep the necessary distance between his vehicle and his pursuer.

Bolan had no real knowledge of the city layout— like any city in Scandinavia, it was more the size of an American small town than a city—but knew that space would be at a premium. And space was what he would need to shake off his pursuers.

The surrounding buildings seemed to hem in Bolan as the streets of the older parts of the city became narrower, and the wooden and stone structures with their ornate decoration became more prevalent. He took a left, cutting off a Škoda sedan whose driver honked the horn angrily at him. The truck had to slow to take the narrower space without taking itself out of the game and that bought Bolan a few more precious yards.

Right now he could have done with a street map on the seat beside him or at least on his smartphone. The navigation system was useless without a reference to feed in, and he couldn't afford the split-second break in concentration to pull the cell from his pocket. He could do with a turn in his luck once again.

The Executioner grinned mirthlessly as he got the break he needed. The traffic flow took him into a newer section of Oslo, and to his right there was a multistory parking garage. It was a desperate maneuver, but the only one he could make. Bolan swung the sedan into a turn that took him across traffic, which squealed to a sudden halt, leaving a pile up behind that blocked portion of the road. He went through the barrier without stopping, the front of the rental car taking a battering from the automatic plastic barrier as it broke across the vehicle's frame.

As he slowed fractionally to take the curve that led up to the first level, he could see the truck weave its way around the carnage and follow in his wake.

This was a dead end in many ways. When he reached the top, Bolan would have to face off with whoever was in the truck; the manner in which they had reached this point would have attracted police attention to the parking garage. His rental car was as useless as the one he had stolen the night before, identified at the house and now marked by the battering it had taken.

And yet, as the soldier continued to ascend, he knew that this was the only way he could isolate the enemy from the innocent populace so there would be no collateral damage, and also the only way he could isolate the enemy from the authorities—who Bolan wanted to be in the dark as much as possible until his mission had been completed.

Under the low roof of the parking garage, despite the sides being open to the air, the sound of the sedan's engine as it protested against the treatment it received sounded deafeningly loud, even within the confines of the car itself. Bolan could not hear the truck at his rear, and cast glances into the rearview mirror to track how close it was to him. He was maintaining enough of a distance to prevent the enemy firing on him, but they were still too close for him to maneuver how he wanted as he gained each level. Looking back, he could see a swarthy, squat figure leaning from the shotgun seat, an MP5 waving erratically as the merc tried to roll with the incline of the building and the shifting balance of the truck's suspension as it cornered too tightly for its size.

Bolan had to admit that the truck driver was good, too much so for Bolan's liking. He could have done with an edge, as there were probably four men in the truck. When he reached the top level, the soldier would need precious seconds to take a defensive position.

All the while he kept his peripheral vision alert for anyone else in the parking garage. Blaring car horns and blazing headlights flashing angrily told him of drivers who had either thrown their cars into Reverse or had braked sharply to prevent collisions. Those people who were out of their cars—on the way to or from the elevators to each level—had the sense to scatter and take cover as the low ceiling of each level amplified the sound, hanging like an oppressive blanket over them.

And then, when the neon horizon had become a narrowing presence before him, it was gone. The cold, slate-gray sky was above him and the sound of his car roared into empty space. He was on the uppermost level, open to the elements.

Open and with nowhere else to run...

There was a smattering of cars on the top level, spread across a surface area that seemed to be as large as a football field. Unlike the levels under cover, few wished to leave their vehicles to the mercy of the elements. There was nowhere he could use as effective cover, but by the same token there were no civilians to get caught in the firefight to come.

The open concrete floor was bordered by a low wall buffered in plastic fenders, about five feet high, hiding from view the sheer drop to the road below. It was a model of safety and with no little irony gave him no area of cover.

He gunned the engine, headed for the far corner of the concrete expanse. Those few vehicles on the top level were clustered toward down ramps, and so he would be completely isolated. But it was the only way to gain the necessary time and ground to execute his single chance.

As he approached the wall at speed, the plastic fender filling his vision, he put the sedan into a skid that slewed it on sideways, with the driver's door toward the wall. The engine stalled, coughed and died, but before the last echo had faded, he was out of the vehicle and using the hood as both cover and a rest for his firing arm.

The truck roared out of the tunnel formed by the up ramp, headed for him without seeming to kill its speed. If they rammed him, they would inevitably pin the soldier against the wall. It would be quick and effective, but probably total their vehicle and hamper their escape.

No, this was to scare him. It wouldn't work; you didn't play chicken with Bolan and expect him to blink.

The soldier had racked the Benelli shotgun, which sat on the ground beside him, and had the micro Uzi SMG cradled in one arm. Judging the distance, he took one of the frag grenades from his web belt and pulled the pin, lobbing the bomb overhand in an arc that was high and short.

It had to be; he didn't want it to detonate in front of the truck and the shrapnel to come back on him. He ducked with satisfaction as he saw it loop over the top of the oncoming truck.

The explosion was loud and concussive, even in the open, with a wrenching sound that told him his aim had been true. The rear of the truck had taken the brunt of the blast, the rear doors and side paneling torn apart by the explosion, the interior peppered with metal shards.

The truck slid sideways, partly from the blast and partly from the sudden jerk of the driver's startled reflexes, the rear tires blown and the steering shot. Its engine stalled in the silence that engulfed them following the detonation.

Bolan looked up, to be greeted by a burst of SMG fire that he returned before ducking out of sight.

The gunners in the rear of the truck had been eliminated by the blast. There were two points of fire, as the driver and the swarthy merc in the shotgun seat had left the remains of the truck. The smell of diesel drifted across to Bolan, and he realized why they had scattered. A crackling and the smell of burning told him that a fire had already broken out.

There was no cover for the two men, but as they ran in opposite directions they at least had the advantage of splitting his gunfire. He could take one down, but leave himself open to the other.

Bolan still had the advantage. He had some cover, and he used it as he looked up to sight the two men. Fire came from each direction, pounding into the bodywork and shattering the sedan's glass. He had enough time to see that the squat figure from the shotgun seat was limping, slowed by injury. The driver was faster and was hugging the wall, hoping that his speed would bring him around to a position where Bolan was exposed faster than the soldier could react.

Nice idea but it didn't work. As the runner hit him with a spray'n'pray blanket, Bolan flattened himself, ignored the chips of concrete and plastic that rained on him, and with cool precision loosed three short blasts that stitched the runner across the torso. He stumbled and fell into the third tap, his head split like a ripe melon.

Before he was even on the concrete, Bolan had turned to face the limping mercenary. He switched from the micro Uzi SMG to the Benelli shotgun, moving across the narrow strip of concrete running between the sedan and the wall, ignoring the splinters of glass that penetrated the tough weave of the blacksuit.

The mercenary fired as he ran, acutely aware that time and lack of cover was against him. His shambling gait and his panic made his firing erratic, and Bolan rolled to let the overhanging chassis of the sedan provide a little more cover.

The merc's fire may have been wild, but it was enough to prevent the soldier from getting a good look at him, and Bolan was running out of distance to fire off a blast before the man was on him. He would have to risk opening himself to enemy fire....

Fate had other ideas. As he was preparing to roll back out, his senses were almost overwhelmed by a blast of heat and smoke as the diesel in the truck finally caught, and the smoking vehicle exploded in a ball of flame.

The sedan rocked from the force of the blast, the heat searing the paint and detonating ammunition in the truck, which fired wildly into the air. Bolan felt the sear through the blacksuit, and cast from his mind the fleeting thought that the blast would turn his cover into a firetrap.

His adversary was thrown sideways into the wall by the force of the blast, the MP5 clattering from his grasp as the impact drove the air from his lungs.

Bolan stood up, his lungs burnt by the hot air of the blast, sighted in and cut loose with the Benelli shotgun. It caught his adversary as he scrabbled for the SMG and pulled it around, the buckshot hitting him in the face and chest before he had a chance to draw a bead and fire.

A plume of black smoke spiraled into the air above the parking garage as the truck continued to burn, drifting clouds of smoke obscuring the view between where Bolan stood and the position of the ramps down into the body of the building. He was acutely aware of how close the sirens now were. He had to evacuate and fast.

His blacksuit was covered with broken glass, but he masked that by taking the heavy overcoat from the backseat of the sedan, shaking off the debris and pulling it around him as he raced toward the elevator. There was an emergency stairwell next to it, and the soldier made for the door. He had stashed the micro Uzi SMG in its holster and put the Benelli shotgun into the suitcase he had dragged from the back of the sedan where it lay with the overcoat.

He took the stairs three at a time, hoping that he was just in front of the arriving emergency services. He paused by the door to the next level down, inching it open to take a peek. The authorities were just speeding up the ramp, with men on foot in their wake, looking to marshal the bewildered civilians to safety.

Bolan slipped through the doorway and moved around parked cars, keeping low until he arrived at a cluster of confused civilians, as they headed in the direction indicated by the approaching authorities.

Moments later he was down the street, weaving through the gathering crowd.

There was still work to be done.

CHAPTER EIGHT

"Striker, you're really going to have to rein in those rental car bills. Hal's going to go ballistic when he sees the expenses so far for this one."

"Yeah, funny. Did you report the vehicle as stolen?"

"Of course. And backdated the report on the local system so it looks like it was taken well before the— uh—accident it suffered...."

Bolan couldn't resist a grin but refrained from further comment. He had wasted little time renting another car, this one under another credit card with a false-yet-verified identity. He was now headed toward the Finland border, his smartphone on the seat beside him as he caught up on events since his enforced flight.

The truck with the GPS was en route for the Karelia region, with a two-and-a-half-hour start. He would be able to make that up with the rental car's greater speed on highways and by taking an occasional catnap instead of hours spent sleeping on the long journey. He figured that the men in the truck ahead would think him out of the game—if not dead, then certainly disabled and unable to track them—and so would not hurry unduly. There was no way of knowing if they were alone or if they had picked up another truck as of yet, but Bolan figured that they would have to call in more bodies and loading space at some point.

He knew that the enemy had added a man to their main team: Erik Manus, who had not been present when the authorities had raided his home, following an anonymous tip regarding his link to the men killed in the parking garage. Bolan was able to get his picture from a website.

"It'll come as no surprise to you that at least two of the dead have so far been identified as being members of Freedom Right," Kurtzman continued. "If you want my opinion, they won't want to risk any more of their men being dragged into combat this side of the border. Any extra transport or personnel will head to the bunker location."

"Can't you pick it up from any exchanges?"

"Striker, I can only work miracles sometimes," the computer wizard replied, exasperated. "I have nothing to trace. If you could have gotten a cell from one of the bodies you left littered across Norway—"

"Point taken," Bolan interrupted. "So no idea how many to expect at the other end…and they'll be trained."

"Precisely. I would imagine they wanted to use the black metal zealots as cannon fodder rather than risk their own men. Kind of backfired on them, right?"

"They couldn't have known anyone was on their tail. They won't make that mistake again, though."

There was plenty for Bolan to think about as he ended the call and concentrated on the road stretching ahead.

His route took him to the border with Finland in the north of Norway, crossing by the Gulf of Bothnia, and then traveling across country to the area where the Karelia region bordered Russia. It was a long drive, and he stopped only twice to take some rest and refreshment, aware all the time of the signal from the GPS he had planted on the truck—plotting its course as it stopped for longer periods, moved with less speed, and he gradually gained ground.

Finland was beautiful; there was no doubt. A land of lakes and 86 percent forest could be little else, and the winding roads that took Bolan through the towering coniferous landscape would have been relaxing at any other time. As it was, he found himself wishing for just one straight stretch on which to put on some speed. His only consolation was that these were the same roads that the truck was negotiating, its handling meaning that, with every klick, he gained a few more precious yards, a few more precious seconds.

Bolan was thankful that he was traveling in the southern regions of the country, where the climate was more temperate than the unforgiving north. He wasn't equipped for serious snow and cold, and was thankful he was away from the land of the midnight sun, as the cover of night may be a useful ally. He was also aware that going off-road could cause problems, as the ground in which the firs grew could be boggy and dangerous. Like Louisiana with added cold, he thought, amused.

All levity was soon dismissed as he reached Karelia and noticed that the GPS tracker had slowed almost to a halt.

HADES AND VISIGOTH stretched their legs, staring around them at the forest that crowded in on them.

"How did those dweebs ever find this in the first place?" Hades asked. "I mean, what were they doing out here?"

"Playing pagans in the woods," Visigoth responded. "Cowardly assholes."

"You don't have to worry about how they found the bunker, just that they did," Seb growled. He was visibly on edge and noticed from the corner of his eye that Manus gestured to the two Norwegians to chill out. Good. Seb was glad someone had some sense. He had enough to worry him now without having to babysit laborers.

They had parked the truck as close to the bunker as it could get. The vehicle could go off-road to a degree, but the land here was treacherous, and if the truck sat too long, its wheels would sink into the soil. There was enough space between the trees to negotiate a path from the forest road, but the deeper they went, the less he wanted to risk it.

His main concern was how long they would have to wait for backup. He had sent coordinates to Estonia, but the trip was as long as that from Norway, and he had had a head start. Seb looked around, smelling the firs and listening for the wildlife that called the forest home. He could never call it that; he felt ill at ease where there were too many hiding places. He couldn't see a way that the guy who had been bugging them could have followed, but the guy had already turned up twice and cost them Milan, if nothing else. Seb would have liked to have finished him personally for that, but the mission took precedence.

"Come on, we've got work to do," he snapped, leading them through the covered path that led to the hidden bunker entrance, dropping down to the concealed port.

Once inside, the smell of death hit them.

"What is that?" Hades asked, gagging.

"That is what's left of the bastards who found this place. If you don't get a grip, then you'll be joining them," Seb snarled.

"Hey, dude, you don't talk to us like that," Visigoth snapped, reaching out and grabbing Seb by the arm.

Before Visigoth had a chance to realize what was happening, Seb slammed him up against the cold wall, his own arm now reversed and up his back, ready to snap like a twig.

"Listen, you do as I say and like it. This is not a game, and I am not playing. Understand?"

"He understands, man," Hades said in a placating manner. "You do, right, Arne? It's only that we haven't got this deep before, and it's new. Just need to get used to it."

Seb let go of Visigoth's arm and stepped back. The Norwegian slumped to the floor, massaging the life back into his aching limb and trying to keep the fear from his face.

"You need to learn quickly," Seb said coldly. "Come on...."

He led them through the complex, the two Norwegians taking in the surroundings with a blank incomprehension that was part fear, part anxiety. For the first time they were wondering—as Arsneth had before them—if they had gotten themselves in too deep. What had happened to Ripper and Hellhammer? They were supposed to rendezvous at Manus's house but had failed to show.

Keeping to the rear was Manus, older than the two musicians, and perhaps a little more worldly wise.

Silently Seb led them through the kitchen area, making a deliberate detour in order to show them what was left of Severance and the Baron in order to bring his point home. He hoped it had worked. By the time they reached the armory, all three Norwegians were grim-faced and quiet.

The silence was broken by a whistle from Manus, unable to contain his surprise when faced with the ordnance they were here to strip.

"What do we do with this?" he asked softly.

"You," Seb replied pointedly, "help us get it loaded and away. Then we put it to some use. That will not be your direct concern."

It flashed through Manus's mind that he and the two young musicians may be left behind, like the rotting meat in the kitchens, once their usefulness had been outlived.

"What do we do now?" he asked.

Seb checked his cell phone and grunted at the lack of signal. "Right now? We wait."

For a miracle, Manus added to himself.

BOLAN LEFT THE RENTAL CAR three klicks from where the GPS signal told him the truck had stopped. It would make intercept impossible, but that was not his aim. He loaded a duffel bag from his case and hoisted it before setting off across the densely packed fir woods. His game plan was simple: ascertain numbers, take them down in the best manner that presented itself, then call in covert U.S. forces to ferry the ordnance—and himself—the hell out.

The ground was thick, muddy and sucked at his boots as he hiked over the terrain—tree roots and the littered ground covering adding to the treachery. He also knew that there was the possibility of hostile wild-life in the region.

Although he had the GPS signal logged and on a map app on his smartphone, he noticed that, as he got deeper into the forest and away from the road, the signal weakened considerably. Good points: the backup the truck driver needed would be as isolated as both the truck and the soldier, giving Bolan at least a level playing field. Bad points: he was isolated from contact with U.S. forces or Stony Man.

Circling through the woods, breathing hard as the terrain sapped the strength from calf muscles already stiffened by the long journey, Bolan came to where the truck had been parked.

The bunker had to be within reasonable walking distance—it had to be in order to transport the ordnance from bunker to truck. It stood alone. Reinforcements had not arrived.

That was good. It gave the soldier time to track their progress to the bunker without being hurried, or forced into a premature interception.

Their trail was easy to follow. The Norwegians were not professionals, and the merc with them had not considered it necessary to make an effort. Was that because he thought they would be undisturbed, or because he wanted to leave a trail for whoever was to rendezvous?

That was a thought. Like the first truck, whoever was to join them would have to trek through the woods. Why give them any help? the soldier thought. He covered the trail even as he tracked it. Make it difficult and he could take down one team before it even reached the bunker.

Having followed the trail to the bunker's entrance, he

could see that the outer doors had been closed. Whoever was inside would be cut off from the immediate outside.

Just as he wanted it. The Executioner tracked back, covering his own trail, and scouted a spot where he had cover and a 360-degree view of the surrounding woods. Climbing a fir, he settled himself on a thick limb, covered by needle and fir, and waited.

DARKNESS WAS CLOSING in when Bolan heard the distant rumble of a truck negotiating the terrain as it came off-road. It was forty-five degrees to the point where the first truck was parked, and as it moved slowly the soldier figured that he had time to intercept the vehicle before the men inside had a chance to exit and spread across the forest.

What would be the better option? Take out the truck as a whole and risk the noise attracting the attention of the men in the bunker? Or wait until the men in the approaching truck went EVA and then pick them off one by one?

Bolan scrambled down the tree and hit the ground running. His path intercepted that of the approaching truck, about the size of the one he had tracked.

Using the intel he'd gleaned from eliminating the first vehicle, the soldier could bank on facing three men, maybe four at most. The truck was solid enough, and he was light on grenades with real firepower.

The moon was bright, and the forest canopy offered patches of cover and patches of light to illuminate any target.

He made his decision and waited for the truck to roll to a halt.

CHAPTER NINE

Three men got out of the truck, warily looking around at the darkening forest. From a distance, indistinguishable grumbles and complaints littered their conversation, their body language wary and yet also signaling their fatigue as they made their way across the fir carpet of the forest floor. The crunching of frozen fir and moss beneath their feet as it gave way to the spongy ground beneath served both to locate them easily and also to mask any similar sounds that Bolan might make as he moved through the trees, closing on them.

They left the truck unlocked and unguarded. Bolan was sure of that from the manner in which they had moved away from it and from the complete stillness that emanated from the vehicle. There was no interior light showing, no movement of the suspension betraying a moving presence within. Bolan knew he could concentrate on the three men as they trudged across the forest floor, trying to pick up the track.

The man in the lead—shorter than the other two, running to fat—carried a tablet that he stared at, his face puzzled in the reflective glow of the screen. He stopped a couple times, changing direction uncertainly to mumbled dissent from the two men in his wake. He had no visible weapon, but a bulge beneath his jacket showed he had some kind of SMG stowed there.

The man at the back was also short but wiry. He had a Steyr firearm slung across his shoulders and hunched miserably into the puffy jacket that did little to bulk him out. The center man carried a slung MAC-10. He had a beard and wore a woolen hat, constantly looking around with darting birdlike motions of his head.

The soldier opted to take care of the middle man first. Divide the other two down the middle and also take out the most alert. In order not to betray his position too greatly, he used the Beretta 93R. Even in this fading light, he had a steady-enough hand, and time enough at that, to take careful aim at a head shot. They were moving slowly, as the man in lead was still puzzling over his on-screen map. Body shots were more effective at range, a safer target. This was being given to him on a plate.

He didn't need a second opinion. Sight, squeeze, one shot... The birdlike turn of the head brought the bearded man around so that he was looking square in Bolan's direction. The slug drilled a hole in the center of his forehead, and he slumped to the fir carpet, already dead.

The effect of the shot was instantaneous. Yelling in fear, anger and warning to each other, the two remaining hardmen scattered. The wiry man at the rear hit the ground, diving around a tree trunk for cover. He rolled and came up firing in the direction of the shot. While the sound of the round was suppressed, the quiet chug had been audible in the quiet, still air.

Bullets chipped wood where Bolan had been seconds before, but the gunfire was too late; the soldier had already moved on.

The fat man had dropped the tablet, tugging open

his jacket to free the SMG stashed inside. He was Bolan's next objective. As the guy struggled to find cover and sight the area where the first shot had come from, Bolan had already circled almost 180 around him, coming up from the rear.

The shots from the Steyr masked the small sounds Bolan made on the forest floor, and he was behind the fat man before he became aware of the soldier's presence. The soft footfalls behind him became audible as the echo of the Steyr died away. The guy tried to roll and bring his weapon around, but was too slow and too late. Bolan had stashed the Beretta in his waistband at the small of his back and fell on the fat man before he could complete his maneuver. His knee drove his adversary onto his front, Bolan ramming an elbow into his skull, driving his face into the moss and fir so that any attempt to shout a warning was muffled in the dirt and mud.

Bolan pulled up his quarry's head again, hearing him suck in breath and choke on the mud that filled his mouth. With both hands he took hold of the guy's head and twisted, pulling up as he did, his knee skewering the fat man's spine.

The crack as his neck snapped resounded in the sudden silence.

Two down, one left.

The wiry gunner yelled something. As Bolan moved away from the second corpse, he could hear the last man moving through the forest. Panic and fear had made him reckless. To gain ground quickly he was ignoring the noise he might make.

Bolan was not so reckless. He could track his prey by the noise he made, and the soldier moved silently through the cover of the forest so that he passed the wiry man and turned, picking him up from behind.

He opted for the micro Uzi SMG, to make it quick, firing as his prey reached his companion's body and stopped dead. Bolan stitched him down the back with a three-shot burst. From stopping dead to falling dead had been a matter of no more than two seconds. There was something that always went against the grain about shooting a man from behind, but circumstances did not always allow for decorum.

Pausing to listen for any sounds that would betray another presence, Bolan tracked back, taking the weapons from the bodies and recovering the tablet. He stowed them in the duffel bag, then stashed that in a tree near the abandoned truck. The MAC-10 he would take with him. The extra firepower of a light SMG could only help. The tablet could contain intel that would be useful when he was clear from this situation.

After completing those tasks, he disabled the truck. Releasing the hood, he ripped cables and flung them away. It was the quickest way to take the truck out of play; there was no time to waste. So far he had been lucky, and the men in the bunker still waited for their companions. Sooner or later, they would be compelled to venture outside.

He wanted to be ready for them.

HADES AND VISIGOTH sat silently, staring into space, waiting. Manus paced the bunker, stopping in rooms, distracting himself by trying to imagine what it had been like to live here. Better than their position now undoubtedly. All three of them had nothing to say, and ignoring the stench and keeping their stomachs was taking all their attention. The manner in which Seb was pacing, and the look in his eye whenever it caught either of the two young musicians, also gave them good reason to keep their peace. Seb was a man who was ready to explode at someone, and neither of them wished to be his target. They just wanted to get the ordnance loaded and return to civilization.

"Screw this," Seb said eventually. "They're either lost or something has happened to them. There's no way of finding out while we're in here," he added, looking at his useless cell in disgust. "We need to get loaded up and out of here. As much as we can." He beckoned to them, and reluctantly they followed him to the armory. Reluctantly because they had to pass the kitchen area, and it took all the willpower either could muster not to gawk at the bloated bodies.

Seb didn't give it a second thought. He yelled for Manus to join them. He was focused on what needed to be done. There was a lot of ordnance—far too much for one truck to take—and so he mentally ticked off an inventory of what would be the important items.

Much of the regular firepower in there was easily obtainable on the outside. SMGs and rifles were not hard to buy. It would save Freedom Right a lot of cash if they could have all the stock—maybe even generate cash if they could sell surplus—and this had been part of the plan. But that had to change. He needed to concentrate on matching that part of the ordnance that was not readily obtainable on the outside to that which was vital to their immediate plans.

Within the armory were heavy-duty carts that were designed to move the weaponry in and out of the bunker. It would take two men to move a fully laden cart.

If Seb stayed in the bunker to load, he figured that between the three of them they could load the truck in about an hour. Manus could be used for a lookout.

"You know the way back to the truck?" he snapped at the two Norwegians, who nodded. Seb couldn't be sure if that was the truth or just fear. He would have to take that chance. He instructed Manus to take an SMG from the armory and take up a position where he could keep watch and also ride shotgun for the two musicians, as a precaution.

Then he turned to the two young men and outlined his plan. That done, he then directed them to help him load the first cart before sending them out into the night, while he returned to his task alone with a second cart, cursing as he did a mission that had been fouled up from the beginning. Only thoughts of the eventual outcome of the mission kept him buoyed as he worked.

WHILE BOLAN WAITED, he pondered the best course of action. He wasn't about to rush the bunker. He had no real idea of the layout beyond a working knowledge of standard USSR design, which gave the people inside one advantage. A second advantage in their favor was that there may be more than the three of them. The soldier had no way of knowing if there had been men stationed there waiting for them. In an enclosed environment like the bunker, three to one was already poor odds. He had no wish for the odds to be upped.

Bolan had already dragged the corpses of the three gunners off the trail they had been taking, covering them so that they could not be easily found or observed. He had also raked over any traces of his presence. Now he was a hundred yards from the concealed bunker entrance, in cover, waiting for something to happen.

When it did, it wasn't quite what he had expected. The entrance to the bunker opened, and he saw Erik Manus come out, tentatively staring around him like a frightened rabbit, inexpertly clutching an SMG.

That made at least one extra gunner. Following close behind were the two black metallers—easily identifiable by their long hair and piercings, even at a distance— who struggled up to level ground, maneuvering a cart that was laden with—again, easily identifiable to the soldier even from a distance—the cream of the bunker's ordnance. Weapons that the Russians would particularly like to retain, and the very weapons that Bolan had been sent to retrieve.

There was no sign of the merc who had been with the two musicians. That would make it one-on-one if he went into the bunker now, and he could take down the two musicians as they returned. The fourth man, Manus, who moved away from the Norwegians and from where Bolan was secreted, looked more of a danger to himself than to the soldier. Manus could wait.

But this course of action would split the ordnance and make it a little more difficult to recover. If Bolan allowed them to load their truck with the prime ordnance, and then took them out of the game, it would enable him to take away the weapons from the bunker before calling Stony Man, and so put some distance between himself and any enemy that was attempting to locate the bunker.

The Executioner made the decision to wait until they had loaded the truck. At a distance he tracked them and watched while they loaded the ordnance from the cart before making their way back. When they were out of sight, he went up to the vehicle and checked the inventory they were planning to transport. From the amount of room it took up, he estimated two more loads from the bunker would fill the rear of the truck. Even then, it would risk the weight sinking the wheels in the muddy forest floor. He would have to act swiftly when they returned with the final load, or else the truck would be trapped here no matter the outcome of the ensuing firefight.

He returned to his observation post near the mouth of the bunker and waited. Shortly the two Norwegians came out again, a little slower this time, with a filled cart that they toiled to drag through the forest to the truck. Bolan didn't bother to follow them this time. Instead, he kept watch on the mouth of the bunker. It was still and silent, and he imagined the mercenary, alone in the armory, loading the last cart that they would be able to fit in the truck's interior.

When the two Norwegians returned to the bunker, they were dragging the cart. By the time they had taken the final load up to the truck they would be exhausted—as, he assumed, would be the merc from loading the carts single-handedly—and so they would deliver the ordnance to him, complete with transport.

By not taking them down until now, he hoped that the odds would be evened up by the toll their exertions had taken on them. There had been no practical way of separating them otherwise. There was still Manus, but all trace of him seemed to have vanished, as though he never existed.

After a short pause the two Norwegians came out from the bunker for the last time, with the mercenary at their rear. He was clutching an MP5, and even from this distance, Bolan could see that he had a wild-eyed look.

Was he suspicious? Or was it just fear?

Get to the truck, take it nice and slow, Bolan thought. Then the takedown will be easy...

It wasn't going to be that way. Suddenly the merc stopped the Norwegians, whispering urgently as he began to move off into the words. Bolan cursed and started to circle through the trees.

For whatever reason the mercenary had been drawn to the location of the dead gunners. If he discovered the bodies and the truck and raised the alarm, then the Norwegians would be panicked.

Bolan would have to take him out of the game silently, before the merc had a chance to raise the alarm, but the distance between them was too great. Bolan had little choice but to run faster and with less caution, casting to one side the need to keep his progress silent. He was aware that his footsteps across the fir were louder; however, the risk should be worth it.

He was within a few yards when the mercenary heard his pursuer and whirled to meet him. A mix of surprise and fear washed over his face, replaced by the diamond-hard gleam of determination born out of the need to survive. As Bolan took a flying leap to make the last yards, the merc leveled his MP5 and let fly a short burst. It should have stitched Bolan across the torso.

Should have. The soldier was too experienced not to have anticipated the move and had deviated from his path at the last second. The fire blasted past his shoulder, so close that he could feel the heat before he slammed into the mercenary as he tried to adjust his aim for a second shot.

The two men went rolling across the moss and fir, sinking into the soft mud. Bolan was acutely aware that the gunfire had to have alerted the Norwegians, and their reaction was unpredictable. He needed to finish this quickly.

As the men grappled, Bolan felt the merc's hands grab for Bolan's throat. Fingers like iron, with the intensity of the desperate, clutched at the tendons of his neck, the thumbs feeling for the windpipe. Bolan was on top, and he rolled, so that they flipped and the mercenary was now uppermost. It enabled the soldier to bring his knee up into the merc's groin, the sudden pain causing the man to loosen his grip, while the momentum of the thrust carried him over Bolan's head.

Before the mercenary had a chance to fully regain his feet, Bolan was on him. The soldier cannoned into the merc and drove him back into a tree, driving the air from his lungs. His adversary gave a strangled gasp as his ribs gave way under the impact. Bolan took hold of the merc's jaw and drove his head back onto the trunk of the tree three times. The man's eyes glazed as his hold on consciousness began to slip.

Bolan brought the Beretta into play and discharged one shot, angled up into the merc's body, the last light draining from his eyes. Bolan let go of the limp torso and turned away at a run, heading for the location where the two Norwegians had returned to their truck. He could hear the engine fire up; there was no loyalty among these terrorists, only fear.

Which was the one thing he didn't want. He had

planned on being able to take them down at least one by one, almost relying on their camaraderie or discipline to keep them in one place. But the Norwegians were not soldiers of any stripe. They were frightened youths out of their depth, which made them—in some ways—more dangerous.

Especially as Bolan's sedan was a hell of a ways off, and it would take him far too long to replace the leads on the disabled truck. He had to stop the truck, even at the risk of disabling it. He could fix it. He couldn't fix losing them; at least, not as easily.

He ran through the forest, zigzagging among the trees as the light of the moon illuminated his path. The engine of the truck gunned as it moved off. It started to grow fainter as Bolan took the MAC-10 from his shoulders and racked the weapon, ready to fire on the run, to take out the rear wheels. The forest resounded to the sound of the truck hammering into a tree and skidding away as the driver panicked, trying to find the way back to the road.

Bolan cut through a clump of trees, the rear of the truck coming into view as it skidded along the path. He had one shot: a burst of SMG fire at the rear right tires. Sparks flew as he hit the bodywork, wood flying as the surrounding trees were sprayed.

But the tires remained intact, and Bolan cursed as the truck went out of his line of sight.

The gamble—and his luck—had failed him this time.

At least it was the truck with the GPS tracker attached. All he had to do now was get back to his vehicle. He would keep a lookout for the fourth man, but chances were that he was as far from here as he could get. Poor bastard would probably get lost and freeze to death.

The cold night suddenly felt a bit colder.

CHAPTER TEN

Bolan reported to Stony Man the events at the bunker, informing them of its exact location. The Farm would arrange for a pickup team to remove what ordnance remained there, but it was left unsaid that the real payload was trundling the highway to Norway. Bolan vowed to keep on the trail and take down the two Norwegians.

After making his way back to the rental car, Bolan had hit the road in the direction he had seen the rogue truck take.

It was nearly half an hour and fifty klicks before he picked up any kind of cell phone signal and was able to follow the GPS. He drove through the night as the target vehicle hit the highway that took them north, headed toward the border with Norway. It was reasonable at this point to assume that they were retracing the route that had brought them to Karelia just a short time before.

It should have been a straightforward task. At the speed he could push the rental car, he was gaining ground, and when the truck appeared to come to a halt, he was relieved. By the time the sun had risen, he was within a few klicks.

Pulling into a service station, the soldier parked and got out of the vehicle, taking in the immediate area. The services consisted of a diner and gas station, with a large parking lot split into two sections. Even at this early hour, both the diner and the gas pumps were busy with long-distance truck drivers, the parking area littered by semitrailers that made a clear view across the lot impossible.

Bolan headed for the diner. The Norwegians had not gotten a look at him, and at this time of the morning, he looked like any other truck driver on a comfort stop. He bought a coffee to go, used the restroom, and bought an English-language newspaper so that he could scope out the store attached to the diner.

There was no sign of the men who—in truth—would have been easily visible among the other truck drivers.

Bolan checked his smartphone as he left, headed for the parking lot. According to the GPS, they were still in the area and had not moved. He was hoping that it would be possible to take them down away from any civilians.

A recon of both parking lots failed to reveal the truck he was tailing, and Bolan started to suspect the worst. A careful survey of the area confirmed that fear. The bad luck that had dogged him at crucial moments had been compounded by the fact that the GPS tracker he had fitted to the truck had worked loose.

Thrown to the roadside and trammeled by passing traffic was a piece of chassis from beneath the truck. It lay there, battered and split. By some quirk of chance, the GPS transmitter was still attached where he had placed it, having escaped damage.

Bolan had reported the find and within minutes had a call from a phlegmatic Brognola. It was not enough to assume that the truck had headed back to Oslo, particularly as the soldier had left a trail in that city that made his presence a risk at this time. The big Fed suggested Bolan head to the nearest NATO base with a U.S. presence, and from there he would be flown to Essen to await developments. In the meantime intel sources would be utilized to trace the missing payload.

Bolan did not suffer from pride. He would have been history long before if this had been the case. He did, however, have a professionalism that smarted at this job not being wrapped up.

Three days later Bolan was in Essen, Germany, at a military base, resupplying and trading intel with the Farm, awaiting the next move with the tension of a coiled spring.

Seventy-two hours full of tension. Then came the chance for its merciful release.

"HIS NAME IS STEIN SUNDBY. Sounds a lot less impressive than Ripper Sodomizer, don't you think?"

"Certainly does, Bear. Have the authorities got anything positive to tie him to the death of Arsneth? Or is it just the word of a bunch of kids and a mysterious guy with a gun?"

"Considering the level of deductive ability they had shown up to that point, I wouldn't have been surprised if they'd settled for that. But, no, they were actually forced to do some work and found DNA links."

"Nice to know *CSI* shows are big in Norway. I didn't think the locals were that lax."

"They're not as a rule. Anything to do with black metal brings up nasty memories, and they'd rather bury it as soon as possible."

"Not at the expense of the truth," Bolan said flatly.

"Our friend Sundby is the only one left standing to take the rap," Kurtzman continued. "You may also be interested to know that Milan Millevich also had DNA traces at the apartment where Arsneth was murdered. As did Seb Illytch, whose body we retrieved from the woods near the bunker. All three men had traces present in the bunker and around the corpses of the two remaining Abaddon Relix youths, who had been there some time."

"Kids shouldn't mess with grown-up issues," Bolan said sadly.

"The important thing is that all bodies were removed along with the remaining ordnance. There was no sign of your fourth man. ID could be Erik Manus—it was his house you followed them to. He's a musician and producer. No real political or terrorist history of any kind."

"Out of his depth, too, and it probably cost him his life," Bolan observed.

"Indeed. By the way, I hear that the Russians have finally pinned down a location for their bunker. They're going to be sorely disappointed at what they find. Or rather don't find."

"That's one consolation. A small one."

"Not really. The mother lode is still out there. But, on a positive note, if we don't know where it is, the chances of the Russians finding it first are remote. And it may be flushed out sooner than you'd think."

"Why?"

"Sundby has a court hearing to set a trial date tomorrow. Hal thinks it's time you went back to Norway."

"He thinks it's safe?"

"Striker, you're going to be there…. When is that ever an indication of 'safe'?"

AFTER HITTING THE HIGHWAY to Norway, Hades and Visigoth had made the arranged rendezvous on the border with a third truck. The vehicle, with four men, had been sent by Freedom Right to split the cache and transport it to two different locations. The original plan had been for the Norwegians and Seb to return to Oslo with some of the ordnance, while the second and third trucks would head for Estonia and the headquarters of the organization.

The two Norwegians arriving alone, and a truck short, had changed all that. They had expected to be greeted by comrades who would sympathize with their plight, which only served to show their naïveté. First, they were dragged from their truck at gunpoint and questioned as to why they had sent no word. Their protestations about a poor cell phone signal were dismissed. Why had they not called when they regained reception?

Again their explanations about not having a contact number were dismissed. Where then was Seb's cell phone? Come to that, where was Seb? And where were the men they had sent as backup?

Their story, garbled as it was by their own fear and exhaustion, did them no favors. They were split up and held under observation while the existing ordnance was split into two loads, and the trucks now set off north, both vehicles headed for Estonia.

After a journey in silence, they were blindfolded as they entered the city of Tallinn, so that their eventual destination could be kept secret. Not that it mattered.

Both young men felt that they would never see the outside world again.

They had been bundled into the basement of a building, locked in a room that had two beds and a table, and left there until fear had softened them up. Hades and Visigoth had spent two nights in that cellar. They had not yet been tortured but feared that would be their fate.

Then they were questioned and cross-questioned relentlessly. They had to understand, they were told, that security was paramount. Could they have been followed from the bunker? How had they been tailed there in the first instance? What had happened to the men sent to them? Where was Seb? What went on in Oslo that had left them short of men to begin with?

It didn't help that they could not answer any of these questions. They had been witness to nothing, and even with Seb's death they only had the impression of sounds to go by.

As the only survivors, with nothing to offer as to why they had been lucky, they looked to be in an untenable position. The whip-thin man with the drawn, hawklike face who came to them last was blunt about this.

"I cannot understand you. You are either cunning and very good actors, or incredibly stupid and extremely lucky. If you are the last, then perhaps we can still have use for you.

"You know what we stand for, by now. Here we are in Tallinn, in the county of Harju. This is the center of Estonia, yet it is also one of the two regions that are populated by foreigners. They have been here for generations at the behest of the scourge known as Communism, and still they will not move.

"We join with the European Union and what does this mean? More people can move in and dilute our purity. We should be looking to strengthen our race, not pollute it.

"We of the Baltic and Scandinavian states recognize one another. We recognize that we are proud, pure people who stand together because we stand alone. That is why we can work with each other to rid our lands of the foreigner. But in order to do that, we must first make the world sit up and take notice. We need a gesture, an action that has meaning. Do you follow me?"

Hades and Visigoth each nodded, though in truth they were too scared to listen properly, and both had lost track of what he was saying to them. His careful rhetoric to set them up as sacrificial lambs was wasted. It was also unnecessary. They would, at that moment, have agreed to anything if they thought it would keep them alive a little longer.

Something the man said penetrated their fog of fear: Ripper was still alive and had been charged with complicity in the murder of Count Arsneth. He had a court appearance to set a trial date this morning. Once set, then action could be planned. Action in which they were to play a vital role.

The prospect of staying alive, no matter that it may be for a dangerous mission, cheered them immensely.

"I will give you this chance to prove yourselves to us," the thin-lipped man continued. "You will go back to Oslo with two of our men and some weapons. Your task is simple. You will take your friend Ripper away from the police and return him to us. He is like you—young, scared—and can reveal too much. But we want him alive."

"So we can be of use to you?" Hades queried, his spirits rising.

Those were quashed by the words that came through a thin, humorless smile.

"No. It is so that you can flush out the one who has caused us all these problems. He must be eliminated before we proceed to our final objective."

BOLAN ARRIVED BACK in Oslo via a NATO ticket, passing through customs without having his baggage checked. That was just as well, since the case he carried had a greater amount of ordnance than the last time he had arrived in the city. He had been caught short before, and that lack had influenced his previous decisions, making choices that perhaps he would not have if greater firepower had been available. He may not have to use the full range. Having it now, however, gave him one less variable to worry about.

Having booked into a hotel, showered and rented a car, he made his way to the courthouse. It was approaching half past eleven, and from the court schedule supplied to him, he knew that Stein Sundby's hearing for a trial date would be directly after the lunch break. That gave Bolan time to conduct a recon of the courthouse before the judge opened the afternoon session.

The building itself had visible security, but the team's body language and interaction with the public suggested that they were rarely in any danger of seeing action. Bolan had little doubt that the uniformed men would be found wanting if called on to act, even if there was prior warning.

There were no extra guards, police or military this day. That was dangerous enough. He would have to ask

Brognola to put some kind of pressure on to make this place secure during the dates when the trial took place.

Once inside the court itself, Bolan found that, despite the age of the building, the refurbishment inside made the room comfortable, and the public gallery evinced a clear view of all of it. Whether that was a good thing was debatable. It would be easy from here to cause some serious collateral damage to judges and defendants; it was also simple for any security to survey the entire room—and, most important, those in it—with ease.

Which was exactly what the soldier did as Sundby was brought before the court. Manacled, he stared morosely and sullenly around the courtroom, speaking only to mutter assent to his own name, and to plead "not guilty" without once looking at the bench.

If he recognized Bolan, Sundby showed no sign. Neither did he show any sign of recognizing anyone else in the room. That meant nothing. Freedom Right could easily have sent men that the erstwhile Ripper had never met. Still, if there was anyone from the terrorist group in the room, they had damn good cover. Bolan, who usually had an instinct for such things, could not pick out anyone from the few people— court reporters, interested parties—scattered around the room.

It was only when the date had been set, and Sundby remanded for five days until his trial began, that the man showed anything other than a studied disinterest. As he was being led away, he looked up and a momentary flicker of disbelief and amusement crossed his face. Almost before it could be noticed, he had set his expression once more.

Almost. Bolan noticed and also heard the sound. It was the door to the public gallery opening.

Casually the soldier got to his feet and made to leave. As he did, he caught from the corner of his eye the latecomer who had caused the flicker of recognition.

It was all he could do to keep such an expression from his own face. There, seated at the rear of the gallery, was the lookout he had last seen running away into the cover of the fir forest.

Erik Manus.

CHAPTER ELEVEN

Oslo was a municipality. It stretched over a vast tract of land that belied the relatively small—around half a million—population. Like many of the cities in Norway, it had large areas that were mountainous forests studded between the urban and suburban areas. That meant that it could be easy for a man to hide during the warmer months, if he really wanted to. These were the colder times of the year, but still Bolan would not have put it past Manus to have found himself a forest refuge. If this was the case, then Bolan could kiss goodbye ever finding Manus if he managed to give the soldier the slip.

Norway was a country of long coastlines, an oddly narrow shape and a population that was low in density. The public transport system was rail based, in places sparse, which could be a problem if a person was trying to tail a man who didn't appear to have a private vehicle and was jumpy.

Manus was unshaved, his jaw and scalp with a two-day growth that showed that wherever he was staying, he was living roughly. He moved quickly, nervous glances over his shoulder and around him betraying the anxiety that he felt. Even in the center of Oslo, where the courthouse was located, there were relatively few people about in the early afternoon, and Bolan had to put considerable distance between himself and his target in order to remain unobserved.

Manus took the train to an area of the city far removed from his empty house. Bolan knew from his intel that it had not been linked to the incident in Arsneth's apartment complex and so was not under observation by the authorities. Manus either did not know that or feared someone else.

Bolan didn't blame him. The two Norwegians who had engineered an escape would have been pumped for every last detail about why their operation had gone wrong. Manus had committed the cardinal sin—desertion—and his cowardice would mark him as a security risk. Two reasons to eliminate him, and he had to know that.

Bolan kept a railcar between himself and his target, and got off the train at the last moment to remain unobserved. As far as he could tell, as he left the station and followed Manus through almost barren streets, they were alone. Freedom Right had not yet caught up with the deserter. He could still be of use to the soldier.

Turning off the street, Manus made his way through a small industrial park. Wherever he went in the world, Bolan found that these areas always had the same basic, easy-to-assemble design, and they all looked the same. That was sad if a person had a sense of aesthetics, but in his case made it easy for him to follow and conceal himself, as he was only too familiar with the way they were laid out.

Despite his care in checking out his environment, Manus did not see Bolan on his tail. Manus did not see Bolan approach as Manus tapped in the entry code to the small side door on a unit. In fact, the first he

knew of Bolan's presence was when the soldier rushed
Manus, bundling him through the door as it opened
and slamming it behind them as Manus tumbled to the
floor. As Bolan stood over him, the music producer
put his hands up to his face, his eyes staring wildly.

Bolan shook his head. "I'm not here to kill you. I
might just save your life, if you're lucky."

"YOU KNOW, I REALLY NEVER wanted to get into this
crap," Manus said as he made them coffee from the
few supplies he had in the small kitchenette.

"Then how did it happen?" the soldier asked, taking the proffered mug.

On the second level of the industrial unit, behind
a security-locked, fire- and soundproofed door was a
recording studio. It stank of tobacco, stale alcohol and
body odor. The recording room was tiled with carpet
felt, many instruments and amplifiers laying under
a tangle of wires and leads, some of which led into
the control booth. In there—where Manus now led
Bolan—was a mixing deck, analog and digital equipment, two swivel chairs and a sunken sofa, with a pil-
low and duvet. Manus pushed them to one side before
sitting down. Bolan sat facing him, in one of the swivel
chairs.

Manus rubbed the stubble on his scalp. "It happened
by accident. Like things do. John Lennon said that life
is what happens while you're making plans. He was
wrong. Life is what happens when you're not paying
attention. That's what happened to me. I like the music.
Who gives a shit about the lyrics? You can't make out
what they are anyway."

Bolan's lip quirked; he felt exactly the same.

Manus continued. "I've got good ears. If you don't like the music, you might not think so, but engineering and producing is not about what you like so much as what you can hear, identify and make more like the sound the band wants. I can do that. And the image makes me laugh. It pisses people off, and I like pissing people off—"

"You've pissed off the wrong people this time," Bolan commented.

Manus gave a sour grin. "I knew some of the bands actually believed the shit they sing, but I didn't know they were truly into the really heavy shit. Asmodeus is a good band…were a good band…and when they talked about me helping them with something—and some guys that were coming from Estonia—then I thought they were just more fanboys with fantasies. Instead I got a couple of guys who looked like they were on the run from a war crimes trial. By then it was too late. I'd seen them. If I said no, I was a marked man."

Bolan wasn't sure how much was true, and how much was a revision of the truth, but there was no mistaking the fear. He could smell it on the producer.

"The police haven't linked you to Asmodeus and Arsneth. Your home is not being watched by them. That's one less thing for you to worry about. Your problem is Freedom Right. I don't need to tell you—but I will anyway—that you ran out on them, and by now they'll know about it from the guys who got away."

"Got away?"

"Two guys with long hair—"

"Hades and Visigoth?"

"Yeah, or whatever their mothers call them. Everyone else was taken down."

Manus looked puzzled. "Everyone? But there was only—"

"The men he must have been expecting turned up. They just didn't get far."

"How do you know that?" Manus asked, then, realizing the stupidity of the question, added, "You were there. And now you've come for me. Make it quick, please."

"Listen, I'm your best chance of staying alive. But I need you to trust me."

"I don't have much of an option, do I?" Manus said softly.

HADES AND VISIGOTH had been let out of the basement. For the first time they walked the streets of Tallinn, able to breathe the air and feel free. They had an escort, of course, but freedom was a relative concept to the captive. Word had reached the Estonian capital that Ripper's trial had been set, and they had readily agreed to the proposal that would save their skins and free their friend.

Now they sat in an airy, sun-filled upper room, feeling optimistic that they could turn around what had seemed to them a hopeless situation and so become heroes of a forthcoming revolution.

The whip-thin Freedom Right leader, whose hawk-like visage they had become familiar with—although they still did not know his name—looked down on them with an indulgence born of experience. There would be no revolution—only a hard, long-drawn-out fight that could well end in defeat. Let them believe in their fantasy, if it was necessary to spur them on.

He placed a laptop in front of them and went over the plan.

"You arrive in Oslo the night before the trial begins. We will have the authorities believe that you have been there longer. Let them search, and when they do not find you, their impotence will be obvious to the world. We have a man placed within the courthouse security who will allow you access to plant the device. The government will have to release your friend, or else they will find the center of their city devastated. Let them see what can be done by my organization.

"You will go with three of my men. They will lay down a diversion while you place the device. The authorities will be looking for a cell that is based in their city, while we will go in, attack and be gone before they realize we are there.

"But first this will have to go," he added, indicating their hair and piercings. "Your appearance must be changed."

"But, dude, this is our identity. This is who we are," Hades said lamely.

Their captor's face hardened as he leaned over them. "No. You have no identity now. You are who we say. That way, you stay alive."

He left the two metalheads to digest that. Outside the room, he found one of his men waiting for him. "Velio? You look concerned," he greeted him.

"Not concerned, Andrus, vengeful," the stocky terrorist replied. "That traitorous Manus has returned to his house. And he's not alone."

Andrus smiled a mirthless grin. "This could be very interesting."

THE HOUSE WAS AS MANUS had left it. He moved around the interior as though it was somewhere he was seeing for the first time. Bolan went ahead and checked the outside. When he had secured the grounds, he returned to the kitchen at the back of the house, where Manus was waiting for him.

"They've got two watchers. One is using the house at the north end of the street. The second is roaming and is working on a fifteen-minute patrol. I figure the back is too dense with forest for a permanent watch, which is why they're using the mobile patrol."

"How the hell do you know that?" Manus asked.

"The house was obvious. That's why I drove past twice—to identify which one. Field glasses always give themselves away if you know what to look for. Do you have neighbors on vacation?"

"Not everyone lives here permanently—too far from the center of town. It's a weekend suburb."

Bolan nodded. "Good. I'd hate to drag anyone else into this. The roaming patrol is easily identified. You just need to watch and be patient."

Manus shrugged. Since the soldier had taken him from the studio, he had meekly allowed himself to be led—first back to Bolan's hotel, while the soldier had equipped himself for what lay ahead, and then by rental car to the very place Manus had tried to avoid. Now that he was here, he felt the pull of the inevitable was too great for resistance.

"What do we do now?" he asked Bolan.

"We wait. If they want a warning shot across the bow, they can have it. You know what you have to do?"

Manus nodded. "It's not like there's any real choice, is there?"

BROGNOLA SAT IN his office, poring over reports on paper and on screen. There were some days when it felt like his entire working existence was devoted to explaining the actions of Bolan, making conciliatory apologies to outraged authorities in far-flung countries, wondering how he could make the expenses incurred by Bolan's actions in populated areas fit the budget Brognola had. There were few in Washington who knew what he really did.

His cell phone buzzed on his desk, and he picked it up.

"Make it quick," he growled. Then, as the big Fed listened, his expression changed from annoyed to concerned.

BOLAN DISCONNECTED HIS smartphone and put it on the kitchen table.

"It looks like your favorite Estonians have just upped the stakes," he told Manus. "If Sundby isn't released to them before the trial begins, they'll detonate a bomb in the center of Oslo that will decimate the city. They've released the ultimatum virally, and some wire services have already picked it up. Your government is saying that it would be impossible, but I think we both know they have the firepower."

"Those cylinders. I don't know much about weapons, but Seb was sure keen to move those before all else."

"With good reason. They have nuclear capability. Small scale, sure, but small scale in nuke terms—"

"Is horrific," Manus finished.

Bolan nodded. "I was going to let them come for you, then use them to find where their headquarters are located. Now that they've put me on the clock, it looks like I'm going to have to force their hand. You know how to use a gun, right? I saw you with one—"

Manus shook his head. "I took it, pretended… I've never used one."

"Then listen very carefully," Bolan said as he opened the duffel bag he had brought with him, taking out a Heckler & Koch MP5. "You're going to get a crash course in using one of these. And these," he added, placing two grenades on the table. "You may well need them."

Bolan had slipped out the back of the house. The lawn fell away sharply to a dense knot of trees that clustered by a brook that ran the length of the street before disappearing into a culvert that ran under the road.

To position men here for surveillance would have been difficult. To effect an escape was not easy. Bolan used the cover of approaching night to head for the cover of the trees. He plunged into the brook, ignoring the cold as it soaked through his boots and the cuff of his blacksuit pants. His ordnance was in the duffel bag, slung high across his shoulders. A Tekna knife in his belt was the only weapon immediately at hand, but as stealth and silence were what he required at this point, that wasn't a problem.

The brook was sluggish, and he was fortunate enough to be moving with the current and so making little noise. When he came to the culvert under the road, he was relieved to find that it was open, with no shutter or grille barring his way and needing removal. He dropped to his knees and crawled quickly through, feeling the water cold on his hands and knees. At least he was able to keep his belly raised and didn't need to crawl flat. When he reached the far end of the drain pipe, Bolan massaged life back to his hands before continuing.

He was now across the street from the target house, coming on the blind side. He looked at his watch: five minutes remained until the roaming patrol came into view. He crossed the street to the house facing him, the back of which connected to the yard of his objective.

There was a six-foot side gate to the rear of the house, which he climbed with ease. A low wall stood at the rear of the yard, fronted with half-grown fir trees.

The soldier scaled the wall slowly. On the far side the yard was empty, and by the light showing at the back of the house, a man was in the kitchen. The house resembled Manus's from the outside, and the brightly lit interior showed that the layout was similar.

Bolan dropped down and ran in a crouch toward the rear of the house. The back wall of the lower story was one long glass sliding door. The light from inside shone onto the lawn. Bolan skirted that area, staying in shadows, the knife now resting easily in his palm. The man in the kitchen was alone.

The man busied himself in there, seemingly oblivious to anything else. He turned away, pulling open the refrigerator and peering inside.

Bolan tried the sliding door. Unlocked. He eased

it open, slipping through the gap and heading for his target.

The soldier had been silent, but the terrorist had enough awareness to sense another presence and turned. His jaw dropped when he was saw Bolan coming for him, and his hand snaked toward the Smith & Wesson pistol holstered on his hip.

He was quick, but Bolan was quicker. One arm curled around the terrorist's neck, pulling him down to meet the upward thrust of the Executioner's hand as it drove the Tekna knife into the cavity below the ribs, twisting hard. The victim's face was rammed into Bolan's shoulder, stifling his cries, while his gun arm was wedged, stopping him from pulling his gun from its resting place.

Bolan felt the man stiffen then relax, and let him slide to the floor. He took the gun from its holster and slipped it into the web belt over his blacksuit before heading for the stairs.

He had no idea how many terrorists were in the house, but he had already taken one out of the game and next had to be the man watching the street.

THE CAR CRUISED past the house for the eighteenth time. Two more and the crew would change shifts, getting some much-needed rest. Muscles would be tired and cramped after so long.

The man watching them from the upper story window put down his field glasses for a moment and rubbed his eyes before staring across at Manus's house without the device. Manus and the mystery man had entered an hour before, and there had been no sign of movement since. All they would need was the word, and they could move in. It should be a simple operation.

He heard the door of the bedroom click softly as it was opened.

"I hope you put cream in my coffee this time and not milk. Since these assholes left us with a well-stocked fridge, we might as well take advantage of it," he muttered, raising the field glasses once more. They were frozen halfway to his face by the time the sound of the strange voice behind him reached his ears.

"No cream this time. You don't deserve it. You should be more observant, if you want to do this job properly."

CHAPTER TWELVE

The terrorist turned quickly after Bolan spoke. Taking in the scene almost unconsciously, Bolan's prey groped behind his back for the Walther pistol he had left on the windowsill, the field glasses falling from his other, now nerveless, hand. As he reached, at the same time he threw himself sideways so as to present a smaller moving target.

Bolan threw the Tekna, the blade pinioning the terrorist's hand to the sill, the gun skittering away from his hopeless grasp. He started to cry out in agony and shock, but the sound was stifled in his throat as the iron edge of Bolan's hand slammed into his Adam's apple, choking back both voice and breath. As he sank to his knees, the soldier slammed a fist into the soft area behind his ear.

The terrorist was out cold. Ideally it would have been good to get some idea from him of how many other people were in the house and when the patrol would return. He would just have to find that out the hard way.

Bolan frisked the unconscious man for weapons, pocketed his cell phone and picked up the Walther.

The gun and the field glasses had landed with dull thumps, muffled by the thick carpet, but still Bolan paused for a moment, listening for any reaction.

There was none. The two terrorists had either been alone in the house, or else there were others who had grown lax through inaction.

Downstairs was clear. There was only this level left to secure. Bolan had seen three other closed doors as he had ascended the open-plan stairs. Bathroom and bedrooms? Probably, but which was which?

Bolan left the unconscious terrorist, knowing from the force with which Bolan had hit him that Bolan had at least twenty minutes before the man would even stir. Outside, on the landing that faced the living room and kitchen area, Bolan walked softly to the first door. Listening, he could hear no noise within. He tried the handle; the door was unlocked. Gently he opened it to reveal an empty bathroom.

He closed the door softly and proceeded to the next one. There had to be at least two more terrorists in this cell, otherwise how could they organize the patrols, the static recon and still find time to rest? Yet there seemed to be no one else here.

The room behind the second door was also silent. He repeated the procedure, only to find that this was a bedroom.

He was about to close the door and move on when he heard faint voices from behind the last door. He made to duck into this room and conceal himself when he was forestalled by the last door opening suddenly and a tall, thin man in shorts stepping out. He was facing away from the soldier, rubbing his head as though only just awake, and muttering in reply to another inhabitant, out of sight.

Bolan was almost hidden when the man looked around. He had to have just caught a glimpse of the soldier—enough before his instincts told him that something was very wrong. Snapped instantly awake, he yelled and dived back into the room. Bolan cursed and stepped out of cover enough to take a shot that took a chunk from the doorjamb but was just a fraction off the beat.

He pulled himself back into the small room, anticipating the flurry of fire that rained down the hallway.

Now he had a problem: he was trapped in this room, with two men able to advance on him.

Slipping the duffel bag off his shoulder, he pulled out a gas grenade. He loosed a couple of shots at an angle beyond the door to dissuade any swift advances while he ferreted nose plugs from a pouch on his web belt and put them into place. Another two covering shots—only a couple left in the magazine now—and he rolled the grenade out along the hallway floor. He heard both men yell a warning and begin to cough as the cloud of gas started to spread up and out, drifting toward them. The soldier fired off the last two shots to keep the gunners back, then took his micro Uzi SMG from the duffel bag.

Stepping out into the hall, he saw the two terrorists clustered around the doorway to the third room. They had MP5s, each pointed at the floor as the men were doubled over, their eyes streaming, both coughing as the gas seared their lungs. They tried to turn and fire but were too incapacitated to respond with speed. Their SMGs were not even level when Bolan had taken them down with two quick bursts that had stitched them both. Before they hit the floor, the soldier advanced toward them.

He stepped over the bodies and sprayed gunfire into

the bedroom. If anyone else had been hiding there, they would most likely have been hit; at least, they would have been driven to find cover and be unable to attack as Bolan stepped into the room, his Uzi SMG leading the way.

It was empty. Bolan moved forward and quickly rummaged through three carryalls that lay on a twin bed. Two contained clothes and toiletries, while the third held ordnance. There were two cell phones lying on a nightstand. He picked them up and stowed them in a slit pocket of the blacksuit. A shattered photo frame lay on the floor, where his random fire had thrust it. It showed a young couple with two small girls.

Looking around again, without the focus of a moment ago, Bolan could see that this was a little girl's bedroom. The group in the photograph had to be the usual residents. The Executioner was thankful that they had not been here when the terrorists had chosen to make this house their base.

But he put the thought out of mind; there was still work to be done.

The cloud of gas hung thickly over the upper level of the house as Bolan surveyed the bedroom for any other useful items of intel, then returned to the first bedroom. He looked for anything that he might have missed, and while he was there, he checked the condition of the unconscious terrorist. The man was still out cold, and with the lungful of gas he had taken in while the brief firefight had raged, it was likely that he would be out for several hours more. Any chance of gathering intel from him was negligible.

Bolan had no idea how long it would be until the members of the patrol were relieved, but if they maintained regular contact, then the lack of response would bring them running. He had to complete his search of the house quickly. Recovering his duffel bag, he hurried to the lower level, where a search of the living room turned up a tablet. He put it in the duffel bag. Along with the three cell phones he had taken, there was a good chance of useful intel being pulled from the devices.

Time to reel in the patrol. Bolan wanted to get Manus to a place of safety as soon as possible and also get to work on downloading the contents of the phones and tablet to Stony Man for analysis. He couldn't do that while two of the terrorists were still out there.

He checked his watch. Forty-three minutes had passed since he had made his way down to the brook. That had been ten minutes since the last circuit he had observed. They were due back this way in seven minutes.

Bolan left the house by the front door and jogged across the road to Manus's house. As he ran up the drive, the front door opened, and he could see Manus peering anxiously at him.

When they were both inside, Bolan explained briefly what had happened, and what he now needed to do. The young producer seemed to take it in, although Bolan could see that the tension was getting the better of him.

"Hang in there," Bolan finished. "I'll arrange it so that you have protection, and at the same time you can tell the authorities everything that you know to show good faith."

"I wish I could trust you on that," Manus said bitterly.

"Listen, when my contact finishes with the authorities here, you'll be surprised that they don't give you the freedom of Oslo. You were roped into this reluctantly, and you've done all you can to extricate yourself. Keep it together, Manus, for just a few minutes more."

Bolan checked his watch: two minutes to go before the terrorists would drive by again. If he had been dubious as to Manus's sincerity at the beginning, the young man was either genuinely terrified or wasted in the music business when he could be winning acting awards.

The Executioner walked to the front door and then out onto the drive. He took the Benelli shotgun from the duffel bag and racked it.

"What the hell are you doing?" Manus asked, half in disbelief and half in horror.

"Ending this quickly," Bolan replied. "There's no need for subtlety now."

His timing was accurate. The car turned onto the end of the street, heading for him, as he reached the middle of the road. The headlights pinned him in their glare. The car seemed to slow for a second, and then picked up speed as Bolan raised the shotgun and aimed directly at the windshield. He cut loose two blasts that took out the windshield and the driver. He stood squarely in the middle of the road, unmoving, while the car slewed to the left and plowed through the hedge and into the front yard of the house directly opposite Manus's.

Even before the car had come to a halt, Bolan moved after it, racking the shotgun again as he approached. There was no sign of life in the car, even though the engine whined uselessly as the dead driver's foot jammed on the gas and the wheels spun in the damp earth of a flower bed.

His shotgun preceding him, Bolan looked in, could see that the second terrorist was also dead, his neck at an unnatural angle where it had hit the frame of the car.

Bolan backed away quickly, returning to Manus's house. The front door was already open, and the soldier beckoned Manus to join him. The young producer rushed out, and they climbed into Bolan's rental car, the soldier pushing Manus to the driver's side.

"You drive. I need to make a call."

"Where am I heading?" Manus asked.

"My hotel—for now," Bolan replied.

While Manus pulled away, Bolan took out his own smartphone and called Stony Man.

"Bear, I'm downloading some intel I've just picked up from Freedom Right. You might tell Hal there's some cleaning up to do…and I'll need him to put in a good word for my friend Mr. Manus…."

BROGNOLA HAD NO IDEA if there was a minister of justice in Norway or what the equivalent post may be or who filled that position. But he soon found out, and when he had, he placed a call to the minister, regardless of any time difference. It was not the most comfortable of conversations under the circumstances, especially when it came to explaining why a quiet residential area of Oslo had become a temporary war zone, and why an American justice department official knew of this before the local authorities.

However, even if the Norwegian was in the dark about the bunker and its contents, the mention of the threat to Oslo made by Freedom Right and the potential firepower that intel had unearthed was enough to cut through any red tape and dispel any air of distrust and political pride that may have been bruised.

Two hours later Erik Manus walked into a police station in the center of Oslo and was surprised to find that he was not greeted as a criminal, which was still his expectation, despite the American's promises. When he was taken to an unmarked building in the center of the city and made welcome by men in suits who were keen to ask him a number of questions—but politely—he only then began to realize the magnitude of what he had unwillingly been coerced into. At that point he also realized how lucky he had been that the American had got to him before the Estonians.

He wondered who the American had actually been…and what he was doing now.

"TALK TO ME, BEAR," Bolan said as he hit the highway once more.

"Your friend Manus is in custody and will be looked after. You think he's genuine? You think he knows anything?"

"He's a stupid young man like the others, but he's a stupid young man who didn't know how to back off without getting himself hurt and so got in too deep. I don't know if he really knows anything, but I'd bet that, if he does, it's something that he doesn't actually know he knows."

"Sheesh, I love it when you go all Scooby-Doo cryptic on me, Striker," Kurtzman said sardonically. "But let's leave that little debate for another day. What I know—and I know that I know—is that the data on the cells and tablet were very interesting indeed. The calls and texts were mostly personal. They seem to keep their communications to a minimum. What we have been able to isolate are many of a more business-like nature—on all three cells—that go to a number we can trace to Tallinn."

"I know it's the capital of Estonia, like Oslo is for Norway, but what is with these racial purists that they like locating themselves where their countries have the highest concentration of immigrants? Does it reinforce their beliefs to do that, or are they just hiding in plain sight?"

"I'd bank on the latter," Bear mused. "Neither city is a nationalist stronghold, so their security services don't go looking there…"

"But we do. Have you got a location?" Bolan asked.

"Without a call in operation, can't trace it. And, no, I don't think you should try just to get a fix. That kind of warning even you can do without. We do have a billing address, though. It's a box number, but I'll give you evens they're within about a quarter-mile radius. The little things always let them down."

"It's a start. Anything else?"

"They seem to operate on a need-to-know basis and keep their cells fairly isolated when on a mission. There was very little relating to the Oslo pronouncement. An address of where the other cell is, maybe? That would have been nice."

"Maybe they're not even there," Bolan suggested.

"They'd have to be. Four days? It's a hell of a job to get people in and set it up in that time."

"Not if they have one man there to rig things, and then move the rest of the men and the ordnance later. The Norwegians were headed up there with the ordnance.

Freedom Right is planning to use one of those Russian nukes and decimate Oslo. They're not concerned with stopping the trial. That's just an excuse to flex their muscle. If it's up there, then they'll bus it down at the last moment."

"It could already have been dropped. Who's to say that they didn't split the ordnance along the way?" Bear asked.

"No one, but think about it. Even if they were met en route, if you were an Estonian, would you trust a couple of kids to deliver a payload like that? Another thing—the reason they used the band in the first place was because they didn't want to risk putting too many men in. They only used the minimum number to track Manus. They haven't got men on the ground…

"The nuke's either there or en route. And it's my job to stop it."

CHAPTER THIRTEEN

As he drove north, Bolan considered the position of Freedom Right. Politically and ideologically, he didn't care; their geographical position was much more urgent.

Estonia was an aggressively developing country, but it had little in the way of mineral wealth, which made it vulnerable. Especially as it was bordered by Latvia and Russia, countries that had an abundance of minerals, and could impose their will if it became relevant.

Finland and Sweden bordered Estonia on the west and north. At one point, Estonia had spent centuries as a part of Sweden before spending most of the twentieth century annexed to the Soviet empire. It had been a slave state for much of its existence and had only recently been able to once again assert itself. That might explain a lot about groups such as Freedom Right.

Easy access to Scandinavia meant that Bolan's theory was the most likely method of attack.

Yet easy access from Russia was what concerned him. The Russian president would be livid that his men had not recovered the ordnance from the bunker. If Bolan and Stony Man knew who was responsible—to the extent of being able to narrow down their location to a quarter-mile radius—then it was a certain bet that the Russian military and intelligence services weren't far behind. And they had the ability to put men on the ground quickly and with greater numbers and speed than the soldier could hope to achieve.

He was up against more than one clock: not just the countdown to Sundby's trial but also the ticking time bomb that was the Russian president's chagrin.

VELIO KROSS WAS FURIOUS. Andrus would not be pleased when the message was relayed. Velio paused outside the room where the Freedom Right leader was sitting with the two Norwegians, running them through their battle plan. Velio's hesitation was partly to compose himself and partly to listen.

Through the plain wood door he could hear Andrus patiently explaining to the young men the route they would take, and where they would rendezvous with the contact. Arvo would accompany them, riding shotgun and ensuring that their lack of experience did not lead them into trouble along the way.

Velio grinned. Trouble was exactly what Arvo would lead them into. And then…

He knocked and entered. The two Norwegians looked expectantly at him, while his leader let a frown of annoyance flicker across his hawklike brow before masking it as the two young men turned back to him. He excused himself at Velio's raised eyebrow and left them to contemplate their mission.

"Well?" he snapped when he had closed the door. "You know I didn't want to be interrupted. God knows it's hard enough to get anything into their heads, but—"

"You'll want to know this, though you won't thank me for it," Velio interrupted before detailing what had happened to the men dispatched to find and secure Manus. The terrorist group's inside man had gained full access to the report, even to the extent of knowing Manus was now in secure custody.

Andrus gritted his teeth in anger. "How much does this idiot know?"

Velio shook his head. "Very little. About as much as those two cretins in there, probably a lot less. Milan and Seb would keep things on need-to-know, and they were just using Manus for accommodations. I doubt he even knew much about the bunker until they took him there. He is not the problem."

Andrus nodded. "True. Who are these men who are ruining our plans at every turn? If they are Americans, then are they CIA or black ops of some kind? And just how many of them are there?"

"Our man can tell us nothing. There is no official conformation of nationality and no record of any personnel liaising with Norwegian forces. It's like they are shadows, and only we can see them."

"They are more than shadows, and they are a king-size pain in the ass. If we are going to carry out our mission with real effectiveness, then we at least need those two idiots to look like they are going to achieve their objective."

For the first time since the news had reached him, Velio allowed himself a small smile. "They really have no notion of what is going on?"

Andrus shook his head. "They are like children. Particularly stupid children, at that…just like that scumbag Russian president…"

"It's the last thing he will expect."

"Exactly. That is why we must press ahead and disregard the threat the Americans may pose. They have been an irritant, but they have not yet completely deflected us from our plan. As long as we can keep them focused on Oslo, then they may yet be obstructive enough to the Norwegians to actually aid us."

"Very good. I shall tell our man in Oslo not to worry."

"Indeed...but send a three-man team to stand at his shoulder. I should hate it if we could not get that fool released—or eliminated—before he opens his stupid mouth too far. I wonder if the Americans are still hunting fruitlessly around Oslo, like the Norwegians?"

"Of course they will be—they have no reason to suspect anything."

BOLAN ARRIVED IN TALLINN exhausted after his drive. He had a directory of hotels in the capital on his smartphone and picked the closest one to the P.O. Box billing address. The closer he was to ground zero, the sooner he could begin his search. But first he needed to grab a few hours' sleep. Otherwise his judgment might become impaired, and he could overlook something vital or make a fatal error.

IT WAS NIGHTTIME when he awoke. The interior of the room was lit by the streetlights outside, yet swathed in shadow. As Bolan rose and looked on the nightlife in this section of the capital, he wondered where he should begin. There was no time to stake out the P.O. Box pickup and follow whoever showed up. He would have to be a little more proactive than that.

The ghost of a smile flitted across his face as he figured out a shortcut.

THE BAR WAS OFF the main drag, down two side streets and an alley that took it beyond the kind of areas frequented by tourists. It was a local bar, for local people, and the low murmur of conversation rumbled beneath the sound of a soccer commentator trying desperately to whip up enthusiasm for a lower-league English game in which players no one had ever heard of—or were likely to hear of—showed why the name, the Beautiful Game, was a misnomer.

As the bartender polished a glass and noted that only a few of the customers were paying attention to the game, he turned his back on the bar in order to kill the TV.

"Don't do that. It's nice to hear something I can easily understand."

The bartender froze then slowly turned to the tall, dark, muscular man facing him and grinning broadly.

"Cooper. I never ever expected to see you here. Get the hell out of my bar."

"Now, is that any way to greet an old comrade?" Bolan asked, ignoring him and leaning on the bar. "I'll have a cold lager, when you're ready," he added.

"Excuse me, I know you are American, but even so you still claim to speak English. So what part of the last sentence did you not understand?"

"Come on, Dostoyevsky. I thought you'd be pleased to see me."

The saturnine man leaned across the bar so that his poker-straight face was almost touching the soldier's.

"Pleased? The last time I saw you, Cooper, I had the pleasure of ending up in a hospital bed for longer than I would have cared. Do you know that my knee aches in cold weather now?"

"It wasn't your knee you injured," Bolan said mildly.

The bartender's face split into a sly grin. "I know. What the hell brings you to this quiet little backwater?"

"Maybe not so quiet…after all, you're here."

"Because of me it's quiet. Look at it, Cooper," Dostoyevsky—bar owner and ex-mercenary—said with a sweep of his arm. "The quiet life, a chance to kick back and relax, to think about life as the world passes me by instead of trying to kick me in the ass."

"You're bored out of your skull," Bolan commented.

"Hell, yes…I was looking forward to retirement, and I invested my fee for the Chechen operation in this. But you know something? I don't think retirement is ready for me."

"Then I may have a question that will kill your boredom."

"As long as it doesn't kill me, as well." The bartender looked at the sedate room of regular customers, nodded and called out to a back room. A young woman with long raven hair, stunning cheekbones and icy blue eyes appeared in the doorway.

"Lana, mind the bar for me," he said in Russian. "I have to catch up with my old friend."

Lana eyed Bolan up and down. With no change in her expression, and without taking her eyes from the soldier, she said, "I thought you promised me those days were over. I don't want to be a widow and hit on by customers who think they could end up owners."

"Ah, it's not like that, woman," Dostoyevsky muttered with a dismissive wave before opening the bar flap and ushering Bolan through.

"It never is," Lana returned coldly, her eyes following Bolan as he went through to the back.

A kitchen for food preparation and glass cleaning

was set up to one side, with the balance of the room fitted out as a comfortable rest area.

"Is it me, or has the temperature dropped several degrees?" Bolan commented as Dostoyevsky bade him to be seated.

"Lana, she worries. That's good. Then she moans. That's not so good. I can live with it," Dostoyevsky answered with a dismissive head shake. "Right now, she will be wondering just what I am. What brings Matt Cooper to Estonia?"

Bolan had thought carefully about how to approach the Russian, and began, "Tell me, are you still a great admirer of your president?"

"I love the bald, power-mad bastard. That's why I live in another country."

"I was kind of hoping you still felt that way," Bolan said, remembering the endless tirades he had endured from the ex-mercenary. "I've got a story that may interest you."

Dostoyevsky sat and listened while Bolan outlined the events that had taken him to Norway in the first instance, and then to Finland and now to Estonia. He was careful to highlight the possible involvement of the Russians, and also the prominence of Freedom Right and their possible location. When he had finished, he sat back and held his hands wide, inviting the Russian to comment.

Dostoyevsky ruminated on the information before answering, seeming to mull over matters in some depth. Finally he nodded and leaned forward. What he said was not exactly what Bolan had expected.

"What kind of armament have you brought with you?" he asked, listening carefully before adding, with a sly grin, "How would you like some explosives and an RPD to add to that? I know where I can lay my hands on some nice heavy-duty ordnance."

The explosives might be useful, but Bolan wondered if the 40 mm machine gun, which had 100-round drums and needed a bipod—or even a tripod—to mount it before use would be practical in what he saw as a get-in-get-out rapid-hit mission. Seeing his hesitation, the Russian shrugged.

"It's up to you, of course, but you can't go wrong with some serious Russian firepower to back you up. Come on," he added, standing, "let's get you some backup."

"You're not wasting time," Bolan said wryly as he stood.

Dostoyevsky shrugged. "You're the one who is in the hurry," he answered in a laconic manner. "I'll tell Lana on the way out."

"She won't like that."

"There is very little she likes but much she will put up with. It's how she is," the ex-mercenary replied with a shrug. "We have much to do...."

LESS THAN A HALF HOUR LATER, in a suburb of Tallinn that was populated by houses built in a timbered Finnish style, Dostoyevsky pulled up before a structure fenced and gated in wrought iron.

"Looks nice, yes? Try to climb that and see how it fries your balls."

"How do we get in then?" Bolan queried.

"We ask nicely," Dostoyevsky replied as he got out of the car and walked across the quiet street.

Bolan followed him, scanning the gates and surrounding fence for any sign of an entry phone. He cast the Russian a querying glance and was answered with another sly smile as Dostoyevsky took out his cell phone and called up a number on his directory.

"It's me.... I know, but circumstances change. I have some business for you." He hung up, and grinned broadly as the gates swung wide before them. "Money is a wonderful thing," he murmured as he ushered Bolan up the drive.

The double doors to the house opened, and they were greeted by a slab of meat in a suit masquerading as security. He directed them through an ornately furnished hall and into an office that was lined with leather-bound books—which looked artificial—on mahogany shelves that matched the desk. Behind the desk sat a desiccated man with a peppered goatee and wraparound shades.

"I like the look, Dimitri," the ex-mercenary said in a conversational tone. "I'll bet you can't see a thing in this light."

"True, but you can't see if I'm looking at you or not," the small man replied in a voice that was as dried as his frame.

They were speaking in Russian, and Bolan's mind raced as he tried to place the man before them. There was something familiar about him, but age had not been kind. It was a few moments before he placed the man as Dimitri Bulganin, an ex-KGB general who had gone missing after the fall of the Soviet empire and had been heard of only sporadically since, both as an "adviser" to third-world dictators and as an arms dealer. It looked like he had settled into a prosperous semiretirement in the relative obscurity of Estonia.

Any photographs of him were decades old now and did not reflect the passing of the years. He was safe here.

While the two Russians exchanged pleasantries and discussed possible purchases of ordnance, Bolan realized why Dostoyevsky had brought him here. Bulganin, because of his trade, would know of anyone in the country interested in large amounts of ordnance. More important in terms of his anonymity and happy retirement, he would not want any undue attention focused on his city of residence.

Bolan waited patiently while the two men discussed the possible purchase of the RPD machine gun and the grenades. When a nominal price had been agreed upon, Dostoyevsky added, almost offhandedly, "By the way, you may be wondering what has prompted a return to action. My friend has something you may wish to hear."

The shriveled old general smiled. His dry, thin lips pulled over his teeth like a grinning skull. "Mr.... Belasko? No, Cooper these days, I believe."

Bolan returned the smile with the same sharklike coldness. "You're very well informed, General Bulganin."

"As are you, Mr. Cooper. Forgive my showing off. I rarely get the chance in this backwater to showboat, as I believe you call it."

"It helps us to know where we stand, General—"

"Please, call me Dimitri. The title is a sad reminder of a glorious past, no more."

Bolan nodded. "Dimitri then. I'm here because of a matter that relates to your old country as well as your new. Allow me to explain."

For the second time that night, Bolan outlined events

that had led him to Tallinn. He could see from the hardening of the old man's expression that he—like Dostoyevsky—had little love for the current Russian regime.

More than that, Bolan could see that the idea of his backwater becoming a focus of counterintelligence activity—as it undoubtedly would if Freedom Right were allowed to carry out their plans—was not a prospect that pleased Bulganin.

When Bolan concluded, the old man nodded decisively and rose to his feet. He walked over to the fake bookshelves and hit a hidden switch. The shelving slid back to reveal a stairwell. There was something old-fashioned about it, and Bulganin shrugged as he caught the soldier's expression.

"You must forgive an old man his indulgences. I like to keep some stock on site, and I like to feel there is a sense of tradition in what I do. If you gentlemen will follow me, we can examine the explosives and machine gun, if you truly wish to buy. If not, we can discuss payment for a less tangible commodity."

"Such as?" Bolan queried.

"Freedom Right, Mr. Cooper. They are customers of mine. I like to keep extensive files on my customers. Friends closer than enemies, I am sure you understand.... I do not appreciate their finding other sources, nor the opprobrium and attention it could bring me. Most unwelcome. For this, I will strike a good bargain with you."

CHAPTER FOURTEEN

"Have you seen much of the country since you arrived here?" Dostoyevsky asked as he swung his sedan around and headed back into the center of the city.

"The airport, your bar, the hardware store," Bolan replied in a dry tone.

Dostoyevsky's blank visage lightened briefly, then he said, "I may not have given you the impression, but I quite like this place. It has a number of beautiful castles scattered about the countryside, which is why the Nazis were so keen to take it from Scandinavia in the Second World War. The fascists love a castle, and they love some feudal history. The Estonians, on the other hand, show too many signs of being under Stalin's heel for so long. They want nothing more than nice and functional. And small. People crammed into the tiniest possible spaces."

"I wouldn't have had you down as an architectural expert," Bolan commented. "There's a point to this, right?"

"Absolutely. With so many large buildings—most of which are in isolation—that have built-in security, why would Freedom Right choose to take a house that is in the middle of a city and is surrounded by newly constructed buildings that are crammed with curious and snooping idiots?"

Bolan said nothing for a moment. The intel Bulganin had given them included an address that was only a few blocks from Bolan's hotel and a couple from Dostoyevsky's bar. The thought that they were operating so close by created problems. Taking down the terrorists without triggering an incident involving police and civilians was unlikely.

If Freedom Right had heavy-duty ordnance on the premises, then the chance of severe collateral damage was increased. Bolan guessed that the group had chosen Tallinn for the simple reason that they wanted to hide in plain sight, and despite the security offered by one of the many castles in isolated locations, this would make comings and goings paradoxically more likely to be reported.

On balance, Bolan could see why they had chosen to stay in the city. He told the Russian this and was met with a wry grin.

"Maybe so, but I tell you something. Our job would be easier if it was somewhere out of the way. I don't want to be firing in two directions, you know?"

They pulled up at the back of the Russian's bar and took the ordnance they had purchased from Bulganin out the trunk of the sedan. Bulganin had not charged them for the intel but had made it a condition that they bought merchandise from him. The Russian had murmured that it was hardly as though he had books to keep and taxes to pay, but Bolan figured that all men love a system, especially those whose very survival had depended on keeping tabs on everything in their lives.

They carried the canvas-wrapped bundles through to the back room of the bar as a second sedan pulled up behind them, and the slab of meat who was Bulganin's bodyguard got out and followed them in.

"Do we really have to have him?" Bolan murmured as the guy stood by the door, looking as though he was standing guard and saying nothing, his face immobile and unreadable.

"Part of the deal."

"There are too many conditions on this," Bolan commented.

"Life is compromise, my friend," his Russian friend stated. "Speaking of which…"

Lana walked through from the bar area and looked them up and down. Her eyes lingered on the slab of meat by the door.

"You said those days were over," she hissed. "Like everything else, you lied."

"I did not lie." The Russian shrugged. "Circumstances change."

"Nothing can justify this change," she snapped, turning on her heel and returning to the bar before the Russian had a chance to reply. He stopped momentarily in his task and watched her go.

"Maybe you should have a few words with her," Bolan suggested.

The Russian shook his head. "There is no time. Besides, she always goes off like this, no matter what. By the time we have resolved this, one way or the other, then she will have come around. Let us just hope that I am here to receive her apology," he finished with a wry smile.

The bodyguard joined them at the table as the Russian dragged back a rug on the floor and opened a small trapdoor, under which he kept boxes containing grenades and SMGs, as well as spare magazines of ammunition and a selection of handguns. As he heaved some of the boxes onto the table, the bodyguard looked at him. His expression didn't change, but the Russian could read him.

"Don't worry, Igor. I have no intention of setting up an operation in competition with your employer. I just like to be prepared in event of emergencies."

The three men supplied themselves, selecting ordnance and checking that their selections were in working order. They continued in silence. Only when they were equipped did Bolan indicate that Dostoyevsky should produce a tablet and call up maps of the locale.

"I love Google Earth," the Russian deadpanned as they studied the location from the bar to the house where Bulganin told them Freedom Right was located. It was a ten-minute walk from the bar to the early twentieth-century three-story house where Freedom Right had their secured headquarters. Situated just off the city center, in an area that had escaped regeneration because of its architectural heritage, the building stood as part of a terrace that ran the length of the street. To the rear, it backed onto the yard and carport of a new apartment building. That would enable them to access the back as well as the front.

Igor spoke, indicating areas on the screen while he did, in a voice that was surprisingly high and clear for his appearance.

"They have watchmen on the top story, always. Working in rotation. The basement is where they have their ordnance—I have delivered here many times for Dimitri. Andrus and Velio have their quarters on the second floor. Central in the building, with metal reinforced doors and walls against blast. They are the brains. Without them, the others are just meatheads. If we isolate or eliminate them, then picking off the rest will be simple. The main thing is to cut off access to the basement. They usually carry only handguns or maybe an SMG in the house. They feel too at ease. We can use that."

Bolan nodded in approval. "I can see why Bulganin wanted you on board," he said.

"Dimitri likes a job done quickly and with a minimum of fuss." Igor shrugged. "May I suggest you take the front, while I cover the back?"

"Why would you want to do that?" Dostoyevsky mused. "Perhaps you would like to put us together so that you can fulfill your own agenda?"

Something that may perhaps have been a smile flickered across Igor's face. "You can have your suspicions. The truth is that I know the building better than you, and I can secure the basement from the rear while you attack the front and move up. Look—" he indicated an area that was blurry on camera "—at the rear of the apartment building there is a service area for trash. The wall there is low. I will go over the wall. There is an old coal cellar delivery door that has a loose bolt. I know that because I loosened it. I can get into the house from here and secure the area they use for ordnance."

"Now why would you want to make it easy to break into your best customer?" the Russian queried.

"Keep your enemies close, your friends closer, like Bulganin said," Bolan answered for Igor. "Am I right?"

"You understand my employer well," Igor agreed. "Now, if we are ready, I suggest we go."

WHILE BOLAN, DOSTOYEVSKY and Igor discussed their forthcoming assault, Bulganin sat in his study under the illumination of a desk lamp, staring into the darkness and brooding. This was a situation that did not reflect well on him, no matter what may occur. Freedom Right had brought attention to Tallinn that he did not want. They had be removed and with as little fuss as possible.

And yet, if the American and Dostoyevsky took them down, the repercussions from any evidence remaining could still be damaging to him.

Damage: that was the very word. Limitation, by association, was the next in his mind.

He picked up the phone.

THE DOOR BURST OPEN and Velio flicked on the light. Andrus sprung upright, his eyes unfocused.

"I know, I know," the Freedom Right second-in-command said, forestalling his commander. "This is important. Bulganin."

"What does that Russian scumbag want?" Andrus growled.

"For a Russian, he's not so bad. Or maybe just cautious. The Americans are here. One of them, at least. With a Russian ex-mercenary in tow. They're taking us down."

"How do they know where we are?"

"What do you think?"

Andrus was already dressed and checking his HK as he replied, "I can guess. At least he had the grace to warn us. Get the stupid Norwegians ready. Evac as soon as possible, red alert on the watch."

As Velio hurried to complete his orders, Andrus

racked his SMG and cursed. In truth, it meant little more than bringing operations forward by a few hours, but at what potential cost?

"ARE YOU CERTAIN his name is really Igor?" Bolan asked as they approached the front of the building on foot.

"Cooper, it may seem strange to your Hollywood-trained mind, but Igor is not just something Bela Lugosi is called in old horror movies. It's actually a name with a great and distinguished history to it."

"But come on, the way he looks…"

Dostoyevsky shrugged. "Fair point. He does fit the part, and Dimitri is not a man without a sense of humor, no matter how twisted."

They came from the main street, walking abreast and making no attempt to hide themselves. As far as they were concerned, they were not expected; attempting subterfuge when there was little cover would only attract the watchmen's attention. Dostoyevsky carried the RPD under a canvas cover, while Bolan had a duster borrowed from the Russian covering his black-suit and hiding the bulk of an HK, a mini Uzi, and a holstered Desert Eagle pistol, as well as a string of smoke and explosive grenades across his web belt. He checked his wristwatch. According to the time, Igor should be, right now, underneath the building they were approaching. He counted off until chaos broke loose.

But when it did, it was not as he expected.

IGOR WALKED BRISKLY through the carport at the rear of the apartment building and hauled the trash cans out of his way, scaling the wall with one heave of the muscles in his arms and shoulders. He had an HK and mini Uzi strung across his chest, and was still wearing his suit. He ignored the ripping of the jacket as he dropped into the yard at the back of the house.

He looked up at the sightless windows. Swiftly he made his way to the trapdoor, which he pried open before dropping into the cellar area. So far, so good. He made his way across the coal cellar to the door leading into the basement area. The door was unlocked, and he opened it cautiously. There was no sound from the other side, and he stepped into the narrow corridor, sliding the HK from his shoulder and into his slablike fist.

Perhaps a little too late. He froze at the sight of the two Estonians who stood at the end of the corridor, covering him with their own SMGs.

"Surprise…" one of them said, grinning.

"MOVE, NOW," ARVO commanded. Hades and Visigoth moved quickly, but with the jerky motion of men who were unsure of exactly what they should be doing. As they passed the open door at the end of the corridor, they could see a suited man being beaten by two Estonians. He had something to do with their sudden mobilization.

"Back way," Arvo snapped, guiding them where Igor had been dragged and out through the cellar. They moved across the yard and up over the wall to the carport, where a black truck was parked.

"Here's one we prepared earlier," the Estonian said as he unlocked the vehicle.

The three men got in, and Hades took the keys from the Estonian, firing up the engine.

"Why the change in plan?" he asked hesitantly. "We're going to get there a day before—"

"No questions, just drive. Things change. You want your friend back, right?"

Hades knew that there was more going on than he and Visigoth had been told but was too scared to probe further as he guided the truck out onto a deserted road. He knew he was right as he heard the distant chatter of SMG fire.

One thing was for sure: the sooner he hit the highway, the safer he would feel.

THE FRONT OF THE HOUSE exploded into life. Literally, for the top story windows were blown out by an avalanche of SMG fire that peppered the street below, and caused Bolan and Dostoyevsky to rush for the nearest cover. There they could cut down the angle and make themselves smaller targets.

It also trapped them and prevented any forward progress unless they could stop the fire from above. It was covering fire, and the soldier was sure that it was cover for an evacuation operation. He had been expecting an explosion from within that would have signaled Igor reaching the basement armory.

Two options: Igor had double-crossed them, or else he had been expected and had been double-crossed by his boss. Bolan could expect nothing less of Bulganin, though he had neither the time nor the inclination to work out his labyrinthine motives. Right now, they were pinned and needed to make some space to attack the front.

Dostoyevsky had unwrapped the RPD machine gun and set it up, using the 100-round drum to lay down covering fire. He sat behind the tripod-mounted weapon, firing steadily and using its bulk as cover as he edged out from the side of the building to get a better angle.

Bolan could see what the Russian was doing and, keeping low, Bolan headed across to the far side of the street, zigzagging to make a harder target while taking two grenades from his web belt. One was an explosive grenade, the other a smoker. He moved along the front of the buildings opposite the house, the gunfire from the top story pocking near by, the windows shattering around him.

The soldier ignored the showers of glass and eyed the third-story windows, estimating the distance. He lobbed the explosive grenade, following it with the smoker before the first bomb had a chance to detonate. He then picked up speed and moved farther down the street and away from the Russian, using the doorway of one house as a makeshift shelter, turning away as both grenades went off within seconds of each other. He could feel the heat of the blast and the shock wave, and hear the crash of glass, framework and masonry as the top of the building crumbled outward onto the street below.

Before the billowing cloud of dust had a chance to settle, he had turned back to the target building and was making for the front entrance. The chatter of SMG fire from above had ceased, as had the steady and regular thump of the RPD. Through the dust cloud he could see the Russian moving to join him, having deserted the RPD in favor of greater mobility. In the sudden silence that followed the blast, the distant sound of the city at night seemed strangely at odds with the clamor that had recently cut through it.

The front of the building appeared empty and deserted. Anyone who had been on the top floor would have been neutralized by the double blow of explosion and choking smoke to follow—Bolan had intended this to drift through the whole of the top floor and drive anyone left up there downward to meet them—but he had expected some kind of rearguard action to be taken up by anyone on the second floor.

The complete lack of any sign of life after the explosions did not, somehow, ring true. There was something wrong, but what it might be would only be revealed when they entered the house.

The Executioner leveled his HK and blew out the ground-floor windows with three bursts that peppered the interior, driving back any unseen foe. He flattened himself against the wall on one side of the door as Dostoyevsky arrived and did likewise on the other.

The two men exchanged glances, and Bolan nodded. The Russian's face was split by a grin that let slip how much he had missed this kind of action, before he stepped out and raised one foot, crashing it against the door to judge resistance before hammering SMG fire into the area of the lock. He crashed his foot a second time, and the door gave way to reveal an unlit corridor.

With a sharp intake of breath, they plunged into the darkness.

CHAPTER FIFTEEN

"Quick, follow me," Andrus gasped as the smoke began to drift down from the top floor and envelop the men on the one below. He beckoned to Velio to follow him as he began to clatter down the stairs, passing men on their way up, carrying SMGs.

The second-in-command had been issuing orders and attempting to rally troops thrown into a state of confusion by the double whammy of the explosion and smoke. He barked a few more commands and then hurried after his chief.

"Where are we going?" he yelled.

"We're getting the hell out of here," Andrus returned. "You think these guys can hold out?"

"There are only two out there as far as I can tell." Velio shrugged. "They have surprise on their side, but we got numbers. We should be able to take them down."

"Yeah? I don't believe we can do that after Norway. We need to safeguard the hardware for the main attack. Come on."

Grabbing his second-in-command and dragging him in his wake, the Freedom Right chief made his way down to the basement and through to the area where Igor had been captured. There were no signs of a struggle here now, and it was so quiet compared to the carnage unfolding above as to be sedate. Andrus led Velio out the same way that the Norwegians had come earlier.

"We shouldn't be leaving them," Velio said with a pang of conscience, looking back over his shoulder as they emerged near the wall at the far end of the yard.

"They know the score. This is a war, and sacrifice is necessary. If we are to achieve our aim, then all must be prepared to sacrifice themselves to the greater good."

Andrus was already halfway over the wall as he spoke. Velio stood at the foot and gave him a cynical look.

"That's easy to say when we're running in the opposite direction of the firefight," he gritted out.

"There's no time to argue here," Andrus told him. "If we are to make a sacrifice, let it come in Moscow. Then the glory will be ours."

Velio hesitated. It was necessary for them to recover the hardware and make for the real target, but still he felt uneasy about leaving his men behind. There were cells across Estonia and many men who would be willing to lay down their lives for Freedom Right—the men in the house behind him were part of this and not alone in their desire—yet still Velio would prefer to stay and engineer a way out.

His hesitancy was a spell broken when Andrus cursed loudly and dropped out of sight into the trash area so thoughtfully—and inadvertently—cleared by Igor just a short while before. Even over the chatter of gunfire behind Velio, he could hear his chief's footsteps as Andrus ran across the carport. There was no point in being caught in a no-man's land here, where Velio was of no use to anyone. Pushing his doubts to one side, he scrambled up and over the wall, hitting the ground running as he followed Andrus.

Unlike the truck bound for Oslo, which had been left in the carport for easy access, the truck containing the bulk of material taken from the bunker had been parked in a garage a half block away.

By the time that the firefight in the house had been resolved—one way or another—the Freedom Right chief and his right-hand man would be well away from the scene and on their way to link up with another cell on the road to Moscow.

BOLAN THREW A SPRAY of gunfire into the darkness to drive back any lurking enemies. There were no cries or sounds of movement to indicate that he had hit anyone. As his eyes adjusted to the dim light, he could see that the passage and the unlit stairwell were deserted.

He indicated to the Russian that they should clear the ground floor first. Smoke from the grenade on the top story was drifting down the stairs, which would incapacitate any troops left above. Those coming up from the basement would be at a disadvantage and so give the upper hand to Bolan and Dostoyevsky. A cleanup on this level was therefore the pressing task.

There were three doors. Bolan took the first, kicking it open with his heavy combat boot and going low while the Russian laid down suppressing fire.

Two men were in the room. They had been detailed to the front window but had been too late to stop Bolan and Dostoyevsky's entry. Now they were trapped. They had waited for a chance to take Bolan and the Russian from the rear but had been unlucky.

Their only way out was the shattered front window, but as one of them dove through, he caught himself on a jagged shard of glass—unnoticed in the commotion—which pierced his abdomen. He screamed as it bit then ripped, a keening sound heard above the chatter of SMG fire as his companion threw himself to one side to avoid the full stream of gunfire from the Russian. He was still hit in several places, his own fire erratic as a result. The bullets streamed harmlessly wide of both men as Bolan took him out for good with one short blast.

The terrorist impaled on the glass turned and tried to fire, but shock and the sudden blood loss made him weak, and his shooting was poor. Dostoyevsky ended him with a short burst.

Down the hallway one of the two remaining doors opened and a man swung out of a room, firing wildly before withdrawing. The Russian had not thought to cover the hallway and was nearly stitched by the shots. He cursed loudly as he swung around and returned fire.

Bolan had one ear listening to what was going on outside. They were in the middle of a city, and it wouldn't be long before the area was swarming with the authorities, all no doubt armed. This was no time for subtlety. He used another explosive grenade, rolling it along the floor and pulling Dostoyevsky into the now secured front room. Both men crouched, mouths open to equalize pressure, as the house rocked from the impact, plaster dust shooting into the air.

Before it could settle, they were on the move. Bolan took the lead, swinging himself to face the shattered doorway of the first room they came to, a clearing burst of fire preceding him. The terrorists in the room were neutralized. One of the three men inside had taken the blast full-on and lay bleeding on the floor. Another had been impaled in the eye by a large splinter of wood ripped from the door by the blast. The third slumped against the far wall, clutching his ribs with one arm while he cradled an HK with the other. His attempt to raise and fire was cut short by the soldier's own burst.

Dostoyevsky, meanwhile, had moved past the Executioner and had focused on the end room, his covering fire taking out one man while another was injured as he exited through a back window. He limped down the yard toward the far wall but only made a couple of steps before the Russian finished the job.

Bolan waited for him at the foot of the stairs as he strode back. "You take the basement, I'll clear the upper floor."

The Russian nodded. Without a word he ventured down the stairs, the SMG crooked in his elbow.

Leaving him to his task, Bolan moved carefully up the stairs, balancing the need for caution with the need for speed. He could hear nothing from inside the house other than the creaking of floorboards and joists put under pressure by grenade damage. He figured that the top floor had been mostly taken out, and this was confirmed by the gaping hole in the ceiling that was visible as he mounted the stairs.

It was deathly quiet as he reached the second-floor landing. Outside he could hear the approaching sound of sirens and the screeching of tires as the authorities negotiated a city block panicked into gridlock.

Four rooms were on this level. Part of the hallway was obstructed by a chunk of the floor above, and the remains of the staircase leading upward. From the basement he heard the brief conversation of two SMGs chattering at each other until one gunner extinguished the other. He hoped it was Dostoyevsky.

Of the rooms on this level, three had no doors left on them. In each, he could see at least one corpse. He picked his way over the rubble and checked the rooms fully, beginning with the nearest.

There was only one dead guy here, tied to a chair that had been thrown onto its side. The body showed signs of contusions and lacerations that spoke of a beating before the 9 mm hole in his temple had finished him off. Igor stared sightlessly at the toes of Bolan's combat boots. The soldier cursed to himself. The bodyguard hadn't been as smart as he had thought, or as Bolan had hoped...unless he had been betrayed by his boss. If that was so, then Bulganin would be due a visit when this was wrapped up.

The second room showed two men who had been injured by falling masonry and pummeled by debris. The last room was empty.

Bolan was aware that his recon had taken him farther and farther from the stairs and an escape route. He was also aware that the one closed door that needed investigating now stood invitingly in front of him.

He raised his SMG, aware that this front-facing room could harbor a deadly enemy. There was no time for careful checks.

The soldier stopped and listened. There was just the slightest shuffle—foot on bare board, disturbed rubble, an ill-fitting door being leaned on—to betray a presence of someone still alive on the other side of the wood. Bolan smiled grimly and bent to pick up a chunk of plaster that lay on the floor. Carefully, making sure that his footfalls were audible, he took steps that carried him to the doorway of the room where Igor remained.

Timing it with the last footfall outside the room, he threw the chunk of plaster over the stairwell, aiming down so that it would hit a stair, bounce and hit another, with at least some resemblance to footsteps. As he did, he darted into the relative cover of the open doorway.

It didn't sound much like a footstep to him, but to a panicked and trigger-happy terrorist, it was close enough. The closed door was swung inward, and a wild-eyed man—barely out of his teens—stepped forward and rained SMG fire into an empty stairwell, his eyes registering surprise before the tension relaxed on his trigger finger.

Bolan doubted that the young man even noticed that the Executioner was actually standing in the doorway. The guy didn't appear to even look up as the soldier stepped out and stitched him across the torso, throwing him back into the room. Following, Bolan sprayed an arc before stepping inside.

Apart from the fresh corpse, it was empty. Like all the rooms on this level, it had been heavily damaged. Given time, Bolan would have liked to root through the debris to see if he could find anything that would be useful intel. The sounds from outside told him that that luxury was to be denied him.

He hurried down the stairs to the ground floor, taking a look through the smashed front door at the street outside—still deserted with the desperate sound of wailing sirens and belligerent car horns betraying a face-off between those seeking to access the area and those seeking to escape it.

Bolan could see through to the back of the house—

now that it had been cleared—and the best access to the open yard might be through the basement. That, at least, would hide them for most of the way as they escaped.

He took the stairs to the basement, yelling the Russian's name into the silence.

"There is no need to shout, Cooper. I have not been deafened by the gunfire. Not yet," Dostoyevsky said as he stepped into view. Motioning to Bolan to follow him, the Russian walked through the low-ceilinged corridor linking the basement rooms, indicating one with a corpse and another that was empty as they walked. "Only one man down here. I suspect that discretion formed the far better part of valor, and they ran. They did leave this, though," he said as they came to the end room.

Bolan looked in: it was the armory, and in it were cases and boxes of ordnance, some of which were marked with Russian or German stamps. These were undoubtedly the merchandise from Bulganin that Igor had delivered, which allowed him to manufacture an entrance.

There were other cases, which had much older, Soviet markings. Bolan went straight to those, opening them and examining the contents.

"Are they what we're looking for?" the Russian queried. "Because if they are, we're going to have to think very swiftly about how we move them out of here."

Bolan shook his head. "They're from that cache but not the serious ordnance. They must have stashed that somewhere else."

"Maybe not stashed—maybe on the move?"

Bolan's brow furrowed. "It'd be a hell of a lot to take out Oslo alone. Unless…"

"Unless they have more than one target, or they really hate Norwegians. But who doesn't?"

"Funny… We can worry about that later. We need to move fast," Bolan stated, one ear on the noise outside. "How do we get out of here?"

"As you happen to ask, you just need to follow me."

Dostoyevsky led Bolan through the corridor and past the door through which Igor had hoped to infiltrate the house before his betrayal. After a few moments they emerged through the old coal cellar and at the far end of the yard.

"It looks like this was no secret, no matter what Igor thought. Half of Tallinn has been using it by the look of it," the Russian remarked as they followed what was now a well-trodden trail that led to the carport on the far side of the wall.

"I suggest that we get the hell out of the area in a hurry. The local police are stupid, but not so stupid that even they couldn't follow that trail."

The streets on the far side of the apartment building were empty, attention diverted elsewhere, and they were far enough ahead of the authorities to have made it back to the Russian's bar before the police had even discovered the route to the carport.

"We may have to neutralize Dimitri before he causes more problems," the Russian remarked as they stripped out of their combat gear.

"He can wait. We've got more pressing matters—if you're with me," Bolan added.

"I haven't had this much fun in ages. Just don't tell

Lana I said that," Dostoyevsky replied with a dismal expression that belied his words.

"Good. I'll need someone I can rely on," Bolan said, clapping him on the shoulder.

"I don't get why we left that much hardware behind," the Russian continued after a pause.

"It's out of Freedom Right's hands," Bolan answered. "Let the Estonian authorities deal with it. They'll be baffled by the Soviet markings, but they can puzzle over that. The hardware we're really after is still missing, and that's serious."

"Some of it will be bound for Oslo, I'm thinking," the Russian mused. "But will they take it all there?"

"I doubt that. But without any kind of intel, we could be looking over half of Scandinavia and Eastern Europe with no idea where the hell to start. We've got only two indicators."

"Two?"

"Sure," Bolan affirmed. "The first is that we know they're headed for Oslo, and they want to make a big impression."

"What about the second?"

"It's a long shot, but…" Bolan rooted out his smartphone and hit a speed-dial number. "We might be out here on our own, but it's always good to have backup," he added with a grin.

"If they're still using that truck, and if the ordnance we want is on it, and if… Cooper, that's a hell of a lot of ifs."

"Maybe it is," Bolan stated as the connection was made, "but maybe we'll get lucky."

"Striker, you're always lucky," Kurtzman's voice said over the air. "You're still alive, right?"

"So far, so good, Bear. Listen…" Bolan explained quickly the events of the evening. Kurtzman listened in silence, until the soldier finished by saying, "Two trucks for sure, but if I'm right, at least one of them in use will be the one I tracked before. Now that GPS tracker is gone, I know, but maybe there was some vehicle identification you can match up from CCTV."

"You know what? Miracles take a little time, Striker. It's one hell of a request, but maybe no more than usual. I'll drag Akira in. I mean, who needs days off anyway? Between us…"

Akira was Akira Tokaido, Stony Man Farm's ace computer hacker.

"Bear, it'll be invaluable. If the vehicle we can track is going to Oslo, it'll make it easier to find. If it isn't, then we need its heading with the remaining ordnance."

"It'll still leave a big hole in your mission. Hal—"

"Can worry about it, Bear. I don't have time. Maybe we can pick up some intel while we mop up one end of the operation."

Bolan finished the call and turned to his companion. "Pack a bag, because we've got a chance. If we're really lucky, then they're taking all the hardware to the same place."

"And if we're not, then I'm thinking that at least it will be easier for us to find them after we clean up the bastards in Oslo. Yes?"

"Damn right."

CHAPTER SIXTEEN

As the Russian maneuvered his sedan through the crowded streets, Bolan felt some relief that they had been able to enter and exit from the target area on foot. To have left the Saab behind would have pointed straight at Dostoyevsky and would also have given them the problem of finding transport to take them back to Oslo.

Negotiating the gridlocked traffic had been difficult—as diversions and panic had caused streams of cars down unfamiliar side streets—but now it was compounded by armed police who had set up a roadblock, and were stopping and questioning every vehicle.

"Officer, what can I do for you?" Dostoyevsky asked smoothly as they were pulled over.

The policeman squinted at him before a light of recognition dawned. "I know you," he said in Russian. "You have the bar that shows English football, right? And the barmaid with the…" His gesture that made his point clear.

"I am indeed, and that will be my wife you describe so accurately," Dostoyevsky replied.

"No offense intended," the policeman sputtered. "You are a lucky man. Hey, your bar is about ten minutes away from the incident—"

"That explains it," the Russian interrupted with mock exasperation. He turned to Bolan, speaking in Russian. "Did I not say it was a slow night? Did I not say I thought I could hear explosions? You said it was on the TV. I told you they only let off flares and fireworks in Italy, not in English games."

Bolan had to admire the Russian's handiwork, especially as it had the desired effect on the policeman.

"So you only heard that? No one came in and said anything to you about what was going on?"

"If anyone came in tonight, I would be too busy forcing them to buy to listen," the Russian said sadly. "That is why we are out now—I promised my friend I would find him a bar not like mine, where maybe he could meet a nice, or not so nice, girl while he was on leave."

"You are a soldier?" the policeman asked.

Bolan nodded, but before he could answer, the Russian chipped in again. "Hey, do not ask him too much—we served together, and you know that I cannot talk about that—so imagine what he cannot talk about," he added with a jerk of his thumb at Bolan.

The policeman accepted the explanation with surprising alacrity, and it was only when they had been safely waved on their way that he looked to the Russian for an explanation.

Dostoyevsky shrugged. "Look, they know I have served. I don't speak about it, but they guess. So they guess wrong, and maybe it suits me to let them keep believing their mistakes."

Bolan shrugged. Considering that the false floor in the trunk of the sedan concealed enough hardware to start a small war, anything that prevented the questioning being turned into a search was fine by him.

Hopefully this luck would hold until they could hit the road to Norway.

HADES, VISIGOTH AND ARVO had a good couple hours' head start and had driven in silence. Hades took the wheel for the first stint, concentrating on the road ahead in the darkness while his mind raced.

Too many people had died from among his own group for his liking—Hades included the dead Finns, as metal meant more to Hades than right-wing politics— and now he and Visigoth had to rescue Ripper from a courthouse. Visigoth was also worried about that— Hades could tell from the way Visigoth said nothing and looked blankly ahead all the time. Normally he wouldn't stop talking.

Ripper was the one with the beliefs; he was the one who had gotten Hades and Visigoth in over their heads. But Ripper was still their friend, and being purely selfish, if Ripper opened his mouth in court, they would all be in the shit over their heads, mouths open and suffocating. The latter being a better reason to get Ripper out than the former, if Hades was honest.

So what if Freedom Right had an inside man? What good was one man on the inside? If a force of trained soldiers were utilized, then maybe they would stand a chance. But Hades and Visigoth were two guys who spent more time playing fast music than exercising, and drank too much beer and smoked too much weed. They were dead men walking.

Hades looked away from the ribbon of road as it unwound ahead of him for as far as he could see. There was nothing else out here, so he could spare the attention. Visigoth sat still looking ahead, his features stony. Leaning against the door frame on the far side of the cab, his mouth slack and drooling while he gently snored, Arvo did not look like a man who was about to lead a paramilitary attack.

Maybe he wasn't. Back in Tallinn, the Freedom Right soldiers had scared the living shit out of Hades, but now that they were away from that atmosphere, Hades had a chance to process what had been yelled at him and Visigoth.

In the back of the truck there was a lot of conventional weaponry, some of it from the bunker they had traveled to. There was also one of the cylinders that Seb had been so keen for them to load before the Americans got him. The thought that Hades and Visigoth had been so close to their own deaths that day still made Hades shudder and momentarily deflected his train of thought.

But not that much. Death and the prospect of it were wonderful for focusing the mind.

If he had understood correctly—through the rush and confusion of fear—then the attack on the courthouse was to be a straight assault and extraction. If that was so, then why did they need this nuclear device?

Why the hell did Freedom Right want to nuke Oslo when they were supposed to be getting back one of their own?

Hades returned his gaze to the road ahead. The only thing that would make sense was if he and Visigoth were being used as a decoy, and Arvo had another directive. Hades and Visigoth were to be a sacrifice while Arvo completed his mission. In which case, Hades and

Visigoth—and Ripper too, for that matter—were as good as dead.

Hades's mouth set hard. If so, then these guys might get a little surprise. In fact Hades was more than a little surprised himself. Maybe now that he knew he had nothing to lose, he suddenly gained the courage to do things that otherwise would have seemed impossible.

At first chance he had to talk to Visigoth without Arvo being able to overhear. The man had to take a piss sometime. Hades would hold Visigoth back when this opportunity came, so that Hades could persuade him. They were still at least eight hours from Oslo.

No one—not even Arvo—had a bladder that strong.

THE WATERY SUN was still low in the sky as it rose over the firs of the Norwegian forest. Bolan and Dostoyevsky had been driving all night, swapping to rest and for the soldier to catch up with the intel that Kurtzman and Tokaido had managed to scare up through hacking every traffic system they could find along the route.

The luck that had been so erratic throughout this mission had taken a turn for the good once more: the truck headed for Norway was the same one that Bolan had originally placed the GPS on, and a vehicle recognition program had been able to pick out that that was the vehicle now headed back toward Oslo.

Bolan had mixed feelings about that. It would make it easier to intercept the terrorists before they had a chance to put their plan into operation in the Norwegian capital; on the other hand, it meant that the rest of the hardware they needed to track down was currently flying under the radar.

"Don't sweat it too much, Striker," Kurtzman answered when Bolan voiced this concern. "We picked up one other truck—very similar to the one you're chasing—that emerged from the same area of Tallinn within twenty minutes of the first. There were no others before the authorities locked down the area, so we can call it a reasonable assumption that this baby has what you're looking for."

"You've picked up a trail?"

"Not yet, but it's just a matter of time. Considering the amount of money Estonia is supposed to be pulling in from their software, you'd think they might invest just a little more in a decent CCTV system for their capital. As it is, the images are so grainy that it's been a bitch to get a recognition app to take. We're filtering and cleaning the pictures, and we should be there shortly. As soon as we are, then we can apply it to every camera we can pick up on every compass point until we make a trail. You leave that to us, Striker, and concentrate on taking down these idiots before they do some serious damage."

"Your friend is right," the Russian said when Kurtzman signed off. "We cannot split ourselves. The sooner we make it hard for these dudes, the sooner we can shoot the other ones a new corn hole."

Bolan looked at him askance. "Just what exactly have you been watching on that satellite dish of yours?"

They continued in silence for some time. There was little traffic at this time of day, only long-distance truckers traversing the northern wastes from isolated city to city. As a result Bolan and the Russian made good time. The flipside was that—as Bolan was all too well aware from Bear's intel—the first truck was also making good time.

"How many men do they have with them?" the

Russian asked at one point. "It would help if maybe we had some idea of who we were going up against."

"I figure that it has to be the two metalheads who were at the bunker. They weren't at the house. At least I never saw them among the dead. They'd have to have at least one terrorist to hold their hand." A raid on the courthouse and an atrocity like the one threatened— which Bolan knew Freedom Right had the hardware to perpetrate—would be too much for the inexperienced musicians on their own.

Bolan had seen them, back in the warehouse. They were not brave, experienced soldiers of any hue. They were amateurs and in all likelihood terrified. However, that would not make Bolan underestimate them. They had a raw courage and bravura, and fueled by the panic of fear, that could make them, in some circumstances, more dangerous than a seasoned warrior. The musicians would be unpredictable and would do things that others would neither expect nor dare to do.

"You are quiet, Cooper," Dostoyevsky murmured.

"Have you ever considered," Bolan said, not answering directly, "that there's nothing more perilous than letting loose a man with tools he doesn't know how to use properly and who has no idea what kind of consequences his ignorance can lead to?"

The Russian gave him a look that was, if possible, even more serious than usual.

"Cooper, I have been thinking of nothing else."

VISIGOTH WAS AT THE WHEEL as they entered Oslo. At the behest of Arvo, Visigoth drove carefully but not so carefully that he would attract attention. He needed to pilot his way across the city to a safehouse that had been established at short notice by sympathizers in the city. The original plan, to drive in on the morning and hit directly, was blown out of the water by American interference. Now they had to hole up for twenty-four hours, knowing that they were in a city that would be approaching lockdown, sweating out Freedom Right's bomb threat deadline.

For Arvo it was about directing the Norwegians one way so that the two metalheads could take attention from his own mission. He was to trigger an explosion, the magnitude of which would announce to the world that Freedom Right was a group to be taken seriously and had the firepower to back up its goals.

For the Norwegians, it was about freeing their friend. Originally because he could incriminate them. Now, knowing that they had already left a trail to damn them far more than any testimony Ripper could give in court, it was about freeing him and fleeing somewhere they could start over and escape a justice that would never believe they had been sucked in beyond anything they could have imagined.

Arvo had no idea how easy it would be for him to seemingly manipulate the young Norwegians. On the journey, Hades had managed to secure a few moments with Visigoth, and had found to Hades's relief that his friend had been having the same doubts and ideas. A few snatched moments of conversation and they had determined that, as soon as they could escape from Arvo, they would continue with the mission in their own way, regardless of what had been intended.

Now they pulled up outside a boarded house that stood near the center of the city, in a street that dated back to the nineteenth century. It was still early in the morning, and there were only a few commuters on the road as they climbed out of the truck. The door to the house opened before Visigoth had locked the truck, and a small man beckoned them in, casting a glance up and down the street as he did so.

"Do you want to make yourself look suspicious?" Arvo grumbled.

"The police have been more conspicuous of late," the small man replied in an even tone. "They are waiting for tomorrow, and they are waiting for you. Is it any wonder I feel nervous?"

"Nervous is one thing. Stupid is another," Arvo snapped. "The last thing we need to do is attract attention at this time. What time is Nils due?"

"His duties end at five thirty. He isn't even at work yet," the small man said, checking his watch. "I think you should chill out a little and take some rest. You'll need it for tomorrow morning."

Reluctantly Arvo agreed. "I suppose so. You two, follow him," he barked at the musicians.

They followed the man out of the room and to the second story, where they were shown into a tiny room, with the door closed on them. They exchanged glances, and Visigoth put his ear to the door before speaking.

"I half expected them to be listening," he said with grim humor. "What the hell are we going to do, man?"

"Get Ripper," Hades said simply.

"How the hell can we do that?"

"This Nils must be the inside man they were telling us about. We listen to what he says and we just do it, man. He'll be giving us all the information we need, and we have hardware. We just need to get rid of Arvo so he can't screw us over," Hades said.

"You know what? I think he has other plans anyway," Visigoth mused. "He's got one of those weird bombs on board. No way were we going to be using that at the courthouse. I don't think we can trust what Nils says, dude."

"Then maybe we don't give him a choice," Hades replied with a sharklike grin.

ON THE GROUND FLOOR Arvo looked out at the truck. "Will that be safe?" he asked the man.

"Figure so," he replied. "This is a quiet street. Nothing happens here. No one's going to even notice the truck is out there. Don't worry about it. We're invisible."

Despite living in the house for almost a year, he had never noticed the CCTV camera mounted on a lamppost at the corner of the street. As it angled around, it caught the rear of the truck full-on, its license plate centrally framed.

CHAPTER SEVENTEEN

By late afternoon Bolan and Dostoyevsky had arrived in the capital. The courthouse was a modern piece of architecture, and one of the few buildings in the center of Oslo not to be at least partially constructed of wood. The nearby stock exchange and university dated back to the nineteenth century and reflected the influence of the architect Grosch from that century.

No so the courthouse. Leaving the Russian's sedan safely locked and secreted in a side street, the two soldiers examined the exterior of the courthouse and the surrounding streets on foot. There was a heavy police and military presence in the area. It was discreet, but if you knew what to look for—as they did—then it was evident. There were unmarked trucks that contained soldiers and surveillance equipment, and although the added personnel did their best to blend in with the regular security around the environs, the sheer weight of their numbers told its own story.

"They look like they could handle three, maybe four men," the Russian remarked. "They've got the numbers—are we really necessary at this end?"

Bolan considered that. "Yeah, and I'll tell you why. They don't have the intel we have about the potential firepower. They don't have our suspicions about an inside man or men. They don't actually know who they're looking for. We do. And I'll tell you something else—they're expecting this to be one attack focused on the courthouse."

"And we're not?"

Bolan shook his head. "They're not going to use that kind of firepower just to bust out a failed terrorist who can't tell anyone anything more than what they already know. This is a diversion. The real attack will be elsewhere."

"Given that the authorities have no knowledge or suspicion of this, and we have nothing more than your hunch," the Russian murmured, "then how do we know where else we should be looking?"

Bolan grinned. "Let's get back to the car, and we'll see what new intel we can scare up."

HADES AND VISIGOTH listened carefully to what Nils had to say. On his arrival at the house, he had eyed them in a manner that suggested they were already history. Both Norwegians had kept stone-faced. Sitting them down, Nils opened a file on his tablet and took them through the schematics of the courthouse, and the one area of possible entry that he would be able to effect for them. He then ran them through the plan for diverting the authorities while they made an escape with Ripper.

Arvo watched the two Norwegians carefully until he was satisfied they had understood—and more important, believed—the plan.

A key part of this was that while Nils, under the guise of being taken hostage, would aid them in freeing and escaping with their companion, the diversionary measure would be taken by Arvo, at a different location. Hearing that, the Norwegians had remained impassive, though both now understood how they were to be sold down the river.

In the room they shared, they waited until they were sure that they were not being observed before exchanging a few brief words.

"You worked it out?" Hades asked.

Visigoth nodded. "Seems clear. Gets you-know-who off our case."

Hades grinned. "We can make this work for us. Nils won't expect anything."

Visigoth shrugged. "If he does, then it'll be too late."

BOLAN AND DOSTOYEVSKY booked a hotel room for the night, securing the sedan in the facility's parking lot. Earlier a call to Stony Man had given them the intel they had been hoping for. Hacking into the traffic control system for Oslo, Akira Tokaido had lifted CCTV images that showed the known vehicle entering the city and was now monitoring its static position on a residential street.

"It was nice of the boys to park so beautifully," the Russian said as he looked again at the video on Bolan's smartphone, which showed the truck facing the camera, the license plate clearly displayed.

Bolan said nothing for a moment. He had watched the time-lapse images of the truck arrive and three men get out. There had been at least one other man who had greeted them. How many more? If there was another cell here, then the notion of dealing just with three or four men was blown. There was no real way of knowing exact numbers.

That was one variable Bolan could have done without. Another was that there was only one vehicle that they could identify. If the courthouse attack was the decoy he suspected, then there would have to be a second vehicle to transport the ordnance to its intended target. He voiced this opinion to the Russian.

"True," Dostoyevsky replied after consideration. "But we have the advantage of knowing where they are based, and also that they will not move until the morning. What is to stop us from mounting an attack that will forestall their actions?"

"Nothing in theory."

"But in fact?"

Bolan grimaced. "It's a heavily residential area. I'd feel happier if I could intercept them when they were in motion, get the truck somewhere a little more isolated. Right now, too many could get hurt if that truck went up."

"Cooper, if it's a nuke, then a klick or two isn't going to make a lot of difference."

"Maybe not. I wonder if they've armed it yet?"

"They'd be really stupid if they had. Which, if you ask me, is another reason to attack now. At least this way, we can get the truck clear or eliminated before they have a chance to arm the weapon."

Bolan sighed. "You're making a convincing argument. We haven't had a chance to recon the area, though. There has to be a second vehicle, and that means maybe a second safehouse. If it's close, then we could be outnumbered."

"Cooper, we can deal with being outnumbered. We can't deal with being nuked. Come on, man, where is your sense of adventure?" The Russian laughed, clapping the soldier on the shoulder.

"I don't do this for a sense of adventure. I do it to keep people safe," Bolan replied. "But maybe this is the best way to do that."

STEIN THAULOW WAS a good soldier, despite a physique that made him seem small and ineffective. He compensated for that by having a devotion and thoroughness that made him consider carefully every eventuality. He had realized—when word from Andrus had reached him about the early arrivals—that it was likely the same American black ops team that had dogged their progress so far would be hot on the tail of Arvo and the Norwegians. To assume anything else would be stupid.

So it was that he had detailed the men in his cell to mount a series of roving patrols for two blocks around the house. There were six men working in shifts, making clockwise and counterclockwise circuits, varying their routes by degrees and keeping in touch via disposable cell phones. The second truck—a white DAF van over twenty years old, taken from and marked with the insignia of a catering company that supplied the stock exchange—was under a tarp in a garage half a klick away.

It would be brought here in the early hours of the morning and the transfer of the nuclear weapon made before Arvo took it back to the garage to await the appointed hour. The original plan had been to make the transfer at the garage when the black truck arrived in Oslo, but that had of necessity been changed, adding an extra risk that Stein was uncomfortable with. This, however, was the best compromise, as at least it would be within the cordon formed by his men.

For his part, he sat with six cell phones on the coffee table in front of him. Each man on watch had the number of a different phone. He could be contacted immediately—and simultaneously—by any of his men.

Arvo was grabbing some sleep. The Norwegians were secured in their room and were also presumably resting. Nils had returned to his own abode. He had briefed the Norwegians well. The only thing Nils had omitted from his game plan was the matter of the loaded 9 mm Beretta he would keep in the small of his back during the fake raid, which he would use to put them out of the game at the right moment.

All Stein could do now was sit, wait and hope that he had covered every eventuality as he watched the clock tick past midnight and closer to the first action of the day: the switch.

That was set for 3:00 a.m.

By the time they had examined the schematics of the area around the street where their target was located, it was long past midnight. Dostoyevsky suggested that this was the perfect time to recon and attack, as there would be few people about, which would also serve to make any military presence that much more noticeable and avoidable.

Bolan could only agree. He also felt it incumbent to add that any security placed around the area where their target was located would also be that much easier to spot.

The two men made their way down the fire escape to the parking lot, so that they would show as little as possible on any in-house CCTV feed. Down in the parking lot there was one camera covering the area of the fire door and where the Russian's sedan was parked—as close to the door as possible, to cover this eventuality.

Bolan walked out alone, his head down and hunched over, looking away from the camera until he calculated he had passed its arc. He ducked behind and underneath its view to reach for the camera. He slipped an opaque plastic trash bag—taken from one of the bins in his hotel room—to cover the lens, securing it with an elastic band.

Satisfied that they would now be unseen, he dropped down and joined the Russian as he exited the stairwell and opened the trunk of his sedan, removing the false floor so that he was able to access the hardware he had stowed beneath.

For reasons of weight and ease of transport, they had elected to carry nothing heavy. Two AK-47s—always Dostoyevsky's rifle of choice from his years of military service— and a pair of MP5s each, with enough magazines to take down a platoon; explosive and smoke grenades; nose plugs and full face masks. As with their last raid, fragmentation grenades were too risky at the range they were aiming for. Bolan had his Desert Eagle, and the Russian toted a 9 mm Walther, handguns that were like extensions of their own arms to them, again with enough magazines to wipe out more men than they expected to face.

Using the fire exit again, they hurried to the roof of the hotel and climbed down the fire escape of the building next door. An earlier recon of the back and front upon arrival for emergency escape routes had furnished them with this option to avoid showing up on the hotel CCTV.

Down on the streets, they took a direct route to the

area of the city where their target was located, deviating from it only when regular patrols came into view, or where there were groups or individuals that they could tell were security. Maybe some of these people were just civilians, but it was better to err on the side of cautious.

When they were closing in on the target area, Bolan reminded Dostoyevsky that they had no idea how many—or how few—enemy they would face.

"Then it is better to be frosty—like permafrost, even…" the Russian said with a grin.

"I swear you're enjoying this," Bolan said ruefully.

"Come on, you'll be telling me next that you aren't. Just like you haven't noticed that this is the second time he's crossed our path in the last twenty minutes," he added.

Bolan had to admit that the Russian was sharp. They were skirting the target area in order to detect potential enemies, and this was the second man that the soldier had seen pass them a second time. On the prior occasion, he couldn't have been 100 percent sure. Now he knew that his battle senses had been on the money.

"At least a two-man circuit, clockwise and counter," he estimated. "I wonder if it's only those two, or—"

"Let us just take a little detour, my friend. I suspect a few minutes of recon could yield interesting results."

Of course they ran the risk of being spotted and intercepted, but it was worth it to see the lay of the land. Taking a circuitous route around the target area, looking for all the world like two tourists searching for a late-night bar and getting lost, they appeared to wander aimlessly, spotting one other man who was circling in a clockwise and counterclockwise manner.

"So what do you think?" Dostoyevsky asked after their mutual agreement on the third man. "If they have three on the street now, then I would guess they have at least that number to relieve these guys. It would, however, take them time to mobilize those men. Six, plus the four we know of..."

"Five to one. Not bad odds if we move now," Bolan said decisively. "You go counterclockwise, move toward the target and synchronize for ten minutes. Then we go from each side." They synchronized their watches. "Keep it tight—best to assume at least one of those three guys had a brain, and they're expecting us."

The Russian grinned, nodded and moved off. Bolan, with less distance to cover, stood back in the shadows and counted off the minutes until he could proceed.

While he did that, a battered white DAF van passed him. He slipped farther into the shadows as the headlights lit the pavement where he had stood a moment before. It might have been nothing, but...

"A catering truck in this part of town at this time of night?" he mused. "Either some guy's borrowed the company's wheels, or..."

It occurred to him that such a truck would be a perfect blind for the second vehicle the terrorists would need.

Keeping track of time be damned. He needed to move now, before it was too late. The soldier left the shadows and made his way across the street, heading directly for the target area. He took out his smartphone and hit the speed-dial key for the Russian's cell phone. They were both switched to silent, but he hoped the vibration would alert Dostoyevsky.

He cursed as it seemed to take ages for the Russian

to answer. Bolan was about to answer his own thoughts when the periphery of his vision caught movement, and instinct made him throw himself down just a fraction of a second before the burst of gunfire ripped the air where his torso had been.

The silence broken, all bets were off, and stealth was impossible. He rolled, bringing up the AK-47 that had been slung under his loose duster, snapping off a volley that drove his assailant back into the dark shadows. His smartphone squawked at him as he snatched it up and scrambled for cover, answering fire kicking up concrete and tarmac fragments at his heels. He whirled and took out the terrorist with a spray into the darkness that got lucky. He heard the man grunt and fall, and there was no answering fire.

He turned back to the target and advanced on the double.

ARVO AND STEIN greeted the white van driver and unlocked the back of the black truck. While the DAF driver kept an uneasy watch beside the vehicle, the two terrorists unloaded the squat gray cylinder with Cyrillic markings and placed it carefully in the back of the white van. Arvo hurried again to the black truck and returned with the second part of the weapon, carefully stowing the triggering mechanism beside the cylinder before closing the back doors and taking the keys from the driver.

"The GPS is set for the garage. The key is this one for the garage door," the DAF driver intoned, showing Arvo the item. "I secured the—"

He was cut short by the sudden sound of gunfire rending the air. For a fraction of a second all three men were frozen. From inside the house, Stein could hear all his cell phones go off. He pushed Arvo toward the DAF.

"Go, don't stop for anything. We'll deal with this, you just get to the garage," Stein said sharply before turning to drag the driver into the house to grab a weapon. Thrusting an HK into his hands, Stein told him to stand guard. While the driver did that, Stein took the stairs two at a time. Fumbling, he unlocked the door to the Norwegians' room.

"What—" Hades began, but was cut short.

Stein threw the truck keys at them. "We're under attack. Take the truck and drive—anywhere, but away from here. We'll deal with this. You just keep your heads down and meet with Nils as arranged. Now go," he yelled, nearly pushing them down the stairs.

Confused and panicked, Hades and Visigoth did as they were told. Hades took the wheel, grinding the transmission as he took the truck—unknowingly—in the opposite direction from Arvo and directly toward Bolan.

Just a few moments before, Arvo had needed no second bidding. Before the door of the house slammed shut, he was roaring away in the white van. He took the corner with a squeal of rubber, and was almost at the end of the adjacent street when he had to swerve to avoid the tall man who stepped into the road with an AK-47 leveled at him.

Arvo ducked as the windshield shattered, keeping the gas pedal floored even as the back windows were shattered, the metal pierced by the AK fire. It was pure luck that neither he nor the device had been hit, and he did not breathe until his adversary was no longer in his rearview mirror.

Far behind him, Dostoyevsky cursed before turning back toward the house. He had failed to halt maybe one terrorist, but at least he could help his partner attend to the remainder.

CHAPTER EIGHTEEN

Bolan ran across the streets, scanning each direction for any sign of movement. A few lights had gone on in upstairs windows, but the citizens of Oslo were wise enough to keep inside while there was gunfire.

On the corner of the target street, two men with SMGs had taken up defensive positions and peppered the street with spray'n'pray as the soldier approached. He dived behind a parked car for cover, his ears ringing from the sound of metal pounded by bullets as the vehicle's bodywork took the brunt of the fire. Glass smashed above his head.

The two gunmen were on either side of the street, and there was no direct line of fire. They had the soldier pinned down unless he could cause some kind of diversion. He was about to launch a smoke grenade to flush them out when his job was done for him by a blast from the far end of the street.

Bolan grinned mirthlessly. Dostoyevsky had made better time than the soldier had any right to expect and had arrived at an opportune moment.

Bolan looked up over the trunk of the car. The two gunmen had moved, driven from their defensive positions by the gunfire from behind them. In spinning to return the fire, they had both made themselves target enough for the soldier to take a shot.

Two short bursts to either side of the street, and they were neutralized. One was taken out immediately, his back stitched by the SMG. The other was only partially immobilized as the gunfire drilled toward him was not as accurate. He spun and fell as the bullets ripped through his side, trying to crawl back to cover.

Bolan did not give him a second chance. Coming from behind at a run, he finished the man with another tap. That made three men—presumably the moving patrol they had noted. This would leave at least three more in the house. Bolan wanted to take at least one alive, if possible, as he needed information—he could see that the black truck had left, and had heard two vehicles leave moments before he had turned the corner.

Cursing the changeable luck that had let him down once more, he gestured to the far end of the street; the Russian visible under the streetlight.

Dostoyevsky understood immediately. Both he and Bolan fired almost simultaneously as they approached the house, taking out the streetlights and plunging the target area into darkness. There had been lights on in the house, but they were now extinguished so that no targets within would be visible.

Bolan sheltered in a doorway opposite the target. The Russian did likewise, a few houses down on the other side.

The soldier was breathing hard, wondering how to communicate to his compatriot the method of attack he wanted to adopt. He reached into the pocket where he had slipped his smartphone, hoping that the Russian would still be in possession of his cell phone.

Before he had a chance to hit the speed-dial digit, he was forestalled by a dull glow that came from within the target house, visible through the ground-floor windows.

Whoever was inside had set the house on fire. With an enemy outside, that was suicide unless there was a back exit.

No time for tactics now. The only thing they could do was to get in, see who or what they could salvage before the whole building went up.

As Bolan moved low across the street, he could see that Dostoyevsky had had the same idea and was a couple paces ahead of him. He could also see a figure moving—dark on dark—behind the upper-story window, and knew by his angle of approach and lack of deviation that the Russian had not seen the movement.

Bolan changed his own course and dived toward the Russian, cannoning into him as he heard the glass shatter in the window above and the bark of an AK-47. They hit the road hard, driving the air from both their bodies as Bolan carried his momentum into a roll, the AK fire harmlessly hitting the street to one side of where they fell.

As they separated and both men scrambled to their feet, they were immediately blown back by the force of a blast. The front of the house crumbled before them, the wood catching tongues of flame that flickered briefly before the blast blew them out, dust billowing in a choking cloud that was thick with flying debris. The house appeared to collapse from the roof down, imploding on itself as the floors were decimated by the explosives that had been stored inside.

The Russian swore loudly in his native language as he sat up and watched the house settle into a pile of rubble, the buildings on either side slowly sagging as the force of the damage spread to them.

"Fanatics," he breathed in English. "We deal with madmen, Cooper."

"We deal with the police unless we move quickly," Bolan said, pulling himself to his feet and grabbing at his partner. "Come on—we still have work to do."

AROUND THE COURTHOUSE security was tight. Armed police and military response units patrolled and made their presence very visible. Everyone passing in and out of the courthouse by any entrance was searched, either by the regular court security or by the military.

Visigoth guided the truck through the traffic that had built up by diversion and roadblock until he was within half a block of the courthouse building. Taking a left, he drove down a side road that took them past armed guards to the entrance used by police and prison vehicles to drop off and collect prisoners from the secured area beneath the court.

In the early hours of the morning, Hades had driven furiously until they were on the outer edge of the city and then parked in a rest area where they could position themselves among other larger trucks. In such a place there was little chance of being questioned, as the authorities knew the majority of truckers used their cabs to sleep rather than pay for hotels or risk leaving their rigs.

Hide in plain sight was a lesson the Norwegians had learned quickly. Once parked, they had taken turns to sleep and watch until it was time to head back for the city and their rendezvous with Nils at the courthouse.

As Visigoth turned into the narrow road leading to

the security barrier, Hades looked out at the military force gathered around. His heart felt like it was trying to escape through his throat, and he was certain that anyone who looked into the truck would see through them, see through their fear.

All he got was a blank sea of faces. He and Visigoth were dressed in serge uniforms supplied by the terrorists. With the musicians' hair cut, their piercings removed and tattoos covered, they looked exactly what those uniforms and the passes they carried proclaimed them to be: laundry delivery men.

When they reached the checkpoint, Nils was waiting for them with another guard. As Hades wound down the window and presented the credentials that the very same man had given him the day before, Nils took them from them and examined them. He turned to his fellow guard.

"New boys, Lars. Papers are all in order, though." He turned to Hades and asked, "You boys want me to go with you? We've got it locked down, so if you're not familiar…"

Hades nodded. "Maybe that would be good, if this isn't a bad time…" He felt his voice ring hollow, although no one else seemed to notice.

"Okay, you boys park up there and bring the hamper. I'll check out and show you where you need to go."

Visigoth parked the truck, and they took a hamper from the back of the vehicle. Ostensibly containing clean laundry for the cells, and ready to pick up the dirty ones, all it contained were a few weapons and explosives. According to the plan they had been fed the previous day, this was the hamper in which they were to hide Ripper.

Looking at the heavy-duty security presence as they followed Nils into the body of the court building, they could see what a crock this plan was, and how easily it would set them up to be cut down by the military.

Even so, they played along with the undercover terrorist as he took them directly to the cell where their companion was waiting to be called. His presence, and the easy manner in which he made small talk with them, was enough to deflect any suspicion, even though they were not walking the normal laundry route. It was only when they reached the holding cells, and came up to the two armed guards standing outside, that they were challenged.

"What gives, Nils?" one of the guards asked suspiciously, his hands tightening nervously on his cradled HK.

"These boys have come to take out the trash," Nils replied easily.

"What?" the other guard queried, confusion written on his face. "But they look like laundry men."

Under other circumstances, the Norwegians might have found it funny. Not now, not with the adrenaline rush of fear pounding through them. Hades flipped back the lid of the hamper, and reached in, pulling out a mini Uzi that he pointed at the puzzled guard.

Nils being with the two strangers, and being so relaxed, had done enough to divert suspicion and dull reactions. As the puzzled guard made to raise his own SMG, Nils stepped forward and punched the other guard in the throat. Not expecting that from someone who he thought an ally, he did not react in time and fell, choking. An elbow behind his ear as he stumbled was sufficient to render him unconscious.

In the moment of confusion this caused the remaining guard, Visigoth stepped in and slammed a punch into the man's face. His head cracked back against the wall and he teetered, dazed, before a second roundhouse blow finished the job.

"Quickly, inside," Nils snapped as he took the key from the guard and opened the cell door, pushing the hamper inside.

This left the Norwegians to pull the disabled guards into the cell and out of sight. That was exactly what the terrorists had expected. Ripper stood up, unsure of what to do, baffled by the sight before him. Nils pushed the hamper across the cell floor, so that it formed a temporary barrier between Ripper and the door, and was about to step out of the room with the Norwegians occupied and unable to stop him, when Nils realized that Hades had dropped the body he was dragging, and had swiftly turned and reached out. Before Nils had a chance to react, Hades had him in a strangling headlock.

As Visigoth dropped his own burden and dragged the fallen man in just enough to close the cell door, Hades rammed Nils's head into the wall, letting him drop so that Hades could take his weapon from him before standing back.

"Get up, asshole," he hissed at the fallen terrorist.

"Hades? Visigoth? What are you—"

"Later, man," Hades snapped, cutting off any further questions.

"Get them to one side and search them," he said to Visigoth.

"Ahead of you, dude," his comrade replied, stripping the two guards of their hardware and throwing it into the hamper. He took their web belts and used them to secure their wrists and ankles, hoping that these would be strong enough to hold the guards.

Nils was on his feet, though visibly shaken and groggy. "What are…you b-boys doing?" he stammered uncertainly.

"I don't know, you double-dealing prick, you tell me," Hades snarled. "You trap us in here, raise the alarm, then as we try to break out, you kill all three of us, right? We're not that stupid, Nils. We had all night to check the weapons you gave us. We didn't trust you guys anyway, but that raid on the safehouse gave us time to confirm that you're a two-timing asshole. Screwed, just like we would have been."

"It's not like that. It's—"

"It's nothing. I don't care what excuses you have. They're all lies. We were supposed to be nothing more than a decoy for whatever Arvo is really doing. Well, fuck that, dude. He can be our decoy."

"Guys, what are you playing at?" Ripper interrupted. "Arvo is a trusted—"

"Arvo is an asswipe, dude. Get real," Hades yelled over him. "You might like playing at this shit, but we don't. We're not playing, not now. They think we're pussies, and they think that about you, too. They used you, they wanted to use us. We've been treated like idiots, and we were. Not now, dude. This asshole—" he waved the 9 mm pistol at its nominal owner "—was supposed to set us up in a rescue bid that went wrong. I got news for you, Nils, it's you that's gone wrong. We're getting out of here, and you're going to help us. Or die. Whichever you want."

The way in which the man was staring at him made

Nils realize that there was no bluff in his words. Despair and fear had given him determination. Nils had a sinking feeling in the pit of his gut, and it showed on his face.

"I thought you might see it that way." Hades nodded. "Now this is what we do..."

BOLAN AND THE RUSSIAN were by the Oslo stock exchange, seated in Dostoyevsky's sedan. Directly in front of them was the white DAF van.

On returning to the hotel in the early hours of the morning, effecting entry by the same method they had left in order to avoid detection, the two warriors had cleaned up, dressing the superficial wounds that were thankfully all they had picked up during the night's action.

Once that was done, Bolan had called Stony Man, bringing them up to speed on what had happened. Not that he needed to have bothered. As part of their monitoring of the Oslo systems, Stony Man was already aware of the results of Bolan's attempt to break into the safehouse.

The CCTV traffic systems around the city had already picked up the black truck and traced it out of town to where it now sat.

"Let it be for now. The action at the courthouse is a diversion. The real action is in a white van. A damaged white van..."

Dostoyevsky's attempts to halt its progress had at least made it conspicuous, as well as confirming for the soldier that his suspicions on first seeing it had been correct. Within half an hour, the Farm had been able to confirm the presence of the vehicle and trace it up to a point where it had vanished off the grid. Somewhere within a two-block radius that was a CCTV blind spot, it had either been parked or stowed away.

The Russian looked at the rising sun. "We could cover that territory easily but getting there? If we leave now, it may already be out and on the road before we hit the map reference."

Bolan agreed. "We stay here. Bear, keep those systems covered, and as soon as it comes back on the radar, let me know. Keep me informed on the black truck, too."

"We cannot be in two places at once, unless we separate," Dostoyevsky mused. "If you want me to keep one angle covered while you chase the other…"

"We stay together. The attack on the court is likely to be by the musicians, the sacrifices. The military should be able to deal with that. They are expecting it, after all. No one else knows about the white van, and no one else knows what it could contain. I'd rather you covered the angles with me there than be elsewhere when I need backup."

"As you wish. We should be ready, then…"

Coffee for the soldier, a shot of vodka for the Russian, and they made their way down to the sedan like everyday tourists.

For what seemed like eons, they drove around the detoured traffic system set up to assist the extra security for the courthouse, waiting for the call that would tell them the white van had been spotted.

"Just a thought, Cooper, but what if they swap vehicles? The van is pretty damaged."

"I figure they won't have the time or the manpower after last night to make that happen. Hell, a temporary windshield would do the job for as long as they need. It's hardly uncommon enough to get them stopped."

"I hope not," the Russian replied, and was cheered some moments later when a call came through. The traffic monitoring system had picked up a van answering the description of the one they were looking for. Stony Man was tracing its progress through the interlinked cameras and relaying the route to Bolan so that he could intercept.

The Russian whistled when he realized where they were headed. "Some bunch of fascists—I thought striking at the heart of the capitalist system was the preserve of the left."

CHAPTER NINETEEN

Arvo had known that he was on his own from the moment that he had roared away from the safehouse. If the crazy bastard who had tried to mow him down was any indication of the type of mercenary the Americans were using on this mission, then not only were they more serious than Andrus and Velio could have dreamed, but the odds were that there was no one left at the safehouse to pass that message to. For Arvo's own part, he had no working cell phone of any kind and was isolated not only from his superiors but also from the Norwegians he was using as a decoy. He could only hope that they would play their part as they had been instructed, and that Nils could still fulfill his end of the deal.

Arvo had been trembling when he had reached the garage. Unlocking the doors and getting the van inside had been a harder task than it should have been. He would have liked to put that down to adrenaline, but in his heart he knew that it was because the American forces had scared the living crap out of him.

He had tried to effect a few repairs to the van with what he could find in the garage. That was partly so that the vehicle would look less conspicuous when he took it out later this morning but also—again if he was honest with himself—because it took his mind off what might be waiting for him.

There had been the makings of tea, a kettle and a small fridge at the back of the garage, and Arvo passed what was left of his downtime watching the minutes tick tortuously by while he occupied himself by drinking cup after cup of tea. It was not how he had seen the glorious revolutionary action unfolding, but he figured, as long as he got the result that he and his superiors wanted, then that would be compensation enough.

Finally it was time, and he threw open the garage door to a glorious wintry morning. The clean and crisp air hit him after the closed-in atmosphere of the garage, and as he pulled the DAF van out into the open, pausing to close the garage behind him, Arvo felt a new sense of optimism swell within him.

According to the radio the events of the night before had not happened. He had figured on a news blackout, especially as the focus was very much on the Sundby trial and the security that surrounded it. The authorities would want nothing that could deflect from the sense of security they were trying to build.

Nonetheless it did amuse him that, if he was concerned about the presence of the American black ops personnel in Oslo, the Norwegians were probably a dozen times more concerned.

It was a pleasant thought to buoy him as he drove steadily through the city toward his target. He had repaired most of the gunfire damage to the van and had fixed a temporary windshield that made him look like a delivery driver striving after a motor vehicle accident rather than a terrorist on the run. He was contravening some road laws, but he was playing on the fact that the authorities would have greater concerns on this day.

He was right about that but had not considered the two soldiers-at-arms who were prowling the city, looking for someone who would be doing exactly as Arvo was. He never noticed the dark sedan as it slipped on to his tail and followed him straight to the stock exchange.

"HE'S BEEN VERY LUCKY to get this far without being intercepted," the Russian growled as he kept two vehicles between his sedan and the white DAF van.

"That's lucky for us, too," Bolan murmured. "I don't want anyone stopping him who doesn't understand what he's carrying."

"Well, I hope you do, because unless we take him down soon, he's going to have a chance to put that thing into action."

"He won't have armed it yet," Bolan asserted. "No way is he going to trust himself driving an armed warhead. He'll do it before he walks away."

"You are, of course, assuming he wants to walk away. If this is some kind of fascist jihad, then there may be the equivalent of a thousand virgins waiting for him. And us, frankly," Dostoyevsky added.

Bolan did not reply. He was sure he had made the right call, but there was no point in arguing the toss. Better that they act as soon as possible and prove it that way.

The white DAF van had passed any number of armed vehicles and men who could have stopped it. On another day, the looks many of them cast the van said that they would have. Arvo rode that luck and turned down a narrow road at the side of the timber-framed building that housed the stock exchange.

It was a beautiful example of Norwegian architecture from a golden age, and to the Estonians that only made it all the sweeter that he would strike here. This was a symbol of the good things about the northern culture debased by Jewish and decadent finance. Perhaps people would realize how debased if it took destruction of such purity to cleanse it.

Dostoyevsky nosed the sedan down the narrow road, pulling up so that he blocked access by his angle of parking. All that he and Bolan could see was some right-wing nutcase who wanted to nuke a load of innocent people for some half-baked theory that belonged in a storybook.

That wasn't going to happen on their watch.

Arvo got out of the van at the far end of the narrow road, where it tapered into a pedestrian exit marked by bright orange cones to prevent through traffic. Down this end of the road was a fire exit door where smokers congregated on their breaks. There were two or three coming in and out as Arvo opened the back doors of the white van. One of them called out something to him, and his reply was greeted with a resigned shrug.

"What's that about?" the Russian wondered.

Bolan's mouth quirked. "Regular catering run, maybe? If that's how they got the van, then that could explain why it wasn't stopped, even with the damage. I wish those smokers would get the hell back inside, though. I don't want anyone getting in the way."

"Collateral damage, my friend. It is never pleasant but sometimes necessary. Look at it this way—two or three lives against thousands," the Russian said grimly as he slid out of the sedan.

"Still prefer to make it zero against thousands," Bolan returned as he, too, left the vehicle and joined the Russian in moving toward the van.

Looking around them as they strode down the street, they could see that the narrow closed-in walls of the buildings on either side gave them some shelter. There were no windows directly overlooking them, and apart from the three people clustered near the van, there was no one else in the street. Arvo had his back to them and was leaning into the rear of the van.

The Russian pulled an HK from the back of his belt, where it had rested hidden by his duster. In one smooth motion he had it extended before him.

"One burst, Cooper, even from here, and I can drop him."

"No," Bolan barked, "not while we can't see what he's doing—"

The risk was that the terrorist would have the triggering mechanism in his grasp and so would be able to effect detonation before they could intervene.

There was another risk: stock exchange clerks sneaking a quick cigarette might just be scared witless enough to yell at two men striding toward them, one of whom had an SMG seemingly pointed at them.

It was too late for Bolan to mention that to the Russian, and besides it had never occurred to Dostoyevsky that they would scream and cause the terrorist to spin.

Arvo had been connecting the trigger and warhead prior to arming it when a piercing scream made his blood freeze. He knew that the idiots who had asked him about sandwiches a moment before could not see what he was doing, and so it had to be something behind him that had terrified them.

He snatched at his own HK, which was resting on the floor of the van beside the gray cylinder. The box that held the triggering mechanism was on the other side, partly programmed.

Bolan had caught a glimpse of the weapon before he had to throw himself sideways to avoid the wild burst of SMG fire from the terrorist, who sprayed in an arc as he brought the weapon around.

The Executioner hit the street hard and rolled along the surface, coming up short against the wooden wall of the building opposite the stock exchange building. Having to maneuver in such a tight space made it hard to get his own weapon into a good position to return fire.

On the other side of the street, Dostoyevsky cursed loudly as a bullet from a volley of gunfire took a chunk out of the arm of his leather duster and scuffed at the flesh beneath. It was a superficial wound but enough to prevent him returning fire.

Arvo took advantage of the lull to scramble around to the front of the van, wrenching open the driver's door and hauling himself in before either of his adversaries could get a decent shot at him. Before him, the three office workers had been mercifully spared stray fire—two had fled back into the building, and the third was now beyond the cones and into the street beyond. There was no doubt that an alarm would now be raised.

Arvo threw the van into Reverse, veering crazily across the road as he hit the gas and tried to build up enough speed to take him past his attackers without their having a chance to stop him.

Both men stood firm, ignoring the wild course Arvo was taking, and aimed at the tires. If they were blown out, they could bring him to a halt before he hit the sedan. A hail of fire shredded the rubber, and sparks flew into the air as metal bit into tarmac. The frame of the van was pitted by SMG fire, but then Bolan paused. The DAF was spun by its own momentum so that the front arced to face him, and Bolan found himself staring into the face of the terrorist.

Without hesitation the soldier let fly a burst that shattered the temporary windshield and made a bloodied mess of the terrorist, his expression obliterated. The van roared, jerked and then stalled, coming to a harmless stop in front of the soldier.

Bolan rounded the back of the vehicle, hauling wide open the back doors and checking the hardware. With relief he could see that the trigger had not been fully attached or activated, and he disconnected those parts which were conjoined. As he did this, Dostoyevsky joined him.

"While we have done good work here, I fear that the authorities may not agree. We should hurry."

Bolan nodded. "One down, but there are still too many of these we need to track down. Can you carry part of this to your car?"

The Russian gave him a look of disdain. "Please, I have carried more than this for Lana."

Despite the urgency, Bolan couldn't resist a grin. "Good, because we're not finished yet. We can't leave this behind, but we can't leave at all until we've mopped up a little."

HADES AND VISIGOTH had the HKs they had taken from the guards concealed under blankets. Hades appeared to be carrying one, while Visigoth had his on the top of the laundry hamper, his hand snaking underneath to grip the weapon while he tried to keep the basket moving steadily.

"Help him, asshole, or I'll blow you a new one," Hades snarled.

Nils bent and took hold of one end of the hamper. It was heavy from the weight of Ripper, concealed inside, and that made it difficult to maneuver. "This is no kind of a plan—" he began through gritted teeth.

"You're right. It is no kind of a plan," Hades interrupted, "but that's probably because we're not terrorists. On the other hand, it's still better than you selling us down the river. And remember, shithead, if we go down in a hail of bullets, you will, too."

Nils said nothing, just kept pushing. So far they had managed to negotiate several yards of corridor without coming across anyone. That had been pure luck. There was no way they would get to the outside without being stopped, and he still hadn't been able to think of a way he could get himself out of this without either side ripping him to shreds in cross fire.

They turned a corner. Ahead of them were three armed guards. They were deep in a conversation, and didn't notice the three men and a laundry hamper until they were almost on them. It was then that the guard who had seen them first turned to face them, looking puzzled.

"Nils? What are you doing, man? Why can't that lazy one push?" he asked, indicating Hades. "If you get caught, then it'll be your balls, especially on a day like this—"

He was halted midharangue by the sound of an alarm piercing the interior of the building. The guard looked up, then at his fellows.

"That's the cells—someone must…" His voice trailed off as he realized what was happening. He was a fraction behind the other two guards, one of whom was yelling at Hades and Visigoth to get down. Both had their SMGs raised.

Caught in the middle, and still slow to react, the guard could only stand mute as fire from both sides blasted by him, somehow miraculously missing him. The two guards fired bursts that went wide of the mark as both Norwegians took evasive action, bringing their own weapons into the open and into play. They were less experienced gunmen but had been more prepared for this and were given an extra edge by their fear and desperation. Their bursts hit home, stitching both guards and putting them out of action.

The guard in the middle stood still, too dazed and confused to react fully. He could only stare dumbly when Nils started forward to grab his HK. Instinctively he pulled it to him, trying to bring it up to aim as Nils wrestled with him.

The confusion did neither man any favors. Hades fired two bursts into them that forced them apart, the guard falling dead while Nils clutched at a wound in his stomach.

"Jeez, man, what did you do that for?" Visigoth yelled. "We've got no hostage without him."

"Dude, we don't have time for that now. Change of plan." He flung open the laundry hamper, grabbing the HK that had fallen between the guard and Nils in the struggle and throwing it to Ripper as he tumbled out of the hamper. "We've just got to run like hell and hope for the best."

With that as the best course of action he could come up with, Hades led his two compatriots on, taking the left fork, but not without stopping to aim a final kick—partly from sheer frustration—at the blood-soaked and dying Nils as he lay on the ground.

"COOPER, THIS IS NOT the best idea you've ever had. I've probably said that before, and to be fair I've probably meant it. But this has just got to be the not-best idea that is worse than all the rest," the Russian gritted out as he guided the sedan into the area around the courthouse. There were armed men and armored trucks all around them, and every second a vehicle seemed to be stopped and searched.

Bolan chuckled. Dostoyevsky was probably right. Bolan was making his comrade-in-arms drive into the heart of a gathering of security personnel and government types, headed toward a prison break, with a disarmed ex-Soviet nuke sitting in the trunk along with enough regular hardware to start a small war. There was no way they could begin to explain what was going on, and there was also no way that Hal Brognola could ever admit to having heard the name Matt Cooper should the ordure hit the fan.

But there was also no way Bolan was going to let a cache of ex-Soviet ordnance head east when there was a chance of getting intel, and no way he was going to leave the corresponding ordnance in the trunk sitting on an Oslo street to be found and puzzled over by anyone else.

So far they had been lucky. The roller coaster was going his way right now, and hopefully he would be able to ride it to the end.

The Russian guided the sedan into the streets leading directly to the courthouse entrance. He cursed as an armed soldier gestured them to stop.

"I hope you have a plan, Cooper," he murmured.

"No," Bolan said simply, eliciting a puzzled glare from the Russian. "I don't think we're going to need one."

As the Russian started to pull over, the area to the rear of the court erupted into life. A siren could be heard, and men began to rush from all points toward the service road leading down the back. The guard who had waved them over listened to his earpiece and then waved them on, yelling at them not to stop and to clear the area.

"I knew something would kick off if we waited long enough," Bolan murmured. "Pull over as soon as you can—we need to extract one of the three for interrogation."

"Why is that?" the Russian queried as he pulled into a space just beyond the immediate area. They were ignored by the men rushing past, and the soldier who had tried to move them on was out of sight.

"Sundby or one of the other two band members—we need all that they know about Freedom Right and the setup in Estonia. Get one out, get him to a safehouse and get our people in."

"Your people," the Russian replied. "You don't set us much of a task, Cooper," he added with mild sarcasm before getting out of the car. As they headed toward the courthouse, he added, "How the hell do they think they're going to get out when it's being closed down like this?"

"I don't think they know. I figure they were set up, and they've bitten the hand that feeds them. They're flying blind, and maybe we can help them."

Bolan led the way down the service road. Chaos reigned as the armed forces tried to squeeze themselves into the cramped area. Bolan and Dostoyevsky were helped by the presence of plainclothes security as well as those in uniform. The air of authority that the two men exuded in the midst of the confusion allowed them to pass almost to the courthouse entrance without question.

Not that anyone around them was in any position to stop men going in. They were far more concerned with stopping anyone coming out. One thing was for sure, as paramedics rushed past and men with gunshot wounds were treated in the midst of an ongoing firefight, the unschooled and desperate Norwegians had caused the chaos.

RIPPER ROARED WITH an almost berserker bloodlust as he forged forward, firing wildly into the space beyond the doorway to the courthouse's yard before dodging back to cover, followed by more careful fire laid down by Hades and Visigoth, providing a background that enabled Ripper to let loose the anger that was stored inside him.

"Man, we're not getting out of here," Visigoth screamed. "There's too many of them to get through."

"We take them with us then," Hades replied. "They're not doing that great, right?"

After cutting down the three guards and the alarm going off, the three Norwegians had made rapid progress toward the exit. Their lack of guile and the fear factor had driven them onward, firing at first sight of a guard. They had cut down men and driven them back toward the exit, while at the same time riding their luck and escaping with no wounds.

Now they were on the threshold, and the sheer weight of numbers held them back. It was a stalemate; something was needed to break that deadlock.

BOLAN AND THE RUSSIAN were able to get close to the front of the battle without being noticed. Because the Norwegians were also nearby, there had been little attempt to use gas or smoke to flush them out. The chances of either drifting across the enclosed yard— being counterproductive—was too strong. That was exactly what Bolan wanted. He indicated to Dostoyevsky that he should insert nose plugs and then produced a smoke grenade that he lobbed into the doorway.

As it went off, it was as though the two intruders were suddenly noticed. Armed men turned toward them, momentarily thrown. Bolan nodded to the Russian, and as the smoke began to spread across the yard, as Bolan had wanted, he and Dostoyevsky struck out around them, clearing a space by unarmed combat. The element of surprise worked in their favor long enough for them to allow the Norwegians to make their move.

Without understanding what was happening, or caring, the three young men took advantage of the confusion, charging into the yard toward the vehicles.

Bolan knew they had no chance of making it. Even in the midst of the confusion, the three men could easily be killed by the mass gathered beyond the immediate smoke-filled area. Bolan let them pass before he turned toward the last man in line. A blow to the back of the head knocked the guy to the ground as the others continued onward into an exchange of gunfire that cut them down.

As the smoke gave Bolan and his comrade cover, they took paramedic jackets from two men who had been taken down in the melee and slipped into them. They loaded the unconscious Norwegian onto a gurney and moved through the throng gathered around the dead bodies of the two remaining Norwegians and those they had had taken out along the way. Bolan barked at them to move, and they automatically complied, hardly noticing the paramedics and the body on the gurney.

As the initial confusion around the breakout rippled toward the road outside the courthouse, Bolan and the Russian and their "patient" were able to escape, with no one thinking to challenge them as they took a casualty away from an ambulance and toward a sedan.

Swiftly they bundled the unconscious Norwegian into the rear of the vehicle and took off.

"Where are we headed?" Dostoyevsky queried, keeping an eye on his rearview mirror.

Bolan took out his smartphone. "Let me find out."

CHAPTER TWENTY

"Do you know how many strings Hal has had to pull?" Kurtzman asked in passing, before adding, "This is global news, Striker, and the Norwegians are already pissed enough at what's been going down."

Bolan decided to save his reply for when he got a blast from Brognola, but the big Fed would more than likely know better.

The safehouse was in the center of the city, occupying the fourth floor of a wooden building used as a social and business center. It had enough comings and goings to hide activities in plain sight, while the floor on which the U.S. and Norway Folk Heritage Exchange Center was located had enough hidden security visible only to the trained eye to keep it locked down when the need may arise.

Bolan and Dostoyevsky carried the semiconscious Sundby from the back of the sedan, making loud jokes about too much alcohol to cover his grogginess as the two comrades hauled him into the building. Three men descended the wooden stairs loudly, joining in the faux good humor as they helped drag Sundby to the safety of their office space. Bolan heard the reassuring click of an electronic lock as they entered.

Two other men were inside. All five were dressed casually but carried themselves in a manner that spoke of military training to the experienced eye of the soldier and the Russian mercenary. They made only the briefest of exchanges before they hauled Sundby away, leaving the two fighters alone with a change of clothes, food and beverages in a comfortably furnished room overlooking the street.

"Grabbing the guy was not a complete waste of time," Dostoyevsky said as he clapped Bolan on the shoulder. "There may still be something we can get from him that will make it worthwhile. Look at it this way—the manner in which the Norwegians were handling the situation would have led to a siege, and there would have been more deaths. At least we probably saved a few police and soldiers from an untimely end at the hands of these."

Bolan looked out the window at the busy Oslo streets below. In a few hours this part of the city had seemingly returned to normal, with no sign of the heavy security presence earlier in the day.

"Maybe you're right," he said at length. "But men died down there, and this guy has given us nothing so far."

"So far," Dostoyevsky replied. "Wasn't it you who said to me that maybe he knows something he doesn't know? It just hasn't been tapped, that's all."

Bolan shrugged. It was scant consolation for all that had gone down. Dostoyevsky's unmarked and unnoticed sedan had been able to pull away from the chaos and get clear of the scene before the cordon had closed, once it had been noted that Sundby was missing. Bolan's call to Stony Man had elicited the address of this safehouse, used by security services from the U.S. Embassy for any activities that needed to be kept from foreign officials.

As Bolan and Dostoyevsky tried to unwind, they were interrupted only twice. The first time was by one of the men who had assisted them into the building. With few words he briefed them on progress: Sundby had been brought round and pumped full of the requisite drugs to force truth from him, but so far he had proven to know very little. Indeed, he seemed remarkably ill informed about the organization that he had allied himself to, although he had brokenly described the circumstances surrounding the deaths of all four members of Abaddon Relix.

It seemed so long ago since Bolan had watched four young men, full of piss and vinegar, making an unlistenable racket that had led to their demise. No matter how awful Bolan felt their music had been, at that moment he fervently wished that they had kept to that alone.

But no matter. There were other things that were of greater urgency. Bolan requested that the men ask Sundby about Estonia, and the people Sundby had dealt with—anything that did not relate to the politics of Freedom Right.

"You figure any incidentals might reveal something he doesn't realize is of importance?" the security man said heavily.

"You are quick. You will go far. I hope…" the Russian murmured with barely concealed sarcasm. His reward was a look that told him the Cold War had never died for some Americans, before the security man left without another word.

The second interruption came shortly afterward from Bolan's smartphone.

"Hal, let me have it," Bolan said, prepared for a wave of criticism from the big Fed.

He was surprised by Brognola's mild tone in reply. Weary, perhaps, might have been the best description.

"Striker, even after all this time I never get really surprised by the uproar you can generate in trying to clean up a town—"

"That's the key word, Hal. Town. You put me in a place where the local authorities cooperate or aren't needed, and I can make it quick and clean. The trouble comes when these guys think they have the full picture, and they think I'm one of the bad guys."

Brognola sighed. "I know. You don't have to tell me. I just get tired of trying to explain this to people higher up the food chain. But it gets better. Our attempts to keep things under wraps have been blown to crap. There's nothing more irritating than a political group that gets ideas above their station and then tries to carry them out."

"Careful, Hal, that's how half the revolutions in human history got underway," Bolan said. It did, at least, elicit a wry chuckle in reply.

"Maybe. Point is that we've got only a small part of the ordnance we wanted, and the very thing we wanted to avoid most of all is happening right now."

"The Russians?" Bolan queried, shooting a glance at Dostoyevsky. The Russian mercenary looked suitably baffled.

"We wanted to keep the ordnance out of Russia's hands, right? Its president was actively putting out unofficial feelers for it, right?"

"Yes…" Bolan said slowly. "So what's changed?"

"Those terrorists are giving him exactly what he wants. They're waltzing it all over to him."

"I don't understand, Hal. They hate him, blame his country for their own being subject to miscegenation. Why would they want to give those weapons back to him?"

"They're not exactly doing that. They announced that the Oslo strike was a dry run to test how seriously they were taken, and that there had been no intention of harming their Norwegian allies—"

"That's quick thinking, I'll give them that," Bolan stated.

"Maybe, but I think they used all their brain cells on that one, because they've announced the real target is Moscow. And they're not bluffing. The trace you requested Stony Man put on them has shown the armory vehicle is taking a route that will lead them right into the heart of the city—"

"Where—knowing they're on their way—the Russian president's boys will be welcoming them with armed military types," Bolan finished, shaking his head.

"Oh, it gets better," Brognola said wryly. "They announced this a couple hours ago, and since then the fiber optics of Europe have been glowing white-hot. I've had the Farm monitor as much as possible, but the traffic is immense. It's possible that every right-wing crackpot terrorist group on the continent has seen the YouTube videos of the bunker and knows what these guys recovered and has figured out what it can do."

"And now they know where it's going to be," Bolan added.

"Exactly. This is the very definition of an open secret. And trouble."

"But right now we have the drop on them, right? No one else knows the route they're taking?"

"Not as far as we know. But once they reach the city, God knows how many of the extremists will be waiting for them."

"Maybe we need to leave now, get to them before they reach the city." He turned to the Russian. "Are you with me?"

"I hate that little bastard for what he has done to my country. Hell, I just hate him anyway. But I am known, Cooper, remember that. If I go back to Russia, and I'm caught, then I'm dead. And that will mean you will be, too. Do you want that?"

Bolan grinned. "That's called occupational hazard. The question is, do you want to go back for this? The money will be good, I can guarantee that, but—"

The Russian waved him away dismissively. "It's never been about the money, you know that. Sure, Lana will like it, and I guess it'll be a good pension if I don't get back. But I know she'd miss having someone to complain to. I also know that I haven't had this much fun since the last time you landed me in hospital."

"That's a yes, then?"

"Two heads are always better than one. Although I have one proviso. We'll need another car. My Saab can't take any more punishment, Cooper, and even the idiots they have running security in this town should be looking for it by now."

"You hear that, Hal?" Bolan said into his smartphone. "You get these guys to cooperate just a little more, and maybe we can get to Freedom Right before anyone else does."

"Wait," the Russian added, holding a finger in the air. "Let us not waste any time."

He strode to the door, opened it and bellowed down the corridor, bringing a puzzled security man in response, who was greeted with the words, "You, talk to my boss in the States. He has something to tell you. You know him, right?"

He pointed the security man toward Bolan, adding to the soldier, "There's no time like now, right?"

CHAPTER TWENTY-ONE

Brognola's authority needed no backup. Within minutes of speaking to him, the security man returned to the room with an older man, seen only in passing when they had first entered the safehouse, who was obviously his superior officer. With a barely disguised irritation at having his authority usurped in his own little kingdom, he informed them that a vehicle would be available for them within thirty minutes, being currently in transit. He visibly swallowed his bile when Dostoyevsky told him where their ordnance was located in the Saab, and to have it transferred. And when Bolan told him that they wanted to talk to Sundby, the man could only answer in a barely controlled, strangled tone that this would not be permissible.

"The prisoner is under my charge and under interrogation by trained personnel," he snapped.

"Who've got nothing useful from him," the Russian pointed out.

"And since when did it have anything to do with our Russian friends?" the security chief directed at Bolan, pointedly ignoring Dostoyevsky.

"It doesn't," Bolan replied coldly. "This man is with me, and he's right. You want this situation resolved by the good guys? So far, it's been brewing under your nose without you having the first idea, so you're in no position to argue, as far as I can see. I have prior knowledge of the prisoner. Do you want me to pull rank on you and make your life difficult, or do we do this the sensible way?"

The security chief held Bolan's stare for a moment, but the flinty eyes of the soldier made him look away. Without a word he indicated they should follow, and in seconds they were in the room where Sundby was seated, secured by straps to a padded chair. He was sweating, his hair plastered to his face, and his eyes were glittering and distant. Bolan ordered the two men in the room who had been questioning the prisoner—and the security chief—to exit the room. After a curious glance at their superior, they departed, only leaving Bolan and the Russian alone in the room with Sundby.

"You know who I am, right?" Bolan said easily, seating himself on the edge of a desk while the Russian stood impassive in the corner. Dostoyevsky wanted to leave the field to Bolan and also was determined to keep an eye out for possible intrusions.

Sundby had trouble focusing, but the faint smile that crossed his lips showed that he had no problems remembering Bolan. He said, in halting tones, "You… you started this ball rolling, dude. You here to hit the home run?"

"You Scandinavians, man—you love us Yanks, but you can never quite get it right." Bolan grinned. "I'll level with you. Estonia is a write-off. Whatever they've told you about Freedom Right when they were interrogating you…they don't know what they're talking about. I do. I was in Tallinn. I left that house in ruins. I took out the Estonian who was supposed to blow Oslo sky-high. Me…and my friend, of course," he added, indicating Dostoyevsky. "There's not much left of Freedom Right."

"Except maybe the Soviet shit, yeah?" Sundby grinned. "And you know that's going home. You wouldn't be here otherwise. Was it you who saved me?"

Bolan nodded, and the Norwegian continued. "What about Hades and Visigoth?"

"Gone. Your own security services got them."

"Not mine," Sundby snapped back coldly. "My people would gladly wipe them out."

"Your people couldn't wipe their own noses," Bolan said. "Freedom Right is one truck and a couple guys. With every terrorist on the mainland chasing them—you really think they're going to hit the mother lode like that?"

Sundby grinned. It twisted into a grimace as he tried to fight the impulse to gloat; the drugs in his system screamed at him to reveal all, and he was too weakened to resist.

"You think they're going to do it alone? There are those who support us, who have already been called into action. You are too late to stop them. They have a schedule that will take them right into the belly of the beast."

Despite himself, Sundby's pride in the organization that had used and abused him overrode any desire to stay silent. Detailed queries about the base of the organization and its structure had been wasted on him. He knew nothing of that. But the questions had been all wrong. The only thing Sundby knew about was the route to Moscow.

Bolan had gambled on psychology. The mercenaries

who had first used Sundby had fired his imagination with the grand plan, sucked him into murder by feeding him details of this plan, including his potential involvement in something so large in scale. It had pandered to his ego, and as far as Freedom Right was concerned, he would be dead and discarded long before the plan became operational. They hadn't expected him to be the survivor while they were long gone.

Bolan and Dostoyevsky left Sundby, exhausted by the effort of trying to deny his monstrous ego, and immediately went down to where the replacement vehicle had arrived. They confirmed that the ordnance had been transferred from the Russian's sedan to their new ride and departed, leaving the frustrated U.S. security men in their wake.

"You think our friend will be up to telling the story a second time?" the Russian asked as he piloted the vehicle out of the city center.

"You think they should know?" Bolan returned.

The Russian shrugged. "I think that maybe it would be better if you told your chief and then he decided whether those idiots should know. At the very least he should jump on them before they do anything stupid. We have enough ground to make up on the truck as it is."

"You drive. I'll speak to Hal," Bolan replied. "And then we'll get a route and make tracks."

"You know, I always wanted to be a long-distance truck driver," the Russian mused ironically. "I guess this is the next best thing."

DOSTOYEVSKY HAD SPOKEN to Bolan of the castles that littered the Estonian landscape and how the isolation of these would provide cover for any organization wishing privacy. Rightly the soldier had surmised that to hide in plain sight was a smarter plan for the leadership of any such organization. Yet the more obvious plan had its advantages for smaller, not-so-important cells with less in the way of hardware to hide.

A damp, derelict seventeenth-century structure thirty klicks outside Tallinn—considered deserted by the locals—was just such a place. One wing of the castle had been covertly restored by the cell, which now lived there, with a gasoline-fueled generator keeping it heated and powered for the six men. They had two trucks and a car under tarps in the old courtyard, and had early warning systems in the form of motion sensors and fiber-optic surveillance cameras set up at points all around the moated castle, with the primary focus being the track that connected the isolated castle with the nearest main road.

Even before Velio had called ahead on his cell phone to announce he and Andrus were nearby, they had been spotted, and men were opening the gates to the courtyard. They had been identified from surveillance cam images and their arrival had been unexpected. A ripple of surprise and panic had spread through the men of the cell. Those who had not been on watch had been roused from their beds, and now all six stood in the courtyard, anxiously awaiting an explanation from their leader.

As Andrus detailed to them what had happened in Tallinn, spinning events so that it seemed as though a last-ditch escape had actually been a glorious rearguard action to defend their assets, Velio wondered at the skill with which his chief drew in the six men whose gaze was rapt. The conviction that Andrus imbued in them would be necessary for the coming future.

During the following day, the cell had worked hard in transferring some of the hardware from the transport truck into the two trucks that stood in the courtyard. When that had been done, the six men had been briefed on their part in the upcoming mission.

"My friends, we stand at the threshold of greatness. I had not chosen which of my soldiers would have the privilege—as Velio and I have the privilege—of being the men who would make this glorious strike on the homeland of our enemies and so set spark to tinder for the revolution. We are all—all of us in Freedom Right—soldiers who stand together and are of equal ranking.

"But this mission requires the kind of experience that is unique to this cell, which is why Velio and myself are here now. Only you have the kind of skills and talents that are necessary. Only you have the ability to respond as required to the speed of the challenge before us. From here, we can spread the word of what is about to take place and then put that plan into operation, with a speed and cunning that will inspire our allies and terrify our enemies."

Velio watched the faces of the men as they listened. There was no doubt that they would happily die for their leader. Velio? He wasn't so sure. He believed in the cause, but recent events had made him wonder if Andrus was really the great leader he had led them all to believe.

Getting their hands on the nuclear weapons had been a coup, especially as other groups would happily have wiped them off the face of the planet to get those now into their possession. But what they had done since, and the way in which they had been so easily swatted back in Tallinn, had made him wonder if Andrus's rhetoric was enough.

Velio listened with half of his attention as Andrus detailed their duties and destinations within Moscow. Much of it Velio knew already. The other half of his attention was focused on something of greater import. He truly believed in the mission and wanted it to work. He was not now so sure of the man who was his leader. So Velio's greater duty, as he saw it, was to find a way whereby he could ensure that the mission could be completed—regardless of where that may leave his erstwhile leader.

Dutifully he followed in Andrus's wake as Velio prepared on a laptop the announcement to the world of the imminent strike. More than that, he sat at Andrus's right hand as word came through of the debacle in Oslo. Initially it was apparent that the ex-Soviet device Arvo was to detonate had either been defused or captured. Then, as news leaked of the siege at the courthouse, it became even more obvious that whatever Arvo had tried in Oslo had gone awry.

The Norwegian authorities had not released information about the nuclear bomb, which made it apparent that the American black ops team had captured it. That impression was reinforced by the revelation that two of the young Norwegians were dead but that Sundby was missing. There had been no word on any of this from the cell in Oslo, and the only conclusion was that they, too, had been taken down by the Americans.

"What was Nils doing, letting them get weapons?" Andrus asked.

"Maybe he had no choice. Maybe the American team has a greater hand in this than we know," Velio replied. "They're everywhere. Who is to say that they did not destroy our cell and substitute one of their own for Nils? How else could Sundby disappear?"

"More to the point, what could they get from him?" Andrus mused.

"Nothing," Velio said flatly. "He knew nothing. We told him nothing. He is a dead end."

"Of course, you are right," Andrus said with renewed confidence. "We must make sure the world sees this how we want."

And as Andrus spun events for his proclamation to the world, Velio once again marveled at his leader's ability to bend the truth to his own ends, while at the same time deciding that this ability to only see what Andrus wanted should not get in the way of the mission, should events dictate that Velio need to take the upper hand.

He shadowed his leader throughout the rest of the preparation process. Finally, when they got ready to leave, they separated. Andrus would ride in one truck, he in another. All three trucks would travel the same route, keeping in visual contact, but they would not stop until they reached the target city, nor would they break a communications silence unless an emergency arose. All that needed to be said had been said, and anything that could attract detection was to be avoided.

The last Velio saw of Andrus was the leader's face staring out of the side window of a truck as it pulled out in front of the other two. Maybe it was his imagination, but Velio could swear that, despite the air of confidence he had exuded to his men, Andrus looked worried.

"AND SO I LOOKED the British prime minister full in the face, and I said to him, 'If you have never wrestled with the bear of life and won, then you have no idea of how to swim with the salmon of truth.' I fixed him with my best stare."

The Russian president sat back on his chaise longue, and sipped at his vodka and cranberry. The slim blonde seated opposite had an expression on her face that was supposed to be awe. The president was not the fool she believed, and he could see that she did not believe him. His glittering eyes met hers, and she cracked.

"You did not, Vlad. You could not. No one would— what did he say?" she asked finally.

"He looked at me as seriously as if I had told him that his mother had cancer, and he said, 'Yeah, I know exactly what you mean,' in the same sincere voice he uses when he tells his people that it is all for their own good."

"No…"

"But yes," he said triumphantly. "He swallowed it whole. He is a bigger fraud and idiot than even his worst enemies would believe." He felt the cell vibrate in his breast pocket, and excused himself as he pulled it out and answered, "Make it quick, I am busy…"

He listened and his face hardened. He stood up, dismissing the blonde with a perfunctory gesture.

"You go now. I will text you later," he said in an offhand way before barking into the cell phone, "You—here now."

He paced the room restlessly for a couple minutes as he waited for his security adviser to arrive. When the man shuffled into the room, the premier gave him no chance to speak first. "They issue threats. This I understand. Your people missed out at the bunker—that I do not understand, by the way, but it is for another time—and this gives you a second chance. Now you tell me that you have missed them in Tallinn, and they are coming here?"

"To be fair, Excellency, the Americans have black ops teams who have excellent intelligence and were just marginally ahead of us, as they were in Finland… and in Norway, and—"

"So what? Why was our intelligence not better? They are our weapons! It is our country they want to attack! It is bad enough that the armaments were taken from under our noses, let alone that we cannot even get them back. What now? Have the Americans got half the Navy SEALs running around northern Europe?"

The security chief sighed, and said hesitantly, "As far as we can see, it may just be one man—"

"One? And you cannot stop him?" The president was apoplectic and for one moment the security chief thought he might avoid censure by virtue of the man dropping dead.

But the moment passed, and the president continued. "When I was in the KGB, we could have crushed such a feeble opposition. One man can be strong as an individual, and in some ways I would like to shake this man by the hand. Not as much as I would like to shake him by his throat, but…"

He shrugged. "One man can move mountains, but we have the manpower to blast the mountain while it is on his back. Why is this not being done?"

"It is possible that he has assistance—"

"Ah, so he is not alone? So there is a team? This is not so bad."

The security chief felt on safer ground. Yet this may have been a mistake. He said, with a smile, "Apparently there are reports that he has a man with him who lives in Tallinn and used to be a Russian military man—"

The president's expression stopped him dead.

Carefully the president formed his words, his voice ominously quiet. "So… It is not bad enough that one lone American runs rings around us. When it appears that he does need help, he uses one of our own. Why, pray, do you think this is amusing?"

"I—I do not," the security chief stammered. "I merely think that it is a sign of our quality that he needs inside help to—to—" His words faded in the cold glare of his superior.

"You do not think at all. That is your problem. When this matter is resolved, then we will have words about your future. They will be all mine, and I promise you that they will not be good. But right now, I want you to do something for me without fucking it up. Do you think you could do that?"

He stared at the security chief, who nodded dumbly.

"Good. Now there is a file for decommissioned KGB officers—those who are not dead—which is on the database. There are some details I wish you to get for me. They are in a secured vault. I will give you the password. You will need to use my personal PC as the password is IP linked. If you do this, and hurry, then perhaps you may have a future. Of sorts."

THE ROOM WAS DARK, shadows in every corner, hiding the three men in suits with conspicuous bulges who sat in large leather chairs. They were silent, slablike and bore a remarkable resemblance to Igor, the man they had replaced. Their employer sat behind his desk, poring over a ledger. To one side of him, a bank of monitors showed the outside of the building, while a computer terminal played soundless news from a Moscow TV station.

One of the phones before him on his desk rang softly. Tapping ash from his cigarette, he grimaced and picked it up.

"How nice to hear from you. It is not often that I get a call from someone as exalted as the president of Russia," he said quietly.

"Dimitri, you are not surprised? No, of course you are not. Tell me, how is my old charge Igor?"

"Pretty good for a dead man, but then of course you knew that. I assume you want information?"

"There is much I would want from you."

"Proof of my death being foremost. However, as long as I have my safe deposit box, my instructions with fourteen sets of solicitors across the globe and my backup files nestling in the inboxes of several interesting outlets—awaiting nothing more than a key word to be activated—you will have to settle for whatever intelligence I can offer you."

"How nice of you to remind me of all that, Dimitri. I see your desire to make a point with the subtlety of a sledgehammer still remains. It was never one of your more endearing characteristics."

Bulganin sighed. "I have no endearing characteristics. That is what has kept me alive. Now cut the crap."

There was a momentary silence at the other end of the line. Bulganin allowed himself a thin smile on his skull-like features. He could almost hear the click of tracers and the whirr of recorders, even though in this digital age that was no longer how it worked. Despite himself he felt a pleasant nostalgia for old times in hearing the Russian president's voice again.

"I could have you killed anyway and damn the consequences. Your house is not that impenetrable."

"Then it is like your mind," Bulganin replied. "Allow me to fill in the blanks for you. Your people were too slow at the bunker, then in Finland and again in Norway. If they made it to here, then they were so late that they haven't arrived yet. You are no doubt wondering why I allowed those boy soldiers to bring your old crap to my town?"

"I assume it was because you wished to steal it from them and sell it back. Probably to me—that would appeal to your sense of humor."

Bulganin nodded to himself. "You are right. That would have been most amusing. But it would have gotten in the way of business. I dislike competition, and the last thing I want is people nosing around here, muddying waters I like to keep tranquil. I was happy for the American to rout them out and drive them away. I allowed Freedom Right to exist here because I could keep an eye on them, and because I like the fact that they bait you.

"But their recklessness does them—any of us—no

favors. I understand that they have picked up one of their remaining cells from near here and are headed your way by road, with their payload split in three. I have some reason to believe that the American and his Russian friend—a dangerous man to be at your side, so be warned—have a trail to follow."

"So I should direct the tardiest of the fools who claim to follow in our tradition to look for a convoy by road? You have other intelligence to back this, of course."

"Of course. As a gift I wil. send it to you. Personally."

"You can do this?" The Russian president sounded surprised, even though he tried to hide the fact.

Bulganin grinned. "You have my number. Why should I not have yours?"

The man let this ride, choosing another tack. "Their target is known to you?"

"Alas, no. Believe me or not, I would actually choose to share that with you. However, my inside man was not privy to the intel before he became collateral damage. You will have to intercept them before they have the chance to show you for themselves."

"Wonderful."

"Indeed. There is one more thing before you go, never to bother me again," he added with an equally heavy emphasis.

"That thing is?"

"Freedom Right has shown a remarkable openness in declaring its intent. I understand that this is part of their point. However, I am not sure if they realize that their trail is so easy to follow or divine from their proclamations. I know of three other groups who have made inquiries about the bunker. I know that these three have sent teams to intercept. They are considerably brighter than the men they chase. Of course I think the American and his hired gun are better. But even they cannot be in three places at once."

"I understand," the Russian president said tightly before disconnecting.

Bulganin sat under the light of the lamp, drawing on his cigarette and looking at the gently humming receiver.

"I hope you do."

CHAPTER TWENTY-TWO

"I thought the whole idea of getting a new car was that we could hit the road and try to catch up with these fools," Dostoyevsky grumbled as he followed the GPS directions to a field twenty kilometers outside Oslo. "Pedal to the metal... You know, that sounds like Bachman-Turner Overdrive? I always suspected you were old-school American rock," he added with a grimace.

"Bachman-Turner Overdrive was a Canadian band," Bolan pointed out. "And pedal to the metal was a good initial plan, until this came in—" he waved the cell at the Russian "—and a good general is adaptable."

"You promote yourself, Cooper? I like your army. Now pretend I am not just a grunt and tell me what the hell has changed your mind."

"Pull over when you reach the open plain, and I'll show you," the soldier said, indicating where he wanted the Russian to halt.

As he parked, Bolan added, "You know, the change may not be a bad thing. The embassy guys think we're on the road. I never got the chance to check this for a tracker, but even if it doesn't have one—"

"Then there was only one route we could take?" the Russian mused. "Makes sense. But that's not your reason for this change, right?"

Bolan shook his head before briefly outlining what

had come through from Stony Man. The black truck from Tallinn had gone off radar for a short while, the assumption being that it had used smaller roads, perhaps holing up somewhere. What had occurred was an unknown quantity, but when it had come back on the radar, it had two other vehicles that followed it in a loose convoy, distant enough to seem separate to the naked eye but discernibly following when taken on a larger map.

"I take it we assume they have spread the ordnance in the interim?" the Russian queried.

Bolan nodded. "I figure if they do that now, then the trucks head to different locations in Moscow without any delay. It also means that if one gets taken down, there are still two others out there."

"Makes our task harder but not impossible. Surely it would be better if we try to take them out while they are still en route rather than wait until they have been absorbed into Moscow traffic?"

"That would be the better option under standard operating circumstances. These are not."

The Russian frowned. "What has changed?"

"We take out one vehicle en route, and there's a possibility that it leaves us trailing the other two. If we were the only chasers, that wouldn't be so bad. But we won't be, and I don't want to leave it wide open for them to jump in while we're occupied. Look at this."

Bolan brought up some emails and video that had been forwarded to him, and it soon became apparent to the Russian that the lower reaches of the internet had been running alive with speculation about Freedom Right, the load they were carrying and the route they would take into the city. There was also much speculation about their targets. The Russian mulled that over.

"How much is just talk, and how much is likely to result in action?"

"You mean, are any of these armchair warriors going to get off their butts and come after us? Not any of these, I'd bet," Bolan said with a grin. "It's the ones who aren't making a noise who are the problem." He pulled up a detailed message from Aaron Kurtzman in which scanned communications had been analyzed, and that analysis from intelligence organizations had in itself been pulled, scanned and analyzed by the Stony Man team. When the Russian had finished reading it, he sat back in the driver's seat, stroking his chin, deep in thought.

"Perhaps it is as well that we did not go back and finish Dimitri when we had the chance. Do you think that he knows his network can be so easily accessed?"

"Guys like Bulganin know that there's no such thing as secrecy anymore. It's only a matter of how long before the leak occurs. I think he made sure that this was going to be a very quick leak. He's a cunning old fox, and he wants this merchandise off the market. Make no mistake, it's still merchandise until it's detonated. Any of the three groups identified could sell it to finance actions rather than use it. No one wants the Russians to get it back."

"I suppose it leaves him a clear marketplace." The Russian shrugged. "But I would have thought seeing the old place go up, especially with the mad one in residence, would have been appealing to him."

"Old scores are one thing. But the start of a European theater of war as opposed to localized conflicts?

Maybe not. It draws too much attention to a businessman who likes to stay in the shadows, and there's always the risk of a scorched earth taking everything away from him. Besides, as you know yourself, Tallinn is not that far from Moscow."

Dostoyevsky laughed bitterly. "So the old guy sits in his library and moves us all around like pieces on a chessboard. Truly the emperor in his war, yes?"

"Perhaps." Bolan shrugged. "We don't have to dance to his tune. We can have a little samba of our own." He paused, figuring that maybe the Russian was rubbing off on him in odd ways. When was the last time—and to whoever else—he had used a phrase like that?

"The important thing is that we accept the intel he offers and use it for our ends, not his. If they intersect, then that's lucky for him."

"I guess so," Dostoyevsky said. "You still haven't told me why we're here rather than anywhere else, though."

Bolan looked at his watch and then up to skies. In the distance, he could hear the rhythmic throb of a chopper approaching.

"We're taking a shortcut. And here it comes now."

THE RUSSIAN HAD BEEN only too pleased to renew his acquaintance with Jack Grimaldi once more, and the pilot had wasted little time in helping Bolan and the Russian load up the hardware from the sedan into the belly of his chopper.

"I figured that you might need a little more ordnance, Sarge, so I took the liberty of calling on one of your contacts before hopping across the Straits to get here."

"Not anyone with connections to Estonia?" Bolan asked pointedly.

"Sarge, really?" Grimaldi treated that question with the contempt it deserved. "I've hopped the Urals to be on standby, and this is how you greet me? I'm up to speed, and you can never be too careful. You just check what I've picked up, select what you want and chill while I deliver you."

Bolan felt more relaxed once they were airborne. The Stony Man pilot had picked up enough hardware to start his own trading post, and it gave the soldier a wide range of weaponry for what would be a tough mission. While the Russian studied the intel that Bolan had been sent about the three groups they knew had set out in pursuit, Bolan used the quiet to reflect on the enemy and possible plans of action.

First and foremost, in skipping ahead of the convoy in order to meet them head-on in Moscow, Bolan was taking two big chances. The first was that the chasing groups would not preempt him by opting for the same course of action Bolan had already dismissed. He doubted that they would want to take the same risk he was eschewing, but this did make the assumption that they all knew they were not alone in chasing the ordnance. They would have to be very stupid not to realize that, but one thing he had noted over the years was that intelligence was not the primary trait of the terrorist.

The second chance he took was that, in waiting until they reached Moscow, he would be moving in the midst of the Russian security forces. They were prepared, they had the same intel that Bolan did, and they would be locking down the city in preparation—though they did not have the firsthand experience of Freedom Right that Bolan and his partner had, and he knew that they would be an inflexible, unwieldy force if past experience was any indication. Dostoyevsky and he would at least have the advantage of speed.

Potential targets were many. That he would discuss with the Russian after he had mulled over the three groups that they knew were in pursuit.

All three were from parts of Eastern Europe. The jihad men were from Chechnya, a Muslim fundamentalist group who wished to link its country with the Middle Eastern states that were in some ways closer culturally.

Like many of their ilk, they were small and worked on a cell basis. Available intel on them showed that they were hard fighters, with a determination that belied the size of the group. The organization was underfunded, so its war chest was likely to be small, but unlike Freedom Right, the group did not include ex-soldiers and mercenaries who were as likely to be influenced by money as by ideology. That made this group particularly dangerous.

White Zion had more in common with Freedom Right. Its members were fascists from the Slavic region who believed in white supremacy and had a desire to ethnically cleanse their land and finish the job that had been halted with the cessation of the Balkan war.

Comprised of a few ideologues and a number of men who were ex-military—some on the run still for war crimes—they had pretensions to mainstream politics and were apt to play down their more hands-on activities. This made them cautious in ways that the jihad group would not be. It meant that enough of a public display in Moscow may just frighten them off. That could be a useful weapon in its own right, the soldier considered.

The biggest threat, in Bolan's opinion, would come from the last group: the Ukraine Democrats. Their name might have sounded like a soccer team, but their record belied the faintly comic moniker. Living next door to Russia, they had never forgiven the mother country for the way that Brezhnev had taken any self-determination from them during the Soviet era of the 1960s and 1970s, sucking them dry of any wealth they may have had and directing it toward Moscow.

Many of the best minds of the region had been forced to migrate against their will, the brain drain being echoed by an economic drain that had seen the country struggle in the post-Soviet era. The Ukraine had some wealth of its own, but much was still tied up, not in Ukrainian hands, but in those of Russian oligarchs whose power derived from old Moscow connections.

This group was right on top of the target area. They hated the Russians with a vengeance. They wanted to free their resources, take back and grab reparations, and exact revenge. If they wanted nothing more than to hijack the Freedom Right train as much as to derail it, it would come as no surprise to Bolan.

They were fanatical, like the jihad men. They had the ex-military and mercenary chops of the Slavs. They were on location without having to travel vast distances. Their objectives were obscured by the fact that either outcome suited part of their purpose.

Of the three groups, they were the ones he would place money on being the primary threat. Combating them would be the core around which he would build his strategy.

"You are lost in thought, my friend. We will soon arrive," the Russian said, breaking Bolan's reverie.

"You've read up on them?" the soldier returned, indicating his cell phone. The Russian nodded, and Bolan continued. "Then before we land, we need to discuss targets. What would be the prime objective?"

The Russian smirked. "You're asking me? You know how I feel—"

"Where would you start?" Bolan finished.

"Exactly…"

"I know. You'd take it all down." Bolan sighed. "They've got the firepower."

"Then we need to think not about what would cause the most damage necessarily, but which would make the biggest impression. What would put them on top of the news feeds, my friend? That is how they will be thinking. That is how we have to think."

Bolan looked out of the chopper as they homed in on the capital, with its forty-nine bridges that spanned the Moskva River along the city's expansive banks. There were eleven million people down there, including a small handful who would try to reduce it to dust.

It was like looking for a speck of sand on a very long beach.

THE JOURNEY HAD BEEN long and tiring. Not just because of the vast distance involved and the conditions of highways that were poorly maintained. To cross borders—even in countries that paid lip service to the alleged openness of European Union territories—was not a simple matter.

To avoid toll roads, border guards and the possibility of being searched—either as a matter of course or as a random selection—it had been necessary to sometimes hit back roads and dirt trails that took them through small villages before returning to the major highways. Perhaps if they had known the sudden panic which these detours had given certain parties—who were hacking into CCTV systems in order to keep on their tail—they may have opted to stay on the hard road. As it was, the desire to make good time and have an easier drive had forced them back into the open.

Now, after what seemed weeks rather than the days they had endured, the three trucks stood in the car park of a truck stop on the edge of Moscow's Sparrow Hills, under the watchful eye of a pole-mounted camera that kept them in its unblinking gaze.

The men from each of the trucks stretched their legs, used the facilities and bought coffee that failed to warm them against the bitter cold. Andrus was silent and withdrawn from his men, staring out over the river, with Luzhniki Stadium and the Luzhnetsky Metro Bridge in clear view, but the Russian Academy of Sciences drawing his attention.

"So, now that we are here, do you think we can really pull this off?" Velio asked quietly as he joined his leader.

Andrus smiled weakly. "I will not try to fool you, of all people. I attempt to inspire the others, but it's a long shot. I really don't know if we can. If our luck holds, then we can make the attack before we are stopped."

"I'm surprised that we haven't encountered any resistance on the way here," Velio mused. "Maybe we've finally shaken off the Americans, or maybe they're happy for us to do this?"

Andrus shrugged. "Maybe… If they could track us down, then the Russians could, too. It is only time. I wonder if they are holding off for some reason of their own, or are they really as crappy as we always thought?"

Velio spit the coffee grounds from his paper cup onto the tarmac. "You could think around in circles forever. The truth is, we are still running free, and if they want to give us slack, then they have poor judgment. Let's do this before the slack tightens into a noose. Don't let doubt get to you. God help me, if it does…"

Andrus was alarmed by the expression in his deputy's eyes. "I believe you would, if you thought I was backing down. No worries, my friend. It's too late to do that now."

He turned and called his men together. Under the mute eye of the camera that went unnoticed by them all, he detailed to each truck crew the location in which they were to plant and time their weapons, and their escape route.

"Make no mistake, there is every chance that we will either be killed in attempting to achieve our mission or in failing to get clear of the capital in good time. We have left behind those who will continue our work, and this will give them the platform they need. If we do not get out, then I thank you for the dedication that you have shown and are about to show. But if we do survive, then we will all meet again in Tallinn and continue with our work. The war goes on, even if the humble soldier is cut down in battle."

Velio joined in the cheer that the small group gave

to Andrus. In the silent reflection of the lens, it looked absurd and exaggerated, but to the men on the ground it was the spur they needed as they went back to their vehicles and left the truck stop, finally parting ways as they each headed toward a destination as yet unknown to the several interested parties with a feed on the CCTV system.

DEEP WITHIN THE KREMLIN, Roman Yeltsin chewed noisily on a pink-iced doughnut with sprinkles and washed it down with a cheap local cola. Despite the money that was now washing over the capital, there were some things that were still difficult to get, and so he hoped that this little job would help get him an overseas posting. He picked up the phone and pushed a yellow button. He did this without taking his eyes off the monitors before him, which showed a bank that stretched over half the wall. Now they showed three trucks split across a number of screens as they headed one east, one west and one north.

"Sir," he mumbled through a mouthful of doughnut. He swallowed hard and just avoided choking as he continued. "I have all three in view. They have just separated.... Yes, sir, from the routes they are taking, I would say that I have a very good idea of where they are headed."

GRIMALDI TOOK THE CHOPPER right to the grounds of the U.S. Embassy and put her down.

"Medical emergency. The ambassador has an allergy, and the antidote—as formulated by his consultant back home in the good old U.S. of A.—has to be flown in as a diplomatic bag to make sure that it arrives with no red tape and saves his ass."

"Seriously? They bought that?" Dostoyevsky asked with wide-eyed amazement. "Even my president is not that mad."

"Hell, no, of course he isn't," Bolan replied easily. "But he knows we'll be here one way or another, and as long as we keep up the pretense, then at least he knows where we are. Better he can keep half an eye on us than none at all. We'll tiptoe around each other until the real shooting starts, then he'll claim outrage if our identities go public. They'd have to kill us first, though."

As the three men left the chopper and entered the embassy, met by the head of security for the complex, it became obvious that they were far from welcome. The ambassador refused to meet them, and the manner in which corridors miraculously emptied before them as staff scuttled away from their presence showed how persona non grata they were.

"It's nothing personal," the security chief said uneasily as he led them into an anteroom. "It's just that the ambassador feels that this had rather been forced on him, and it makes things uncomfortable with the locals."

"It would," Bolan said calmly. "And of course it's been forced on him. He'd be an idiot to have agreed. But sometimes shit just happens. You let us unload our weapons, give us transport and let Jack here take off, and you can wash your hands of the whole affair."

The security chief merely nodded. He had the look of a man who wanted to say plenty but wasn't sure just where to start. He left them alone for a few minutes, then returned and beckoned them out to the yard where Jack's chopper, aptly named Dragonslayer, sat. The security chief and two of his men stood mutely, watching Bolan and the Russian get kitted up, before leading them back toward a service entrance to the main building. He opened a door and they were out on a central Moscow side street. He tossed them a set of keys.

"Škoda," he snapped. "Best I could do."

Bolan and the Russian merc looked at the vehicle. When they turned back, the door to the embassy had been closed.

"You know, if I were you, I would wonder why I worked with assholes like that, Cooper," the Russian said mildly as they got into the Škoda and fired it up. Overhead, they could hear the blades of Dragonslayer as Jack took her up and back to where she was more welcome.

"Sometimes I wonder myself," Bolan muttered as he took out his smartphone. "But then I have guys like this—hey, Bear, are you a friendly voice?"

"Certainly are, Striker," came Kurtzman's warm tones. "I take it our diplomatic corps have been less than diplomatic?"

"I would have expected nothing less. Me and my partner are mobile. Where should we be headed?"

"I have three vehicles heading in different directions. No clear target as yet. Take your pick."

"What about any hangers-on?"

"Radio silence. The three groups we know of are keeping their heads down. The Russians? Lots of hot air, but I think that might be just to confuse us. It looks like they're covering ground with no real ideas. I don't believe them."

"Neither do I. We'll have to treat it like jungle warfare down here. Better that way." Bolan grinned mirthlessly.

Dostoyevsky piloted the Škoda through the crazy Moscow traffic. They moved across roads where there were no markings and seemingly no order, away from the richer and regenerated area where the department stores and embassies were clustered, and through an area where the social housing blocks of the late Soviet era loomed grim and foreboding on the skyline. The streets in this area all looked the same, and it was easy to lose bearings as the concrete stood gray and decaying, with men hanging around the entrances to each block, eyeing the Škoda as it passed.

"This hasn't changed since I was a young man," the Russian remarked bitterly. "It was supposed to change when the old guard left. What a crock of shit that turned out to be. The few friends of the old guard who were smart enough to adapt have had the best of the pickings. If I had come out of the army and stayed, then I would be one of those men. I think that if they could get rid of the cancer without killing the patient, then I would not be so averse to these cretins we chase."

Bolan looked at the human desolation set against drab decay and remembered the district in which he had grown up, along with the reasons that had made him join the services and set first foot on this career. The people here didn't deserve what they were getting from the attention-seeking Russian president, who cared more about overseas leaders than his own people. And they didn't deserve the threat of nuclear contamination that was hanging over them.

"This is your city," Bolan said at length. "You know which way each truck has gone. What kind of target does that suggest to you?"

"Cooper, I have an idea."

"Run it by me."

The Russian laughed. "I haven't bothered. We're already on our way. You know the GUM store, right?"

Bolan nodded. Dostoyevsky was referring to the State Department store found in many cities in the former Soviet Union. The one in Moscow was now a shopping mall.

"They wouldn't pick that," the Russian continued, "as it's too difficult to approach easily. But Vladimir Shukhov, the man who built it—he was a big man in constructivist architecture, and he built a tower at the turn of the 1920s. It was a radio tower. A beautiful thing, and how it survived the brutality of Stalin is a mystery. It's a huge symbol of the Russian people, even though the assholes in charge now want to tear it down. Maybe our boys can spare them the bother."

"Why? What purpose—"

Dostoyevsky chuckled. "Even the UN wants to save it for the Russian people. You'll understand when you see it, Cooper."

CHAPTER TWENTY-THREE

Moscow was a strange city in the twenty-first century. Much of its shape and construction were medieval. It clustered around the river in tightly packed streets that, up until shortly before the October Revolution, were populated by mud and wood houses. Even though mass rebuilding had taken place under the Communist regime, the shape of the city remained. Any development outward took the shape of concentric circles radiating from the original design. It was only in recent years that it had started to echo London, and develop in radial fashion along the roads that fed into and out of the city itself.

In some other ways Moscow was very similar to London. Although parts of each had suffered during war, unlike many other major cities in Europe and the western reaches of Asia, they had not had the heart ripped from them to necessitate wholesale rebuilding and redesign. After the Great Fire of London, Christopher Wren had proposed that the twisting nature of small streets that had grown in London be torn down wholesale to make way for intersecting straight roads of almost Roman design. His death, preceded by the intransigence of the bankers who had controlled London's finances, had put a stop to that.

Three hundred years later, in the midst of a con-

structivist revolution in design and thinking, Josef
Stalin had desired to do something similar to Moscow.
Wielding a power that Wren did not have, Stalin had
ripped up tracts of the city and placed long intersecting concrete roads through the heart of what remained,
the new constructivist architecture intended to replace
the old Moscow.

The irony that the fifteenth-century Kremlin was
his power base would have been ignored by Stalin, and
other matters—from in-fighting to finance to war—
would stop the development in its tracks by the late
1930s. But not before he had set in place the three
freeways that dominated the roadscape of Moscow. A
fourth was due to be complete, to cover the spread of
the city and make those areas as accessible as the rest,
but the inevitable red tape that followed a bureaucracy
with as rich a tradition as Russia had slowed it.

Stalin and Wren—an unlikely meeting of minds,
but one that did cross the soldier's as he sat beside
Dostoyevsky while the Russian negotiated the third
freeway, coming onto long straight stretches of road before detouring into mazes that suddenly became, once
again, the long straights. When Bolan was in London,
he liked the odd juxtaposition of the old and new; it
contrasted well with the order of New York and Washington, where grid systems imposed order as opposed
to the chaos of the English capital.

Right now, what was charming in one country was
a damned annoyance in another. The arcane nature of
Moscow was slowing them. Bolan studied his smartphone, tracing the progress of the truck they now pur-
sued. They were gaining ground, but only because they

were approaching the same target from different angles and were rapidly converging.

"How far?" Bolan asked.

"Not far, but the question should be how long," Dostoyevsky replied. "In this traffic system?" He swerved around a cab, throwing an insult in his native language to the driver.

"At least it's like New York in some ways," Bolan murmured. "Skip it," he added, catching the quizzical glance the Russian threw him. "Just get us there as quick as you can."

He looked into the backseat. All their ordnance was stowed in two duffel bags, so that they could cut and run, leaving the Škoda behind without losing hardware. It had made choosing what they took from Dragonslayer a hard call. There was some ordnance that was obvious: HKs and spare magazines, mini Uzis as well, explosive and smoke grenades, handguns—a 9 mm Walther for Dostoyevsky and a Desert Eagle .357 for the soldier—but then there was the less obvious. A machine gun like the RPD would have been useful but too heavy to easily transport. Mines or plastic explosives could have been employed but would have been awkward. In the end they had settled for Benelli combat shotguns, the destructive option of buckshot being something that may come in handy. They also carried night vision monocles, nose plugs and full masks, fiber-optic cameras with small receivers, and motion detectors and surveillance mics. The intel equipment may help in getting the lay of the land before attack. Considering the weaponry they had to retrieve, caution was as important as speed.

Bolan's appreciation of architecture heightened as the Shukhov Tower came into view. Hyperboloid in design, it was not the only one that the great constructivist architect had designed. It was, however, one of the few still standing, and far and away the jewel in his collection. That was what it looked like, even in daylight: gold filigree structures flowing upward, leading to a silver head that looked too ornate, too beautiful, to be part of such a functional tradition.

"Yeah, I see why it's a symbolic target," he stated. Then, as his view came back to earth via the road ahead and the screen on his smartphone, he added, "And it looks like we're just in time."

"And not the only ones," the Russian said grimly as the fight started without them.

"Do we take them now, or do we wait until they have shown us the weapon?" asked the slab-faced colonel, squirming uncomfortably in civilian clothes and seated next to a suave intelligence agent.

"Neither," the agent replied smoothly. "We wait for the intervention, and then we take them all. Your men are in place?"

"Yes," the colonel stated. "We have cars at all four compass points, each with three men. Fourteen including ourselves. It is too many."

"Safety in numbers, I would have thought," the agent murmured as he watched the black truck pull up at the foot of the tower. It was still an attraction and manned even though this was a quiet day. There were enough people around to make him wonder where and how the Freedom Right people would plant the device.

This did not concern the colonel, who was still

bridling at taking orders from someone younger and—in his view—dumber.

"Safety in numbers…ha…too easy to get in each other's way, killed by friendly fire. Anyway, what intervention?"

"According to our sources…" He trailed off as he realized that Freedom Right would just leave the truck. There was no need for them to plant the device, for, as far as they knew, they weren't being tailed by anyone.

"Scratch that, we take them now," he said urgently as he watched two men get out of the truck while a third appeared through the rear door, closing them behind him and nodding to the others. "They've already done it…."

The colonel yelled orders into his communication device and started to open his door when he was cut short by a car that roared past, nearly taking off the door and his arm with it. He yelled abuse at the driver and then fell silent as he understood what the intelligence agent had meant.

The car roared up to where the truck was parked, the sudden violent sound making the three terrorists from the truck turn. It took them a fraction of a second to realize what was happening, for which time they were frozen as the car squealed on a hand brake turn to bring it sideways to them.

As it shuddered to a halt and the doors were flung open, five men exited, waving HKs and Uzis, yelling in Russian for the three men to get down on the ground. It was as if the sound of voices snapped them from their shock.

The three Estonians, who had all come from the

castle, scattered, taking their own SMGs from concealment in their jackets, firing wild bursts before they could aim, just to buy time to find shelter from what they knew was to come.

Behind them the few tourists, who had come to see the tower at this hour, yelled and screamed in fear as they tried to run from the gunfire. Farther back the tower personnel reacted to these cries for help by closing the doors and locking themselves safely inside.

From all sides, a dozen men ran onto the narrow street, all armed with MAC-10s. They were thickset, in civilian clothes, but running like military men. They barked at the passersby to hit the ground, but in the already panicked confusion, that only added to the pandemonium.

"They must not shoot up the truck. Tell them that," the intelligence agent yelled at the colonel as he scrambled from the car, running after the colonel as he rushed to join his men.

"Prick," the colonel breathed to himself. The priority was to secure the area, clear the civilians, and pick off the terrorists and these new bastards—whoever the hell they were—and not necessarily in that order. He shouldered his MAC-10 and directed two short blasts toward the car slewed across the street.

The Estonians were pinned down between the truck they had intended to leave behind and the building that was their target. Without either of their leaders, they were helpless drones, having no real idea of how they would get themselves out of this situation. All they knew was that they needed to keep the truck in place and clear of interference. Having each found some cover behind parked vehicles, they concentrated their fire on keeping back their attackers while they counted down time.

THE SECOND GROUP of terrorists was equally determined. The five men from jihad, picked because of their iron will and determination, would do what it took to secure this batch of weapons for themselves. The sudden appearance of a seemingly random task force was not going to deter them. They turned and clustered, directing their fire toward the men who were rushing in from all points.

The Muslim terrorists might not have had much cover, but they were not as exposed as the Russian task force, who had hit the ground with the sole intention of stopping the terrorist attack with speed. The last thing they had expected was a second attack force, and they found themselves running into a hail of fire from two sources, as the Estonians also sought to drive them back.

In the short time before they backtracked enough to take cover, the task force had lost half of its number, at least two of which were friendly fire casualties.

"Take cover. Uri, Valeri, get around the back of the tower and take out the people we came for. The rest of you, keep these others contained so you can put a grenade in their car—"

"No, you can't do that so close to the truck!" the intelligence agent screamed.

The colonel turned on him, his slablike face mottled with fury. "Don't tell me what I can do. You knew these assholes would be here?" He waved his MAC-10 at the jihad fighters. "You didn't think to tell me after you crowd the area so we already cut each other down?"

The agent tried to muster all the authority he could. "I am in charge here. The president has given us provenance over the army, and you must—"

"I must do nothing, you waste-of-space prick," the colonel growled. He raised the MAC-10 and tapped a short burst into the intelligence agent. The man's face, as he died, registered an almost comical shock and fury.

"Friendly fire," the colonel spit as the corpse fell away from him. He turned his attention back to the firefight in front of him. Now he felt he could concentrate on sorting out this mess.

"PULL IN HERE," Bolan ordered as they saw the whole scene unfold before them as they approached. Dostoyevsky guided the Škoda into a stop and killed the engine while Bolan leaned over the back and pulled over the two duffel bags, handing one to his partner.

"Come on, let's go!" he said as they got out of the car.

People rushing toward them, looking back with panic, their cell phones either recording the events on camera or putting them in touch with the authorities.

No need for the latter. Bolan was already sure they were here. The appearance of men from all points as a firefight developed between the truck and the car told him that. There was something military about them.

The two warriors moved against the shallow tide of people, weaving between them to get closer to the action. As they neared, moving to the side of the street, using buildings to shelter and conceal them as much as possible, they saw the firefight develop into a pitched battle between three separate factions.

Three men crouched beside the target truck holding their position. Four men had been moving around a car, one of them now down. And in positions of cover was a group of at least half a dozen that Bolan had tagged as military. Another three had been mowed down in the initial onslaught, and the survivors had taken up defensive positions. Their leader was only about a hundred yards away. They had watched him take out the man next to him.

"There is trouble in the ranks," Dostoyevsky said dryly. "I suspect that the intelligence services are trying to ride roughshod on the military, and it has not gone down well. We have an interesting three-point problem. Would it be worth trying to take one of those out before we tackle the other two?"

"That would be great," Bolan replied in an equally dry tone.

The Russian grinned. "Follow me, say nothing—your accent would betray you."

Keeping low and swinging an HK into the crook of his arm, pointed down, the Russian moved toward the military man. Bolan did likewise, wondering what his partner had up his sleeve. What he got was unexpected and yet typical Dostoyevsky.

"Colonel, we meet again. Report, please," the Russian snapped as he slid into cover beside the colonel, whose face registered something approaching surprise.

"By Stalin's mustache, I never expected to see you again," he murmured. "You work for his people, I suppose?" He indicated the dead intelligence man. "Friendly fire," he added as an afterthought.

"I saw. I don't blame you. He was a prick," Dostoyevsky said simply. "Most of the president's men are, which is why they still hire men like myself and my colleague, even though the general would prefer we died like him."

The colonel grunted, and then gave them a precise and pointed commentary on what had occurred, why he thought the operation had been badly handled and the situation they were in now. Dostoyevsky listened intently, and when the colonel had finished, he spoke with authority.

"We can redeem this. Pull your men back and allow us to mop up. Two men will not get in each other's way."

"What about this damned weapon that gives the president a hard-on?"

"When we are done, we will call you back and you can deliver his toy." He grinned. "I won't even mind you taking the credit this time."

The colonel's granite eyes studied the Russian, searching for a sign of betrayal. They found nothing, and he gave the order for his men to withdraw to safer ground. As he also made to rendezvous with the remains of his unit, he nodded briefly to Dostoyevsky.

"I never took your credit, and I won't this time. You know that," he muttered before leaving.

When he had slipped away through the parked cars to where he had located his men, Bolan looked long and hard at the Russian.

"Remind me never to play poker against you," he said simply before issuing directions and outlining his own plan. The Russian nodded, and without another word, the two men parted company.

ONE OF THE JIHAD MEN had been felled by SMG fire that had come from the Russian military in that initial burst of activity before they had been driven back. The remaining four were using the car doors as cover, and although the vehicle was now riddled with shot and they stood in a sea of broken glass, it had been enough to keep them protected while returning fire and, as they saw it, drive the Russians back. Grim faced, they now turned their attention to the truck.

One of them tried to move toward it, but he was met with a hail of fire. He hunkered back against the car, feeling the HK fire thud into the bodywork around him but just about keeping him safe. His lips parted in a thin smile. He had failed to progress in distance, but his men now knew where the three Estonians were located.

He barked orders for his men to circle and engage, laying down fire that would cover him as he ran for the truck. He trusted that the Estonians would not dare to fire too close to the weapon. The area around it formed, he hoped, a kind of protective ring. Once inside that, then he was home free.

Stepping from cover and pouring rapid fire in the directions identified, the three jihad men moved quickly across the tarmac toward points they had identified as cover.

Immediately two of them were cut down by chattering bursts that chopped across the fire they laid down. It came from behind them, where they thought they were clear, and they were down before they had a chance to identify the location.

The third man whirled, throwing himself to the ground and rolling back toward the cover of his own car, just as his commander moved, then hesitated and looked back. He watched a grenade as it arced through the air and landed on the tarmac, bouncing once and rattling against the underside of the car's chassis.

His curse died on his lips as the grenade detonated, the car disappearing in a plume of flame and smoke. There was little of him left. The terrorist who had tried to roll back to cover felt the scorching blast, shards of metal from the explosion ripping into him. He was alive but unable to move, as he saw a tall, gaunt man step out of cover and level a gun at him. In his last moments he thought of the virgins waiting for him after death and was relieved that an enemy would be so merciful as to end his suffering quickly.

From their positions of cover, the three Estonians saw the jihad terrorists move out from the car, look amazed, and were then flattened by the blast from the grenade. The Estonians heard the chatter of fire cease as the other gunman was cut down, and then in the sudden silence that was ruined only by the licking of flames in the air, heard the short burst that ended the last terrorist's suffering.

The Estonians were in visual contact with one another, but had no practical way of quickly communicating. They would be forced to act independently and react, rather than plan.

The problem was that none of them had been in combat for some time, and they were rusty; they knew they were up against men who were not. They were hesitant, yet at the same time knew that this was a sure way to die.

They did not see Bolan and Dostoyevsky as they skirted the parked vehicles, moving so that they kept a barrier between themselves and the enemy until they were in a location where they had an angle of fire covering all three identified terrorist positions.

Time was tight. The colonel would be getting hell over his comm system after the car detonation and had possibly already discovered that he had been duped. Bolan and the Russian had to secure the truck and get it away. Any issues with the weapons inside could be handled once they were clear.

Two of the terrorist positions were far enough from the truck to allow them to use grenades from a distance. Both men had accurate-enough throwing arms to land in the target zone. A direct hit was not a necessity. Flushing them out would be enough.

The grenades detonated almost simultaneously. The ground shook with the force of the blasts as Bolan and his partner raced from cover, crouching and firing on the run at intervals toward the remaining position, spraying the area where the grenades had landed.

The two Estonians in the blast range had been silenced, either dead or too injured to move and return fire. That left just the one man, who was forced from his position by the hail of gunfire that peppered his cover, decimating it and the ground around him. He tried to run, but there was nowhere to hide, and he was mowed down quickly.

Knowing that they needed to claim the truck and clear the area before the Russian military on site closed in, or reinforcements arrived, Bolan wrenched open the back doors of the truck.

For one moment the world lurched sickeningly to a stop. Several of the nuclear devices were stacked in the back of the vehicle, their trigger mechanisms attached and blinking blandly at him.

Shaking himself from the shock, the soldier clambered in and pulled the doors shut while the Russian threw himself into the driver's seat. The ignition was easily dispensed with by a man with the right knowledge, but even Dostoyevsky's nerveless fingers fumbled slightly under the pressure. He looked up, expecting to see men approaching and a hail of fire greet him. As the engine fired, the road ahead was still empty.

He threw the vehicle into gear and pulled away from the tower with a squeal of tires on road. The vehicle was thrown into a tight turn, pitching Bolan across the weapons in the rear of the truck, as the Russian saw the remains of the military detachment run toward him, yelling and firing their weapons. The glass at the passenger side of the cab starred, and the Russian swore loudly as he slammed the truck into a higher gear and hit the gas.

In the back of the truck, ignoring the fire that took out the small back windows and dented the rear doors with a hammering that echoed through the interior, Bolan set to work deactivating the weapons. It was a simple task if you knew what to do. The thing that really caused him concern was the time set on the trigger.

"Move it! They haven't given us much time," he yelled at Dostoyevsky.

"We haven't given ourselves much time," the Russian returned. "Colonel Rostov was always a mean bastard, and he'll want my balls now that I've deceived him."

Bolan wanted to ask how he knew and recognized the colonel, but that would have to wait. He paused momentarily and slipped his smartphone from its secure place in his blacksuit.

"The other two trucks have stopped moving. The closest one is only a klick or two away. Presnensky District, Third Ring Road. Mean anything?"

The Russian laughed hollowly. "They are consistent in their thinking, I'll grant them that. Moscow City they call it—the new Moscow International Business Center. A showpiece."

"Not unless we get there damned quick," Bolan said grimly, returning to his task.

CHAPTER TWENTY-FOUR

The president sat behind his desk. On his laptop, he watched footage of the firefight taken from CCTV. His face openly betrayed his dissatisfaction, and the security chief seated opposite squirmed in his seat. His eyes met the flinty gaze of the boss.

"This is it?" the Russian president said mildly. When his tone was that soft, then it was time to run for cover.

The security chief nodded.

"So you have no idea why two men…two men… took out eight terrorists, pulled the wool over the eyes of the military and then escaped with the hardware?"

"To be fair, sir, we had already taken out one of the terrorists ourselves, so it was really only four of—"

The premier crashed his fist onto the keyboard of his laptop. "It doesn't matter how many they killed or we killed, you moron. The very fact that they could do this—in the middle of Moscow—is the point. Do you know where they are headed now?"

"We believe so, sir."

The president shook his head sadly. "'We believe so,' is it? For this you have control of how many men?" He stood, taking his laptop and throwing it at the security chief. "Idiot—you should be on their asses right now. You should be blasting the living shit out of them." He came out from behind his desk, and for a moment the security chief believed that his boss would shoot him where he sat. Instead, he strode right past him, calling over his shoulder, "Come on. If a job is worth doing, then you have to do it yourself around here."

BY THE TIME BOLAN had finished dismantling the trigger mechanisms on all the devices in the truck, Dostoyevsky had piloted the vehicle around Third Ring Road and was on top of the construction site that was the Moscow International Business District. A large part of it in the Presnensky District was now complete, and some parts were already occupied, but there was one corner that was still largely a building site. As the Russian negotiated the entrance, Bolan could plainly see that this was where the action was going down.

Their journey had been remarkable for being free of trouble. Apart from the usual Moscow traffic flow, which was like open warfare, they had not been obstructed by any intervention from the authorities, which was what both Bolan and his partner had been expecting. There had been no marked or unmarked vehicles in pursuit, no roadblocks established and no air traffic that was seemingly intent on tracking them.

"I don't like it when it is this quiet," Dostoyevsky commented. "That is the time when they usually hit you with the sucker punch."

"They can track us by CCTV," Bolan replied. "My guess is that they'll look to intercept us when we reach the business park. They'll know what we're doing and probably already have people there."

The sight that greeted them, as the Russian drove through the populated area of the MIBC, gave them confirmation of his theory.

By the entrance to the MIBC, business was being conducted as though nothing was wrong. However, as the truck raced through the parked traffic and the milling throng of people, scattering them, it became clear that pedestrians and vehicles seemed more anxious to move away from the less-developed area of the park. Even over the roar of the truck's engine as the Russian propelled the truck on, it became clear that a firefight had developed.

Turning a corner, Dostoyevsky hit the brake hard, pitching Bolan forward even as the Russian yelled a warning.

"What the—ah, hell," the soldier muttered as his question was bitten off, answered by what he could see before him.

Directly in front of them was a partially constructed office building. The first four stories were up, with some girder structure already erected for the remaining two stories. Those floors that had been built had window spaces but no frames, and on the ground there was a large bay where the glass front of the reception area would eventually have been completed.

Right now this was being used as a garage for two vehicles that were parked at right angles within the airy interior of the building's base. One was a 4x4 with smoked-glass windows that were starred by gunfire. The side of the vehicle was also pitted in the same way.

The other vehicle was the one that really took their attention. It was another truck much like the one they sat in, and it had the rear doors flung open, with some cylinders, of the same type as they were carrying, lying on the dusty concrete floor. The lower story itself seemed to be empty; the upper floors were filled with smoke that drifted out on the breeze. Further there were signs both of combat within the building and also without. Bolan studied the ongoing engagement with a scattered number of non-uniformed Russians in positions of cover among the construction equipment and materials around the half-built block.

"Two problems here," Bolan summarized as they watched the activity unfold. "First thing is to get the outside cleared, and the second is to neutralize the threat within."

"That simple, eh?" the Russian said with a wry smile. "I doubt I can pull the same trick as last time."

Bolan looked at the locations of the Russian military detachment, scattered along the front of the building.

"I don't think you'll have to...they aren't interested in going in, only in containment."

"There are more on the way then. We have little time."

"Exactly. We need to clear them out, and then go in hard and fast. There's no one on the ground, so if we can keep them up top, then we can snatch the hardware from under their nose."

Dostoyevsky's grin broadened. "I like your thinking. What do you want me to do?"

VELIO PULLED HIS MEN back so that they were in the corner of the second story. He directed one of them to keep a containing fire trained on the men who were scattered on the ground below. At all costs he had to stop them from getting into the building while the truck stood unprotected. In the meantime he sent another of his men up the bare concrete stairwell to flush out the enemy above. They had been driven up a story by the sheer intensity of fire poured at them by the Freedom Right fighters, but Velio was aware that the ammunition supplies carried by his men had to now be running low, and Velio must kill off this threat before they found themselves outgunned.

It had seemed a simple task when they had arrived on site. The blast area from the devices would take out an area larger than the MIBC itself, so planting their truck in the midst of the already functional area would have been an unnecessary risk. Better by far to take it to an area where there was less chance of being disturbed. Velio knew from their research that there was a section of the center that had not yet been completed, and finding a building with an open front where they could just drive in was, it seemed, perfect. They could conceal the vehicle, set the timers and then just melt away.

The last thing they had expected was for the orange 4x4 that followed them into the MIBC to keep on their tail all the way to the building site at the rear of the park.

"That orange thing is tailing us," the truck driver stated, but Velio was dismissive.

"It cannot be. We would have seen something that stupid before. Who the hell would tail us in something so conspicuous? Keep going."

The driver took the truck into the empty frontage and came to a halt. Velio had him convinced, though it nagged at him, the manner in which the orange vehicle had suddenly appeared in their wake and had stuck so close as they entered the MIBC. What if it had been waiting to pick them up, using intel to track them until they were closing in on their target?

He dismissed that as paranoia and joined the rest of the men in helping Velio to unload the cylinders from the rear of the truck.

"Why don't we just leave them here?" one of his compatriots grumbled.

"It'll be easier to set them up if we have some space," Velio replied. "Besides, who's going to interrupt us?"

The words died on his lips as the orange 4x4 gunned its engine and roared across the building site, weaving past deserted construction equipment as it came from behind a row of temporary construction huts, headed straight for the opening.

With a yell to his men, Velio left the cylinders and grabbed a weapon, opening fire on the 4x4 as it roared into the gap, slewing sideways. The gunfire was returned from the vehicle, driving the Freedom Right men backward to seek cover as it raked the empty floor space around the truck, pitting the side of it and ricocheting around the interior.

The hail of fire and the need to seek cover or get mowed down did the one thing that Velio would not have wished for: it drove his men away from the truck and its hardware, and back toward the rear of the building to avoid getting shot. He knew that this would allow the intruders to snatch the weapons from under his nose. That was the last thing he wanted, but until he could at least attain some kind of cover, his men were dead before they could fight back.

The 4x4 might have been a hide-in-plain-sight obtrusive color, but beneath the garish paint job, it was bulletproofed, as was the smoked glass. The Freedom Right men had poured heavy SMG fire at it, but all they had done was star the glass and take chunks of orange from the paintwork. Otherwise the vehicle was unharmed, and the opposition terrorists were able to fire from the slits made at the top of their windows with some kind of impunity.

The Freedom Right fighters were forced back to the concrete emergency stairs that had already been put in place, with the far side doors of the 4x4 opening to let out two men who tried to edge around to the deserted truck, when they were given a glimmer of hope—but not one without its own severe conditions.

From outside the building, another rain of fire slashed into the enclosed space, sparking and ricocheting from the truck, the 4x4, the floor and walls. It drove the two men who had left the orange 4x4 back toward where the Freedom Right men had been trying to shelter. The sheer weight of firepower pouring into the building had forced them up, and they were now rushing toward the front of the building to return fire.

Velio directed his three men to take up positions at the window spaces, identifying and attempting to take down whoever was outside. Meantime he opted to cover the stairwell, figuring that under such a barrage, the terrorists who had tried to rob them would find themselves in the same position. If they had to come up, they would be forced into his line of fire. If they stayed here, they would be cut down.

When the first canister landed on the floor, its choking smoke spreading quickly and driving his men back from the windows, Velio realized things would not be as simple as he had hoped. As the smoke blew across the floor toward him, he was forced to retreat. Unable to see through tear-filled eyes, he was nothing more than a sitting target himself.

Through the smoke, the four men from the 4x4 had blasted their way up the stairwell, laying down a suppressing fire, and had fought their way past the choking cloud, opting to go upward to escape the blind fire that the Freedom Right men had poured at them.

And after the smoke had cleared enough for Velio to regroup his men, they were on another level. The task set him now was to neutralize the men in the orange 4x4 while knocking out the men on the grounds outside.

Only by doing that could he set up the hardware below and then at least try to get the hell out.

When he had set this in motion, something happened to confuse him even more than events so far....

THE RUSSIAN COMMANDER was content. He had already heard of Colonel Rostov's mistake and was looking forward to gloating when Rostov arrived with the remains of his detachment. The commander had received word that not only was the colonel on his way but another detachment of military had also been dispatched, under the personal direction of the president. He was looking forward to proving himself in front of the man and humiliating an old foe.

Maybe that was why—with his men seemingly secure and the terrorists pinned inside the construction—he was a little too relaxed. His men formed an arc around the front of the building. To the rear, there was an earth mound and a deep ditch that had been dug for pipes and cables. The only way in and out was by the open front, and he had that covered.

He wasn't expecting an attack from the rear.

The first grenade detonated in the middle of the

arc, causing more confusion than damage. One man was injured, but more were forced from cover. That was exactly what the mystery attacker had wanted, as chattering SMG fire from two directions took down the men who had broken cover.

The Russian commander yelled into his comm unit for his men to keep in cover, and turn to identify and return fire. His words were drowned by the second and third grenades, which went off at each end of the arc, causing more confusion, forcing them toward a middle ground.

Just as Bolan had hoped, the break from cover had been all the invitation that the two groups of terrorists trapped in the building had needed. They opened fire on the Russians as they rushed into the open, and the Russians themselves were torn between returning this fire and answering the blasts that Bolan and Dostoyevsky were hitting them with from behind.

Caught in this cross fire, the ranks of the military were rapidly reduced, and even the gunfire they could return dropped to virtually nothing as the remaining men, including their commander, sought to regroup and take cover. If nothing else they needed to hold their ground until the expected reinforcements arrived to bolster their numbers. All thoughts of glory—so prominent just a few minutes before—were driven from the Russian commander's head as he sought grimly to draw his men together and hold on.

Bolan left Dostoyevsky to keep the remaining Russians pinned down from the rear while he ran across open space—keeping low and using the smoke and confusion as cover—to where a front-end loader stood idle. Hot-wiring the earth-moving vehicle was straightforward, and the cab gave him some shelter as he fired it up and turned toward the open front of the building.

Flipping the giant shovel so that it came down and formed a barrier between the cab and any incoming fire, he powered over the open ground between his starting point and the half-finished building. Gunfire from the Russians sparked from the frame of the cab, but Bolan ignored it. The chances of him being hit were low, and he trusted Dostoyevsky to keep him covered.

Which was exactly what the Russian did. He had taken note of the angles of fire from the upper stories of the building and had adjusted his own fire so that it channeled the Russians into a space that was narrow enough for him to lob one of his last grenades into. The blast took out the remaining Russians. Not all were fatalities, but those who escaped the worst were too badly injured or shocked to be an immediate threat.

Satisfied that he had done all he could, Dostoyevsky drew back, hurrying to where he had left the truck. He could hear the terrorists in the building switch their full force onto the front-end loader but trusted that his partner had gotten his angles right and could deflect the fire until he was inside the building. Meanwhile Dostoyevsky had a task of his own to fulfill.

There was no sign of any life on the mall as he reached the black truck. Neither was there any sound that would indicate a large number of military personnel approaching. Good. They might just have the time. He clambered into the cab and hit the ignition, piloting the vehicle past the remains of the Russians and toward the half-finished building. There was no fire directed at him. The terrorists inside had a more immediate problem.

BOLAN RAMMED THE front-end loader into the side of the orange 4x4, tilting it so that it almost rolled onto its side, the vehicle jamming under the hydraulic lifts of the shovel arms. Bolan had made it with no collateral damage, the heavy metal shovel taking the brunt of any fire. He killed the diesel engine and jumped down. He could see that there was only one way to move up and down inside the building: the concrete stairwell that had been built at the rear of the building. The lift shafts for the elevators were nothing more than empty spaces in the wall. Knock out the stairs, and your enemy is contained. All they would be able to do is fire at Bolan and the Russian as they drove away.

Those observations ran through the Executioner's head even as he ran toward the stairwell, his HK in one hand and a grenade in the other. He sprayed a burst of suppressing fire into the stairwell to forestall anyone who may be venturing down, then lobbed the grenade halfway up, moving back quickly and taking cover as the blast ripped a chunk out of the back wall and caused the unfinished stairwell to partially collapse. The concrete dust added to the remains of the smoke canister made it hard for Bolan to breathe easily. He retrieved the nose plugs that he'd stashed in a slit pocket of his blacksuit and was relieved when he was able to breathe again with greater ease.

He could hear the men moving on the levels above him, prowling as they searched for a way to get down. The damage to the stairwell made it impassable, but there was still a chance that they would try to use the window openings to make the drop to the ground. He'd keep an eye out for that possibility.

As he unloaded the remainder of the gray cylinders and the timing devices, he heard some desultory gunfire from above, and allowed himself a slight smile. If any of them had tried this, they hadn't banked on their own enemies within the building being as keen to stop them as he would have been.

That train of thought was interrupted by the arrival of Dostoyevsky, who brought the truck as far into the building as the front-end loader and the wrecked 4x4 would allow. Without comment he got out and opened the back of their vehicle, aiding the soldier as he began to load the hardware into the rear space.

They worked fast and in silence, aware that time was at a premium. Right now they had only to worry about the terrorists above them. Before too long they would have Russian military detachments descending on them. Bolan and the Russian needed to be clear before more military arrived, yet had no idea how long that would be.

Sweating with effort and anxiety, they finished loading the truck and slammed the doors, Bolan silently thankful that the Freedom Right terrorists had not had time to set the timers. At least he would be spared that task as they tried to make time to the last rendezvous.

The Russian fired up the truck and rammed it into Reverse, spinning it so that the wheels bit into the loose earth, throwing up a shower of dirt that covered the windshield momentarily.

From the upper floors of the building, both White Zion terrorists and Freedom Right fighters fired at them, trying to hit the tires to stop them. Velio directed his men's fire, listening to the echo from above and knowing that this part of the battle was ultimately lost and that he had failed. Before long, there would be more Russians, and they would have to go down fighting. Capture, and what would inevitably follow, was unthinkable.

It was a depressing thought to continue as the target truck weaved around the obstacles of the construction site and out of view.

"TELL ME WHERE, COOPER," Dostoyevsky said through gritted teeth as he took the truck into what traffic was left in the otherwise deserted park.

Bolan took out his smartphone. He cursed softly to himself. "I wonder which one of the other terrorist groups we've left battling it out with the Estonians?"

The Russian shrugged. "Who cares? My president won't when his men get their hands on them."

Bolan was not so sure. Both he and his partner were battle weary, and working against the clock. Even assuming they reached the last target and were able to recover the hardware, they would still have to find a way of getting it—and themselves—out of Moscow in one piece. Because of the circumstances, Bolan still had no clear plan for that, only a number of possible options spinning in his brain.

The terrorist group he figured had the most experience and would present the greatest challenge was the Ukraine Democrats, their innocuous name hiding the most vicious and experienced fighters of their opponents. The last thing Bolan would have wanted was to go up against them as the last in line.

Maybe the Russian was right. Who cared? They just had to keep fighting. But not before they got out of the business district.

Dostoyevsky slowed the truck as they came to the exit, swearing to himself with relief at the lack of any roadblocks. He swung the truck onto Third Ring Road and hit the accelerator, the sound of distant sirens and the throb of a helicopter headed for the MIBC spurring him on.

The military reinforcements were getting closer. He and the American still had some kind of head start, but they were fast running out of time.

CHAPTER TWENTY-FIVE

The battle was over. The Russian leader strode among the ruins of the half-constructed building, surveying the bodies of the dead terrorists that littered the second and third stories. He had arrived by helicopter, which had landed on the roof, and he had made his way, at the head of a phalanx of men, from the unfinished top, down the stairwell to the third and then second levels.

Finding himself unable to progress to the bottom, he signaled his displeasure with a grunt and ran up to the top, ordering the chopper to take him to the remains of the military detachment and the reinforcements that had arrived just too late to be of any use.

He was met by the security chief and by the unit commander—a man who wore the look of someone wishing he was anywhere else. The president fixed him with a glare that should have struck him down and, without a word, paced heavily into the deserted lower level, past the front-end loader and toward the empty truck. He sniffed heavily as he peered inside, then looked back at the earthmover, gave an ironic snort of a laugh and let fly with a stream of invectives that did not stop for thirty seconds.

When he was finished, he spit on the ground and turned to the security chief and unit commander. He spoke softly but with a flat tone that barely suppressed his anger.

"We will talk of what happened here later. Two men? Unbelievable… We still have one chance, yes?" He paused.

The security chief eagerly agreed.

"Good. You had better make the most of this. Remember what used to happen to failures in the bad old days? There was a point to that."

He strode past the front-end loader, aiming a desultory kick at it as he passed, and went immediately to the waiting chopper. Under his orders, it was already warming up to take to the air as the security chief scrambled to follow.

This was the final countdown.

"They must have a death wish," the Russian said flatly as he hit the accelerator and piloted a weaving path through the central Moscow traffic.

"With these weapons, their chances of getting clear are pretty slim anyway, so why not?" Bolan shrugged. "Suicide missions for the greater glory are nothing new."

"True, but they usually have at least a chance, a plan of some kind, for getting into the target area for their attack. Only a fool would come to Moscow and think they could bomb Red Square and the Kremlin."

"I don't think they will. Sure, they want to hit close to the Kremlin, but remember the power of these babies," Bolan said, casting a glance to the rear of the truck. "Look, they want something symbolic. It doesn't get any more symbolic in Moscow than the Kremlin. The trackers have them going that way, but they don't have to be heading directly into the belly of the beast."

"Of course…they can go next door to the beast and still make their point."

Bolan considered their course of action as Dostoyevsky sped through the new Moscow, headed into the heart of the old. In the last decade almost one-third of this sector had been knocked down, rebuilt and remodeled. This both modernized the old and furnished luxury apartment buildings and nightlife for the oligarchs who had taken Communist incompetence and fashioned it into new Capitalist wealth.

While that was true, there was still a great beating heart at the center of the city that defied the modernizers, at least for the present. It was into this heart that Freedom Right intended to strike. They did not need to hit the Kremlin or Red Square full-on.

An equally potent target was the Seven Sisters in Kudrinskaya Square, which overlooked both the mayor of Moscow's headquarters, which had once been the Comecon building, and the government building from which the whole of Russia was administered. Hit those, and the heart would be taken out of the city and the country.

As Dostoyevsky took them into the old quarter that housed these institutions, away from the concrete and glass of the modern and into the constructivist vision of the recent past, Bolan felt not just the buildings close in on them but also the weight of history.

He could feel the iron fist of the KGB and the Joint State Political Directorate tighten around his throat. It was more than phantoms that they had to outrun, even assuming they could get the last of the weapons, a task that immediately took center stage as they came within view of the Seven Sisters, and found a truck much like their own headed directly for them....

ANDRUS HAD TRIED not to let his nerves show as his men took the mobile armory through the newer sections of the city, around the second ring and then through a maze of freeways and older roads in order to come to the mayor's building by a roundabout route.

They were careful to check that they were not being followed, doubling back on themselves to catch anyone in pursuit. It was only when they were certain that they drove the last short hop between the mayor's building and the Seven Sisters.

When the truck came to a halt, Andrus sat silent for a few moments, catching his breath and steeling himself for what was about to come. He had been prepared for this moment, but still it was overwhelming.

This was the blow at the heart of the hated Russia that he had planned for so long; this was the moment when his movement would be taken seriously. The only shame was that he doubted they would get away to glory in the moment. No matter. His name would live on in martyrdom, and there would be many ready to follow in his wake.

"Is there a problem?" the driver asked anxiously.

Andrus smiled weakly. "No problem. Just remembering the moment when we sowed the seed of our triumph." The smile on the driver's face made it a worthwhile lie.

The four Estonians got out of the truck, and while three of them spread out and kept watch, Andrus opened the rear doors and climbed inside. Before him was a row of cylinders, beside them the trigger mechanisms, old-fashioned LED timers blank and waiting to be activated. Outside, in the watery sun of late afternoon, the streets were thronged with Muscovites going about their everyday business, taking no notice of the black truck that had pulled to the curb, and barely registering the three men who lounged on the street corner and along the sidewalk. Their HKs were concealed under dusters that were entirely suited to the brisk climate of the season.

In the rear of the truck, Andrus began his task, laboriously attaching triggers to cylinders and programming in the code for the detonation countdown.

As long as there were no interruptions, he should be able to complete the task quickly.

"VISUAL CONTACT. I've got two."

He looked just like anyone else on the street using his cell phone. As the man spoke into the handset, he gesticulated as though having an argument. It marked him in the crowd for his compatriot who was walking in the opposite direction. Both men were in their late thirties, and both had the iron-hard faces of mercenaries. They wore expensive suits and carried briefcases, like businessmen between meetings.

Listening in on the conference call were two other men, who sat waiting a block away in a tan Mercedes sedan. They also wore expensive clothes and granite expressions. They could have been oligarchs resting between conferences to decide the fate of nations, or they could have been exactly what they were: hired guns.

The Ukraine Democrats had money behind them; and as well as men who believed in the cause, they had the cash to hire the best mercenaries in their particular fields. In this case, the two men on the sidewalk were dedicated to the cause, while the two in the sedan were not so bothered about the ideology but liked the dollars.

It helped that the men had moved in similar circles during their working lives, and so understood each other. Surveillance had been the specialty of the men in the Mercedes, and they had picked up on the convoy of trucks in the same way as Stony Man.

Just as Bolan had received a feed on the progress of each truck, so they had delivered an identical feed to their employers. Their advantage was that they had opted to take down one truck and liberate the merchandise, so they had the luxury of time to keep track at a distance and choose their moment.

As the cameras on the cell phones picked up the street scene from two separate angles and relayed them to the men in the Mercedes, they were able to see the three Freedom Right men—two from one camera, the third in the frame of the other—and the area around the truck. They were able to place their compatriots and judge the moment for attack.

"Hold your positions. Move when we come in sight," murmured one of the suits, tracking both terrorists on his tablet. As he spoke, his partner slipped the Mercedes into gear and pulled smoothly away from the sidewalk, slipping into the flow of traffic. He maneuvered quickly between the streams of cars, coming round to move into position in the lane closest to where the truck was parked.

Watching, the two mercenaries on the street waited until the Mercedes was almost level and then made their move.

Despite the adrenaline and anxiety that pounded through them, the Freedom Right guards were not as alert as they had believed. They were right about not being followed, yet it had not occurred to them that there were other ways of being tracked.

That was a fatal error. Two of them were puzzled and then shocked as each of them was suddenly faced by a suited businessman who stopped, slipped his phone into a jacket pocket and with the same fluid motion opened the briefcase he was carrying, letting it fall to the floor, to reveal a MAC-10 in hand. Before their blunted reactions had a chance to snap into focus, a tap on the trigger had brought a burst that stitched each man and took him out of the game.

The sudden violent explosions threw Kudrinskaya Square into chaos, as screaming civilians collided with one another—those close wanting to get away from the action, those farther away drawn in by morbid curiosity.

In this confusion, the Freedom Right fighter nearest the truck moved in, trying to pinpoint in the crowd the two men who had taken out his compatriots. In the midst of a jostling, panicked throng it was impossible to pick them out, and in concentrating, he failed to spot the Mercedes slow as the traffic was halted by people spilling into the road. By the time he had realized what was happening, both occupants were out of the vehicle, and one of them had a Beretta leveled at his gut.

Two silenced shots drilled into him, forcing him to the ground. He saw his attackers step past him, but pain numbed him from grabbing his weapon and preventing them from wrenching open the rear of the truck. He saw them bodily drag Andrus from the interior, pulling him backward so that he fell to the ground, his face upward as the Beretta coughed out a round from point-blank range, ending ignominiously his dream before he had completed priming the weapons.

The last thing the fighter saw as his vision narrowed to a black tunnel was the two men who had taken down his compatriots climb into the front of the truck, while the two men from the Mercedes climbed into the rear and slammed the doors shut, then the engine firing and echoing in his head as everything went black.

"DAMMIT, THE ASSHOLE has already started priming the bombs—how do we stop it?" one of the mercenaries yelled, panic rising as he saw himself vaporized in a small nuclear detonation.

"Look at the timers—how long do we have?" the driver asked as he plowed through the milling crowd, driving a wedge between those alert enough to move out of the way or bumping ominously against those who were not quick enough, throwing them into the crowd.

"I don't know—I don't—wait…" the mercenary stammered, staring at the timers and seeing nothing that made sense to him in his fear. He was pushed out of the way by his compatriot, who studied the dials.

"He's set time, but not date. That still reads a row of zeros," he stated.

"Don't leave it—it will automatically default. Set it for next year. It'll just happily tick away until then. Don't try and disconnect, it may be booby-trapped," he added hurriedly.

In the back of the truck, the mercenary carefully set the date on the three devices that Andrus had already primed and then heaved a sigh of relief as he sat back on his haunches. "Thanks for that," he whispered. "Now let's just get out of here."

His wish was not to be easily granted. The driver swung the truck out of Kudrinskaya Square and onto a stretch of road that was clearer than the chaos in the square itself. Yet he slammed his foot on the gas, and as the vehicle lurched forward, his jaw dropped and he swore loudly.

Headed straight toward him at high speed was a truck identical to the one they had just taken.

"I AM THINKING that at least we won't have to deal with two opposing enemies this time," the Russian said wryly. "How long since you played a game of chicken, Cooper?"

"Not long enough," the soldier replied, his mind racing. It was obvious that Freedom Right and the rival terrorist group had already crossed swords, with the Estonians losing out. There was no other reason why the truck should be leaving the scene. Bolan and his partner had the Russian authorities at their back and a moving target in front of them.

A target that, if it did not move and quick, would wipe both crews and half of Moscow off the map, and spread a cloud of death over hundreds of miles.

Bolan realized this. The Russian realized it, too. But did the men coming toward them?

As the two vehicles neared, it seemed as though the world around them melted away so that there was nothing except the identical trucks closing in on each other, head-on and walled in to the same lane by the traffic that flowed around them. Dostoyevsky's stare was blank and unreadable, unblinking as he maintained his speed.

Sweat beaded his brow and that of Bolan's as he leaned over the seat. Both men were thinking the same thing: one of the trucks would have to turn away, but there was little space in the flow around them. Even if the drivers flanking them wanted to get out of the way, the situation was unfolding so rapidly that it was hard to know how many any realized what was happening.

"Not enough time to brake now," the Russian whispered.

The soldier said nothing. He was braced for what seemed to be the inevitable, when without any warning—or even a sense of relief—he was flung sideways as the Russian skewed the wheel of the truck, hard on the tail of the opposing vehicle as it had found a gap and had flung itself into the space.

Neither man had the chance to heave a sigh of relief as they hammered the gas in hot pursuit of the truck as it plowed against the flow of traffic.

As VEHICLES SCATTERED before the mercenaries, the driver cursed long and loudly, trying to cut through the flow and gain ground on the truck on their tail.

"Who are they? Who the hell are they?" he kept repeating.

Behind them, the Russian nosed his truck up against the rear fender of the mercenaries' vehicle, trying to deflect them off the road and up onto the sidewalk. Behind him, Bolan cradled an Uzi.

"Careful," Bolan murmured. "If that hits a building and goes up—"

"Don't worry, Cooper. I have no wish to die without a fight. If I had wanted to ram them, I would have. Now this, on the other hand—"

Dostoyevsky threw the truck into an open space that had suddenly appeared as a number of drivers coming toward them had, in desperation, cut across the oncoming traffic. Using that gap, the Russian took the initiative and hit the accelerator, taking his truck in front of the vehicle they had been tailing, boxing it in as he passed, so that the driver, attempting to pull out, hit metal on metal, raising sparks and veering wildly, had to fight to control his vehicle.

"Hit the brake and we take them down," Bolan told him.

"Where to then?" the Russian asked.

"I'll let you know. Keep your cell open…"

"Okay. And—now," the Russian yelled, hitting the brake so that his truck slowed quickly, but just enough to stop the collision being more than jarring. Bolan braced himself and was out of the truck before the impact had died away.

The mercenaries had been prepared, but even so, they were thrown against the frame of the truck, buying Bolan and the Russian just that fraction of a second that they needed.

And they needed it more than they knew.

"DISTURBANCE OVER BY Kudrinskaya Square," the security chief yelled over the noise of the chopper. "Two trucks this time, both the same as the one we are pursuing."

The Russian leader, who had taken control of the chopper, grinned like a shark. "Government building…

Assholes. Let us take them out of the game." He chuckled as he swung the chopper around.

The security chief heaved a sigh of relief. The men on the ground had lost the truck on CCTV as it raced along Third Ring Road, a defective camera furnishing a gap in which the truck had seemingly disappeared, leaving the pursuing vehicles chasing thin air. Up above his increasingly irate boss had wrestled the controls of the chopper from his pilot and had been circling over the city, growing more and more restless.

Now he had a purpose. He turned the chopper and angled it downward so that it swooped into the gaps between the skyscrapers, moving into the old quarter where the lower level of the buildings enabled him to get closer to the streets beneath, scanning the traffic for any sign of the two trucks.

He yelled in triumph as he saw them below, jockeying for position against the flow of vehicles. His yell turned to one of anger as he saw one pull out and bring the other to a forced stop.

Two men jumped out, clutching SMGs and heading for the truck behind them.

"Bastards—where are your men?" the Russian leader roared at the security chief. "Get them here now—or do we have to go down ourselves?"

BOLAN AND DOSTOYEVSKY ran down the sides of their truck, keeping tight as they used the vehicle for cover. As they got the truck behind into their sights, Bolan put a blast of gunfire through the windshield of the truck, angling his fire upward so that it would hit the roof of the cab, not shoot through to the rear.

He had no idea yet how many men were inside, but

it was necessary to take out as many as possible to cut the numbers. As he fired, his partner moved past him toward the rear of the vehicle. Bolan put a burst of gunfire into the side door as cover, and as Dostoyevsky attained the rear, the Executioner saw the back doors of the enemy's vehicle swing open.

On either side of the trucks, the traffic flow had frozen, jammed up by drivers halting and fleeing in the face of the developing firefight. There was just enough space for Dostoyevsky to step between two cars and get an angle that enabled him to fire at the mercenaries as they spilled out of the truck.

One of them hit the ground immediately, stitched from shoulder to waist. The Russian used the cars as cover and moved around so that he could see the prone mercenary. A second tap eliminated any threat that remained.

The other mercenary who had spilled from the back had disappeared. The Russian cursed and moved toward the rear of the truck, ducking below the vehicle behind to give himself cover.

A second man came into view. He was close to the side of the truck, moving stealthily up to take down Bolan, who had pulled open the cab door to complete his task. One of the mercenaries was dead; the other was mortally wounded. Bolan had pulled out the dead man and was leaning across to haul out the semiconscious mercenary and clear space behind the wheel. For a moment, that left him exposed and unable to respond as the man creeping up on him leveled his SMG.

"Cooper!" Dostoyevsky yelled, his warning drowned by the tap on his SMG that stitched the mercenary along his spine. As the man dropped, Bolan came into view, his Uzi leveled at the empty space.

"You owe me one." The Russian grinned. He looked up as a chopper swooped overhead. "I'll collect later. Let's go."

Bolan clambered into the cab of his truck, punching out the remainder of the windshield as he fired up the stalled engine. The Russian ran past him and pulled the first truck out into a gap in the traffic jam. The big American followed him, pulling his smartphone from its secure place and hitting a speed-dial number.

"Bear, I need the U.S. Embassy to play ball and quick. This is way out of control."

"Striker, the ambassador has complained to the Department of State, and Hal is talking to them now. He's a dickwad, and we've got a real problem."

Bolan cursed to himself, then gritted out, "Keep at it, Bear. I've got half the Russian army on my back, and we need some shelter."

"Striker, leave this with me. I'll talk to Hal, and maybe I've got an idea. I'll be as quick as possible—you need to buy me some time."

"Bear, I'll try, but the numbers are falling…."

"THEY'VE TAKEN OUT another four men and have two of these vehicles now," the Russian president said, unable to keep the admiration out of his voice. "If I had men like them, instead of the cretins I have…" He shook his head sadly, then yelled over the noise of the chopper, "I want men to intercept them. Use as many as necessary, and mark off points where we can divert them. I want to take those trucks without damage. Isolate them and take them down." He cast a glance over his shoulder at the security chief.

The security chief quailed under his leader's glare, wincing as the man added, "You think you can do that without screwing up again?"

CHAPTER TWENTY-SIX

Bolan kept tight on the tail of the Russian as he negotiated his way through the dense Moscow traffic. It moved fast when it could or else came to a dead stop when obstructions occurred. In the richer sections of the new city—where there were numerous apartment buildings and upmarket department stores—much of that was due to the lack of parking spaces and the narrow streets.

Drivers would halt suddenly, waiting for a car to vacate one of the precious spaces, and then take it, ignoring the chaos caused in their wake. It made trying to keep moving and evade whatever might be on your tail a daunting task.

Fortunately Dostoyevsky was used to that kind of traffic—even though he had repeatedly remarked, usually between curses, that it had gotten a whole lot worse in the years he had been gone—and so now on occasion mounted the sidewalks, scattering pedestrians who yelled curses at the Russian and then Bolan who followed suit.

Normally the soldier would be averse to the kind of attention this type of driving would bring on him when trying to escape but figured that it was far too late now for that kind of worry. If nothing else, the Russian military and police forces on their tail would be practicing exactly the same kind of action. At least this way they kept moving and stayed one jump ahead.

Or did they? Despite the chaos they had caused, it seemed odd that they had not encountered any head-on resistance.

"Cooper, I can't just keep driving. We need to head somewhere," the Russian said over the cell phone link.

"We can't rely on the embassy," Bolan replied. "We need to head out to open ground—if nothing else, I might be able to get Jack to pick us up."

"And get shot down by the military's flyboys?" the Russian queried.

"Without causing a major international incident?" Bolan replied.

"Cooper, you think my president would care? How could the U.S. government explain it? He would have nothing to worry about."

Bolan did not answer. He knew that any liability would be denied and that he would be yet another face-less soldier of fortune to the world. Grimaldi's flying might just about be the only thing to get them out. "It's our only chance right now," he snapped. "Let's do it."

The Russian responded by cutting across three lanes of traffic headed in different directions, and headed for the first ring. Right now they had landed themselves in the center of the city by the Kremlin. The problem was how to get out without being stopped.

As they drove, Bolan considered what he knew of the traffic system in Moscow and what its layout meant to their chances of escape. They had been lucky that their last round of combat had been far quicker and easier than he had feared. They had been able to take the enemy by surprise at a point when they had emerged from a firefight and had not been expecting an ambush.

That had bought Bolan and Dostoyevsky some time and enabled them to outrun the military they had been certain were on their tail. The chopper that had swooped over them had been proof of that. Looking up when he had the chance, he could see that it was still shadowing them, keeping them under observation from a distance. If it wasn't marshaling forces that were chasing them, then what was its purpose?

Roads in Moscow. Bolan recalled that they tended to run in straight lines and concentric circles, radiating out from the center. Dostoyevsky was negotiating the straight lines and the grid that they formed wherever possible, to avoid getting trapped on a ring, but it was not as simple as they could have wished.

The Bulvarnoye Koltso was the first ring, which they were now circling. It formed a horseshoe shape around the Bielo Gorod, in the sixteenth-century White Town area, and came to an abrupt halt at the Yauza River. It was the farthest into the city that they could go, and it was imperative that they get beyond that and onto the Sadovoye Koltso, the Garden Ring, which formed the boundary of an old version of the city, long since overrun.

The Third Ring, which they had already used, was much more recent, being only a decade old. It had been built to alleviate the congestion of the newly rich city, and as they had found earlier, it was already failing in that task.

Despite its relative newness, it was one of the most-used roads in Moscow, which was why a Fourth Ring was already under construction. They could have done with it being ready now, but as it was, they still would have had to jump across it and use the concentric road system to reach the MKAD—the acronym coming from the Russian equivalent of the Moscow Automotive Ring Road, built in the 1950s, which still defined the outer limits of the city. Beyond, the spread of the city was unplanned, but even there the road systems followed a concentric pattern.

It made them easy to follow, but in the same way it made it simple for anyone to follow them and intercept. That was what Bolan was beginning to expect. The only way out that he could see was to head for the open land on the outside of the MKAD, and get Grimaldi to swoop in and pick them up. Dragonslayer had the firepower to go head-to-head with another armed chopper. Missiles would be a different matter. They would be at the mercy of ground-to-air, but at least there would still be a chance.

To do that, they had to get past the rings. The question Bolan asked himself was, would the Russians give them that leeway?

THE RUSSIAN LEADER took his chopper higher, leaving the two trucks carving up traffic and leaving a trail of mayhem in the inner section of the city. It seemed to him that the Americans—he spared himself a wry smile as he thought of the strenuous denial he had received from the State Department in Washington that morning—were trying to keep moving while they worked out what they could do.

He knew the ambassador and knew what a moral coward the man was. That man would do anything to avoid getting involved. The Russian leader was amused as he recalled the stammering explanation given to him of why a chopper had landed on the embassy grounds and how he could see the fear in the ambassador's eyes. He knew that there was no way that the ambassador would allow them back into his embassy when he knew he was being watched. That left them few options.

"Are the roadblocks in place?" he yelled.

"Yes, sir," the security chief shouted in return, over the noise of the rotors.

"Good. Let us go and wait for them." He pulled back, and the chopper veered off toward the edge of the city.

Below him, the three internal rings and MKAD were marked and delineated by armored vehicles and police patrol cars that now sat ominously at points that would lead the two trucks into a path which would take them only to one place: a deserted airstrip that had been built and then abandoned some thirty years before in the Naro-Fominsky Districts.

This group of rural settlements had been absorbed into the administrative and suburban spread of Moscow. There, isolated from any interference and prying eyes, and with a large open space in which to maneuver and take down an enemy, the Russian president planned to personally lead the attack that would finish off these intruders.

Of course he argued with himself, perhaps leniency was an option. After all, had they not saved Moscow from the threat posed by Freedom Right and also saved his own men the trouble of taking down three other terrorist groups? Battles in which, frankly, his own forces had been found wanting?

The latter thought hardened him. He could not

admit to the weakness that this admission engendered. He would recover the weapons, and these intruders would die.

It would be interesting to see what response the U.S. State Department would have to that.

DOSTOYEVSKY CURSED LOUDLY as he made another abrupt turn and headed away from the exit off the Sadovoye Koltso. He had tried to get them off this ring and onto the straight roads that would take them out past the third ring for the last two exits, and on each he had turned at the last moment, deterred by the sight of the military waiting patiently.

"Cooper, I don't think they want us to get out of the city," he said over the cell phone link. "You'd better come up with another plan."

"Let me speak to my contact," the soldier replied. "We have to keep moving for now."

"The gas won't last forever," the Russian reminded him before Bolan put him on hold and hit the speed-dial digit for Stony Man.

"Bear, you'd better have good news," Bolan said.

"Maybe," Kurtzman replied. "Forget our people. That ambassador is a damned disgrace. Jack is standing by, but I won't send him in without cover of some kind—"

"Well, if our people won't back us up, then where the hell can we get that?" Bolan asked tersely.

"I'm working on it, but in the meantime, I can tell you what's going down your end."

"We're being herded, I know that much."

"And how," the computer wizard agreed. "There are roadblocks on every exit on each ring and at junctions on the grids between. You're being funneled out to a region called Naro-Fominsky, a rural area. There's an old airfield there, and the CCTV running out of the city is showing a lot of military activity out that way."

"Sounds perfect for Jack, I guess, if we can blast our way through."

"Negative, Striker. You haven't seen how many of these bastards there are. They could take you out—"

"Yeah? Remember what we're carrying, Bear. They've got to be careful or else they're going to reduce Moscow to a heap of smoking rubble with a deadly breeze. They can't fire on us at will."

"Maybe, but they'll give you no place to run, and they'll have no reason not to shoot Jack out of the sky."

"What else can we do?" Bolan murmured. "I'm open to suggestions."

"Take the first open exit—move along but not too quickly. Just give me some time to play with, Striker."

"Okay, Bear, I'll go with you on this. But we're running on empty here." He disconnected and got the link with his partner open. He quickly ran through what he had been told.

"At least they can't blow us off the ring, I guess," he said sardonically. "This will confuse them, especially when we play ball," he added as he came to a turnoff that was unblocked. "Here we go...."

HAL BROGNOLA SAT opposite the Secretary of State and tried to hold his temper. He took a deep breath.

"With the greatest respect, I have to say that your attitude is not constructive. The ambassador in Moscow is doing nothing to assist—"

"You perhaps need to remember that officially your

group does not exist. I had never heard of you before today, and the information about what you do was rather sketchy. I was informed that you deal directly with the President. I'm only involved because the President is in high-level talks and is unavailable to anyone for the rest of the day. He told me to deal with whatever problem you have.

"And I must say," the secretary continued, "that your men have put the ambassador in a difficult position at a very sensitive time. We have several deals that we are—"

"Again, with respect, if we don't get our hands on the hardware our men are carrying, or if the Russian president gets his hands on them, there might not be a situation where a deal can be struck."

The secretary smiled in a manner so patronizing that the big Fed had trouble reining in his temper. "I think you overstate the case."

Brognola thought of the number of times he had overseen such situations in the past and how close the world had come to war or annihilation if not for the intervention of his people. But this was not the time to argue; he took another tack.

"I never experienced this kind of intransigence from your predecessor," he said softly. "She appreciated the work that we have to do and that sometimes you have to step outside the box."

"Well, she's not here, is she? You have to deal with me now, and this doesn't happen on my watch. The ambassador is doing the right thing. I can do no more than trust his judgment and back him. There is an American way, and we must follow it."

"Perhaps one day, Mr. Secretary, I can introduce

you to an American who has done a hell of a lot for this country and might not entirely agree with you."

"I very much doubt that. Good day." The secretary turned to the papers on his desk, ignoring the man still seated before him.

Brognola bit back what came to mind, nodded briefly and left without a word. It was only when he was outside that he swore softly to himself and pulled out his cell phone. He hit a speed-dial key.

"Bear, it's not good," he said softly. "The secretary is backing the ambassador and hamstringing us. How are things?"

He listened while Kurtzman gave him a quick rundown. He listened intently. "Striker needs help, Bear, and we need cover to get Jack in there. I've taken the official and standard routes…"

"I hear you, Hal. I have an idea and a contact. But it's not official, and you wouldn't like it."

"Would the secretary like it?" Brognola queried.

"He would hate it, Hal."

Brognola grinned. "Then do it, Bear. Just don't tell me what it is."

THE RUSSIAN LED BOLAN down a street that was much quieter than it should have been at that time of day. There was a flow of traffic along what was usually a main artery, but it was flowing easily with gaps between the vehicles.

"They're keeping the numbers down, Cooper, trying to make it look like nothing is wrong but giving themselves a more open field. That is the Russian mind for you—cover all the possibilities and screw up on every level," he said via the cell phone link.

"Maybe. I figure the roadblocks would just keep some drivers out anyway, but you could be right about them thinking we won't catch on to what they're doing."

"It doesn't matter if they do or they don't, we're just doing it anyway. Your boys had better come through with something before we reach open country, because I don't give much for our chances."

They took another turn, moving away from a roadblock and down a long freeway that took them onto the third ring. They traveled for ten minutes, passing two turnoffs where military vehicles lurked ominously.

Bolan felt confined and ill at ease. He was used to being proactive, but right now he was unable to take the initiative. The cargo the two trucks carried was too fragile to be caught in any kind of combat. Yet how else could they break free of the straitjacket that the Russians had imposed upon them?

His smartphone registered a call. He switched off the link to Dostoyevsky. "Speak to me, Bear. Make it good."

"It is. I can't tell you exactly what's going down, but you'll have to trust me and follow what happens."

"You're the man. I'm sure it'll all make sense in the end."

"Good. I'm tracking your progress on the Moscow CCTV systems, and my friends are doing the same. You need to head back toward the Bulvarnoye Koltso, Striker. We're taking you to the heart of Moscow."

THE CHOPPER TOUCHED DOWN on the airfield, and the Russian leader jumped from it. Before he had moved through the downdraft of the rotors, he had been joined by a squadron of military commanders.

As he moved toward the command post that had been set up in the old conning tower, he listened to updates from his men on their detachments and where they were positioned. The overall commander of the operation outlined the plan for isolating the trucks within the confines of the field and using foam to slow them before utilizing nerve gas to neutralize the two Americans.

"This is good. We will not endanger the hardware they are carrying?" the president asked.

"No, sir. That cannot happen. Even if they turn the vehicles over or crash them into each other, the foam we use will act as a cushion."

"Good. Then all we have to do is wait." He led the ranking officers into the conning tower where men were monitoring the CCTV systems. They looked up as the president entered, and from their expressions, he knew that things were not good. He strode past them and looked for himself. His jaw dropped.

"Why are they headed back to Red Square?"

THE TRUCKS DROVE across the city. Dostoyevsky picked up the pace as they moved past roadblocked areas.

"I hope you know what you're doing, Cooper," he muttered as he watched the military personnel stir, bemused by seeing their targets double back on themselves. "You know they'll come after us if they realize something is wrong?"

"That's why we're moving fast," the soldier replied. "And, no, I don't know what I'm doing, but I figure I know someone who does. Trust me."

"I do, but it's not like I've got a choice," the Russian returned.

Bolan switched from the cell phone link as a call came through. "Bear, talk to me...."

"You'll be coming up to a blocked turnoff in about a thousand yards. Take it. Just keep going, with a weapon in hand. Then follow the bikers. Radio silence until the action is completed. Good luck, Striker."

The connection died, and Bolan relayed instructions to the Russian. As suicidal as it sounded in bare terms, Dostoyevsky trusted his partner enough to agree.

Bolan reached the turnoff, took a deep breath and swung his truck toward the roadblock, stomping his accelerator as he headed directly for the barrier, the personnel on the military vehicles momentarily frozen in shock.

The Russian did the same, bracing himself for a barrage of gunfire. When it came, it was from a completely unexpected source.

SEVEN MEN ON MOTORCYCLES came from different directions. They had left their base and separated, taking alternate routes to bring them to this point. Their thick bomber jackets hid the HKs they had stowed beneath them, and the web belts that carried spare ammunition and grenades.

Before embarkation, they had studied the roadblock that was picked by their commander as the point of contact. Their routes had been chosen so that they would come at the roadblock from as many angles as the roads allowed.

So it came to be as they wove their way through the streets, mounting the sidewalks and parting pedestrians to beat traffic jams, to synchronize their arrivals on the scene. They emerged from all points as the two trucks converged on the roadblock.

The military personnel on the other hand—with their target vehicles coming toward them, yet knowing they were under orders not to fire on the trucks—remained frozen, unsure of what to do in order to halt their prey.

That hesitation cost them dearly. They were taken completely off guard as the bikers roared toward them, HKs firing short bursts to take down personnel who were in the open, and to drive those in their vehicles into diverting their attention away from the trucks.

Circling, two of the riders threw grenades into the middle of the clustered vehicles that formed the roadblock. The explosions sounded as one, rocking the vehicles and shattering the bodywork on one of the armored cars. The personnel inside were killed instantly, while the flying shrapnel from the blast took more men out of the game.

One of the bikers was cut down by chattering SMG fire from the soldiers who finally gathered their wits in time, but for the most part, the bikers moved too quickly and had the military too much on the defensive for them to be in any real danger.

They rode rings around them, picking them off and driving the remainder back to the cover of vehicles that had been put out of action. Three of the bikers rode interference between the remainder of the military men and the two trucks as Bolan and Dostoyevsky drove past, in the gap made by the blasted vehicles.

Two of the riders fell in alongside the trucks. The rider in front, level with the Russian, turned his head toward the driver. His crash helmet was jet-black glass and impenetrable, but there was no mistaking his intent as he gestured that the Russian follow him. Picking up speed, he moved off into the lead. Dostoyevsky hit the accelerator to follow; behind him, Bolan and his biker escort did likewise. They had already left the remains of the roadblock in their wake, and the riders who had decimated the Russians had melted away down side streets.

"Where in hell are we going, Cooper?" Dostoyevsky called across the cell phone link.

"Just follow him. We don't have much choice," Bolan replied. But all the same, he wondered what the hell was going on. Kurtzman had called in a favor from somewhere. Right now it looked as though they were headed back toward the center of Moscow and the area where the embassies were located.

Had Brognola managed to turn the ambassador around?

That thought was driven from his mind as he followed Dostoyevsky through the service gates of a building he did not recognize. He killed the engine and got out as four riders roared through, stopping and dismounting to close the doors.

The riders took off their helmets to reveal six Nordic men. Bolan followed their gaze as a middle-aged man came out from the main building. He walked straight toward Bolan and held out his hand to the soldier and to Dostoyevsky, who had joined him.

"One of you is the man they call Striker, yes? I think we owe you one."

"Thanks," Bolan replied cautiously. "Maybe you do, but I'm afraid I don't actually know where we are."

The man smilcd. "You are in the Norwegian embassy, not on Russian soil. Your friend Mr. Kurtzman has an interesting address book. This is, as you say, off the record, but we like to repay favors in kind."

"ARE YOU SURE that bastard won't just shoot us down?" Dostoyevsky asked the Norwegian ambassador as they walked toward Dragonslayer, where Jack Grimaldi stood waiting.

"The Russian president is a hotheaded and—shall we say—erratic personality, but he is not stupid. Our country has a rather large deal with Gazprom going through. You have seen, perhaps, how construction has come to a halt here. Russia is asset rich but needs cash. Your friend Mr. Grimaldi is delivering a diplomatic bag, one which is essential to the finalization of the deal between our two countries." The ambassador grinned broadly.

"I can only thank you for what you have done," Bolan said quietly. "With those weapons out of circulation—"

"Oslo would not be the fine city it is today," the ambassador interrupted. "I think our government would have preferred you to work with us, not independently, but that does not change the worth of your actions."

Bolan shook hands once more with the ambassador.

"If there were more men in my own government who had the same pragmatism, then maybe it would make my job a whole lot easier. Not just mine," he added, thinking of the big Fed.

Kurtzman had one hell of an explanation due. Bolan was hoping he might be around to see that. It should be interesting.

* * * * *

Don Pendleton
TRIPLECROSS

An American body found in a devastated Indian village raises suspicions of conspiracy

Tensions erupt between Pakistan and India after an Indian village is massacred and bodies from both parties' troops are found in the rubble. But when neither country claims responsibility for the attack, and an American businessman is found among the dead, a warning flag is raised in the White House. While StonyMan's Phoenix Force hunts down the rogue armies overseas, Able Team must uncover why a U.S. mining company representative was at the massacre, and eliminate the deadly role the company plays in this game of war.

STONY MAN®

Available June wherever books and ebooks are sold.

The
Don Pendleton's
Executioner
PATRIOT STRIKE

Superpatriots decide Texas should secede with a bang

After the murder of a Texas Ranger, Mack Bolan is called in to investigate. Working under the radar with the dead Ranger's sister, he quickly learns that rumors of missing fissile material falling into the wrong hands are true. The terrorists, die-hard Americans, are plotting to use the dirty bomb to remove Texas from the Union. As the countdown to D-day begins, the only option is to take the bait of the superpatriots and shut them down from the inside. You don't mess with Texas. Unless you're the Executioner.

GOLD EAGLE®

Available April wherever books and ebooks are sold.

The Don Pendleton's®
Executioner®
PIRATE OFFENSIVE

Danger abounds on the open waters as pirates embark on a fervent rampage

A group of ruthless pirates have taken control of the seas. Armed with powerful weaponry, they have become unstoppable—unless Mack Bolan can put an end to their reign. Using a cargo ship as bait, Bolan attempts to lure out the pirates. But when his plan backfires, Bolan realizes that he's going to need more than bait and brawn to seek out and destroy the pirate fleet. The hunt has begun and, like the pirates, the Executioner is taking no prisoners.

GOLD EAGLE®

Available May wherever books and ebooks are sold.

Handwritten: OO5261 1842

JAMES AXLER
DEATH LANDS®
End Program

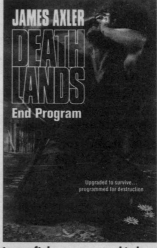

Upgraded to survive...
programmed for destruction

Newfound hope quickly deteriorates into a fight to save mankind

Built upon a predark military installation, Progress, California, could be the utopia Ryan Cawdor and companions have been seeking. Compared to the Deathlands, the tortured remains of a nuke-altered civilization, Progress represents a fresh start. The successful replacement of Ryan's missing eye nearly convinces the group that their days of hell are over—until they discover the high tech in Progress is actually designed to destroy, not enhance, civilization. The companions must find a way to stop Ryan from becoming a willing pawn in the eradication of mankind....

Available May wherever books and ebooks are sold.